UN*hinged*

UN*hinged*

LOVE'S WORTH SERIES #1

Copyright © 2019 by Brigit Rosé
All rights reserved.

Published by
TWO REALMS PUBLISHING LLC
HTTPS://TWO-REALMS-PUBLISHING-LLC.COM/
ISBN: 978-1-955106-16-0

Cover and Interior Design: We Got You Covered Book Design

TWOREALMS
PUBLISHING

Printed in the United States of America

UNhinged

LOVE'S WORTH SERIES
BOOK ONE

BRIGIT ROSÉ

I started this romance forever ago and really pushed through the last month to get it done. During which time I started a new relationship. I know what you're thinking and yes, I am a little crazy. But that's why we work so well together, he's kind of crazy too. And I mean that in the nicest way possible. After all, he doesn't read books. Don't think he listens to them either.

Despite all that, he is one of the most supportive men I know! He has been so patient while I busted my behind to finish this novel and get it out to you, my romance lovelies, in a timely fashion. So with part of the hard work out of the way, I dedicate this book, my first of many more to come (no pun intended), to my ever-loving boyfriend.

You know who you are.

Though, if he never reads this, I guess he'll never know.

one

"ARE YOU SURE THIS LOOKS okay?" Ezzie tossed her dark hair over her shoulder and ran her hands down the tight black dress. It hugged her hips and showed off her curvaceous body. If this thing couldn't show her crush, she was a woman, nothing would. She remembered the first time she met Luke.

Ezzie hopped down the last step and spotted a head of brown hair. Finally, her brother was home. She hugged him around the waist and raised an eyebrow. His smell was all off. It was too... clean. "Are you wearing a new cologne?"

"Um?" He looked over his shoulder.

She yanked her arms back. Whoever this guy was, he was most definitely not her brother. Their similarity in stature and hair color ended there. "Oh my god! I am so sorry. I thought you were Nate. Wait, who are you? And what are you doing inside my house?"

He turned around and faced her. "I'm Luke and I was invited. You would be?"

"I see you've met my little sister." Nate grinned and ruffled Ezzie's head.

She swatted her brother's hand. Running her fingers through her hair, she took a good look at Luke and swallowed. His deep set, chocolate brown eyes

1

met hers and her stomach did a somersault. Wow. Just wow. He was gorgeous from head to toe. His broad shoulders almost appeared too big for the rest of his lean cut body, but his height evened it all out. Clearing her throat, she offered her hand. "I'm Ezzie."

Luke placed his hand in hers. "Nice to meet you."

Her hand tingled from his touch. Pulling her hand back, she nodded. The knock on the door snapped her out of la-la land. Had to be Logan. Perfect timing.

"You expecting someone?" Nate stepped toward the door.

Ezzie jumped in front of him. That was so not happening! "Yeah. My boyfriend."

"Boyfriend?" Luke and Nate spat out simultaneously.

"You're fourteen! How the hell do you have a boyfriend?" Nate tacked on.

Her brother's reaction didn't surprise her. Not one bit. She half-glanced at Luke and something flashed in those eyes of his, but as quick as she swore it was there, it had disappeared. Whatever, she didn't have time to analyze it. Laying her hand on the doorknob, she rolled her eyes. "Um, it's this thing where two people who like each other decide they want to have a relationship. You should try it sometime. Anyway, got to go."

Ezzie stared at herself in the mirror. That was four years ago. She hadn't changed a whole lot since then. Maybe she'd filled out some more, but she'd always appeared a little older than her true age. If only she could get Luke to see her as more than a little sister. So, what if he was her brother's best friend? Or that the two of them had roomed together for the last four years and planned to do so for another three. Damn it, she was eighteen years old. She had to tell Luke how she felt before she left for college. In less than three months they would be thousands of miles apart. She'd waited long enough.

Matt squeezed her shoulders. "For the millionth time, yes. Honey, if he still sees a baby girl with you wearing this, he's either gay or not interested."

Her best friend meant well, but sometimes she really wished he'd lie to her. Then again, maybe not. "Break it down for me why don't you."

"I've sworn to be nothing but utterly truthful."

She flopped back on her bed and blew out an exasperated breath. If things went according to plan, tomorrow night her life would drastically change. It wouldn't be her first time, but it would be the first time it meant something more.

Matt flicked out his pinky and held it out. "Remember?"

"Of course, I do." Ezzie smiled and hooked her pinky finger in his. She loved her small-as-hell hometown, but people weren't exactly ready to saddle up to an openly gay teenager. Matt had been the new kid in school. Well, they'd all been new. Freshmen. Fresh meat for the grinder. She'd stood up to a couple of juniors picking on him. Bam! Instant best friend.

"Good, then do me a favor. If he turns out to be an idiot, promise me you'll come stay with my parents and me in Santa Barbara. We can spend the summer there and then head to L.A. for our new place and college." They'd both be starting at the University of SoCal in the fall.

"I promise. But it's going to work out." She sat up to seal the deal. They kissed each other on the cheeks like aristocrats. It had started as a personal joke and over time it became the way they made the ultimate commitment to one another.

"If you say so." Matt attempted to look positive, but appeared skeptical at best. He'd never been very good at faking it.

Whatever. She was positive enough for both of them. Jumping to her feet, she stood in front of the mirror one last time. She swept her hair to the side for Matt to unzip the back of the slinky black dress. It had to work. "Yep. I do. Now, help me out of this thing."

"Ezzie, can you come here please?" her mother croaked from down the hall.

Crikey, her mother sounded awful. She hoped they hadn't come down with something. Ezzie poked her head out her bedroom door. "In a minute, Mom."

Luke boxed up the last of his books. He scanned the empty shelves of the bookcase. Hard to believe he'd been there four years. Hell, hard to believe it was finally over. A couple months to relax and then he'd move on to law school. He glanced over his shoulder at his roommate. "You going to start packing? Or are you waiting for the fairies to get to it?"

"Dude, graduation may be tomorrow night, but we still don't leave for like a week. Besides, I might be able to get my mom and sister to do it for me."

"You're pathetic." God, she'd be here, wouldn't she? Neither of their families planned to leave Virginia Beach for several days. Great. How many days would he have to avoid her? Too many. Maybe he could convince his parents it'd be better if they headed home sooner rather than later. Something to consider.

The last time Ezzie had been there, he'd realized how much she'd grown since the first time they'd met. She'd certainly matured in all the right places. He'd done everything he could to spend as little time as possible around her. She was his best friend's sister for crying out loud. The last thing he should've been doing was lusting after the girl. And none of the chicks he'd slept with compared to how perfect he imagined her to be. Damn it. Luke dragged a hand through his short hair. He was screwed.

A football sailed through the air and landed with a thud in the box he'd just stacked his books in. Frowning, he picked it up and tossed it back at his roommate. "What the hell man?"

"You tell me. You're the one who disappeared."

"I'm just thinking." *About things I really shouldn't.* And if Nate knew about what, he'd probably kick his ass. Maybe he should kick his own ass and get it over with. The good news, there was no possible chance they'd be alone together. All he had to do was get through the next few days and then home to Salt Lake City. His best friend's family lived three hours from his, but no big deal. He'd only ever traveled to Green River a few times.

"I gathered that much. You know, I truly think you need to party after dinner tomorrow night. Loosen up and have some fun."

Luke opened his mouth to respond, only to be interrupted by the sound of his roommate's phone going off. He listened as Nate answered the phone. Of course, it was his sister. Ezzie had been running a marathon in his brain for the last ten minutes. Her phone call added to the compilation of thoughts banging around in his head. She would likely slap him if she had any idea of the images of her that often played on repeat in his mind.

"No, yeah. I get it. It's okay. We'll do something when they get here and I'll pick you up at the airport tonight. All right, see you then." Nate hung up the phone.

Tonight? Had he heard him correctly? Why would he pick her up tonight? Hadn't they all planned to fly in tomorrow morning? Luke set the box on the floor and dropped down on his bed. "What's up?"

"Apparently my parents both have food poisoning. They can't fly out for a few days, but they insisted Ezzie be here for my graduation. She's coming in tonight."

"What?" Not good. Not good at all. Nate eyed him and Luke knew exactly what he would ask before the words even left his mouth.

"She's got her own hotel room, but I don't want her there alone unless absolutely necessary. Think you could help me keep an eye on her?"

Fuck me. Luke gripped the back of his neck. He shouldn't be trusted around Nate's sister. Agreeing would be the stupidest thing he could do, but he had no choice. If he didn't agree, Nate would know something was up. The images that swirled in his head were not brother appropriate. Leaning forward on his knees, he kept his eyes to the ground and his expression hidden. "Yeah."

Luke stood near the baggage claim at Norfolk International Airport. How had he gotten roped into going along to pick up Nate's sister? Simple. He'd wanted to see her. So, when Nate asked, he'd acquiesced. Sure. Why not? A little bit of sexual torture never killed anyone. Man, he was an idiot. If he hadn't known better, he'd swear he had one of those signs above his head. And it clearly flashed "Dumbest Man Alive."

He watched as Nate shifted back and forth on the balls of his feet. Nate was anxious. Not like he blamed him. Luke paced in small circles around the two suitcases they'd collected fifteen minutes ago. Damn it, he was antsy too. Ezzie should've been off the plane by now. Where the hell was she?

The small hairs on the nape of his neck stood on end. A sweet perfume filled his nostrils. Pausing mid-step, he lifted his eyes. His gaze stopped on the most beautiful creature he'd ever seen. Long brown hair. Dazzling blue eyes. Legs for days. Natural hourglass figure. Hip-hugging jeans, which perfectly accentuated her curves. A baby tee and denim jacket revealed exquisite skin he was certain would be soft to the touch. Man, oh, man. Staying away from her was going to be harder than he'd anticipated. Luke chanced a quick glance at the front of his pants. Whew! No tent for him. At least that stayed in check.

Ezzie closed the distance between the three of them and smiled broadly. "Hey guys."

"What took you so long?" Frowning, Nate crossed his arms, the annoyance of how long they'd stood there written clearly on his face.

"Sorry. I spent a few extra minutes talking to my seatmate. Lost track of time. My bad."

Seatmate? Man, he hoped it was another female. For some reason the idea of her chatting up a random dude infuriated him. Gee, probably because he was attracted to her. *Shut up.* He had to get that shit out of his head right now. Deep breath. Nate was peeved enough for the both of them.

Luke stepped forward and Ezzie walked into his open arms as if it was the most natural thing on earth. He had a good six inches or more on her. Her head pressed into his chest. Luke dropped his head into the crook of her neck and quietly inhaled. She felt damn good against him like this. "It's good to see you."

"You too."

"How 'bout you share the love over here?" her brother chimed in and raised an eyebrow at the scenario before him.

Smirking, Ezzie pulled away all too soon and hugged her brother. "I'm happy to see you too."

Had he really wrapped his arms around his best friend's sister? What the hell was wrong with him? But man, she'd felt perfect, like she'd been right where she was meant to be. Which was crazy. Yeah, they'd known each other for a few years and they'd always gotten along. It wasn't until earlier this year; he'd viewed her any differently. Most definitely similar to the way he saw her now. Okay, maybe he'd always seen her that way, but she was fourteen when they first met. God, he really had to get that shit out of his head. Luke peeked at his best friend. Looked like he was in the clear, for the moment. Too close for comfort.

"Can we go? I'm exhausted. And knowing you, packing hasn't even been started. Something I'd like to do before Mom and Dad get here in a few days." Ezzie glanced between her brother and Luke.

"Yeah. Let me grab your—" Nate paused mid-sentence and pointed to a small tattoo playing peek-a-boo on Ezzie's left hip. "What the hell is that?"

She peered over her shoulder. "What?"

"That thing on your hip?!"

"I'm pretty sure it's a tattoo." Ezzie snickered and rolled her eyes.

Yeah, he was certain it was a tattoo, one he longed to see more of. From what he could tell, it appeared to be a butterfly. Maybe a fairy? Luke glimpsed at Nate, who'd practically blown a gasket at the mere word "tattoo." Quite amusing, considering they'd each gotten one themselves. Something they'd done after passing one of their more massive exams. Hmm, when had she gotten the tattoo? She'd turned eighteen in, what, April? Sometime in the last couple of months. What had spawned the desire? How had she decided on the concept?

"Why would you desecrate your body like that?" Nate grabbed one of the suitcases at his feet.

"Two words: Kettle, black. Now, while I'd love to continue discussing what I do with *my* body with you; how about we do something a little less disturbing? Hmm, shall we?" With that, Ezzie spun on her heel and sauntered toward the doors.

Luke chuckled. He couldn't help himself. Not many people had the audacity to really call Nate on his shit. Instead of standing there and enjoying a good laugh, he grabbed a suitcase and followed after Ezzie. Soon enough, Nate would do the same.

"I'm telling you, he did. Luke hugged me." Ezzie giggled as Matt pulled his best *nun uh, no way* voice. He called it his girlfriend voice. It always made her laugh, especially when the face followed. Too bad she couldn't see him right then; still, she could absolutely imagine the fake jaw-drop with the wide emerald-green eyes.

"Okay. Let me stop. Was it before or after your brother?"

She tugged the brush through her hair one last time and set it on the bathroom counter top. With her nightly check list complete, she turned out the light and traipsed into the bedroom. "Before. I even think he sniffed me."

"Really? Sounds like the odds are favorable."

"Guess it's a good thing you got me this room. By the way, thank you for that. It's really beautiful." Screw beautiful! The room was magnificent! Not only had he managed to swing her a reservation at The Boardwalk Resort, but he'd gone full out and booked her a queen suite. She paraded over to the sliding glass door. The ocean view she had was certainly nothing to complain about. The way the night sky reflected off the deep blue of the sea was breathtaking.

"Yeah, well ... I figured the two of you deserved the whole shah-bang."

A small snicker escaped. She wouldn't have used the word *shah-bang* under any circumstances. But she absolutely understood what he meant. This place was definitely better than the one her parents had originally planned for them to stay at and she certainly wouldn't have had a suite.

"I'm just not entirely sure how I'm going to get him here. From what my brother's girlfriend says there are supposed to be a lot of parties going on. I can't pinpoint which one he's likely to go to."

"Did you ask Becca?"

"Of course, I did, but she wasn't sure. She only said there was a couple she and Nate intended to hit after dinner."

Hmm, what if she wore the dress to dinner? Would her brother have a heart attack? Hell, Becca's or Luke's parents could have a heart attack. No. She needed something more inconspicuous.

"Do you think Nate will have asked Luke to help babysit you?"

Ezzie snorted. She loathed the word choice, but Matt was on to something. Her brother would've absolutely asked Luke to keep an eye on her. She loved Nate, but he was beyond overprotective sometimes. It stood to reason, especially given his reaction to her tattoo, he'd ask his best friend to act as a pseudo-brother. "I'm going with yes."

"Then I have an idea. After all, you've made some friends there. Becca and Nate plan to head off together once dinner is over, right?"

"That's what she said." Good thing her brother's girlfriend adored her. And happened to know part of the truth. Ezzie hadn't gone out and explained her seduction plan to Becca, but she had mentioned her attraction to Luke. And how it could be mutual. Becca played the friend card and had given her a good dose of reality. But she'd known about Luke's reputation for a couple of years. So, what if he'd been labeled a player? Truthfully, she believed there was more to him than anyone really knew.

"Okay. Tell them you have plans, but need a ride back to the hotel to change before you meet your girls. Luke takes you and waits to drop you off so he knows where you're at and who you're with. You just have to seduce him after you change."

There was a knock on the front door to the suite. "That could work. Listen, sounds like room service is here. I'll talk to you later."

"Let me know how it goes. *Ciao.*" The line went dead.

Ezzie hung up and set her cell phone on the night stand. She glanced at the silk robes hanging on a couple of wall pegs, yet sauntered into the living room without one. So, what if room service got a little bit of a show? Her satin night gown came to her feet. It covered all the important stuff. Without looking out the peephole and confirming her suspicions, she opened the door.

Luke stood on the other side. He had a dress bag in his hand. "You, um, left this in the car."

"Um, thank you." Both the skimpy black dress and the dress she planned to wear to the graduation ceremony were in there. In her hurry to get inside the hotel and checked in, she must've forgotten it. Though she could've collected the bag tomorrow morning, he'd brought it up to her room. Ezzie stared at Luke. Why?

He swallowed and his gaze left her face. Even in jeans and a t-shirt Luke was sexy as hell. Who knew how long he'd been up; still he smelled like fresh clean air. She felt, more than saw, as his eyes raked the length of her body. Two could certainly play that game. Biting on her bottom lip, she allowed herself a moment to admire how much his body had physically changed in the course of three months. Dark brown hair. Soft chocolate-brown eyes. Thick thighs. Broad, defined shoulders. Plus, the strong jaw-line.

Then there was his chest. No fat there. Only pure unadulterated, heart-pounding, muscle. His t-shirt clung to his perfectly-developed six-pack rather well. The elevator doors dinged and must've brought him back to reality. Quickly his eyes found hers. As if he'd caught her red-handed, the smallest hint of a smile pulled at the corner of his mouth. Luke cleared his throat and regained his composure. "I thought you might need this and Nate was on the phone with your parents."

"Um, oh, yeah. Right. I was supposed to call them when I landed. Slipped my mind." Which was entirely true. She'd called Matt once she'd gotten in the hotel to tell him about the girl she'd met on the plane and to share all she could about her arrival. Ezzie held her hand out for the bag. Luke looked at her hand as if he had no idea what to do with it.

The room service attendant chose that moment to roll up with her food.

"Miss Donovan, your meal as requested. Would you like for me to bring it inside?"

"Yes, please. In the living room, if you don't mind. Thank you." She stepped back and held the door open enough for him to wheel the cart all the way in. She should probably get the attendant a tip, but her purse was in the bedroom. Briefly she peeked at Luke. He'd perched himself just inside the room and watched the room service attendant like a predator protecting his own. Interesting. Ezzie slipped into the bedroom and grabbed a five-dollar bill from her purse. By the time she'd returned, both room service and Luke had gone and her dress bag was draped over the back of the couch. *Well, damn.*

He'd spent half the night tossing and turning with a raging hard-on. All night long a sea-green satin nightgown danced around in his mind. Luke hadn't been able to get the image of Ezzie in the doorway of her hotel suite out of his head. God, he hadn't even been able to stop himself from checking her out. Her long, brown hair had shimmered in the light. Bright sapphire-blue eyes had gawked back at him. And those beautiful full lips of hers had practically cried out for a kiss. Even if his gaze hadn't stopped there, at least he'd stopped himself on that front.

Instead, his eyes had traced their way along her exquisite neckline to her collarbone, then over the swell of her breasts where his gaze lingered for far too long. Had he stared? No, not at all. Maybe a little. What would it feel like to have his hand on one of her breasts? He bet the skin would be smooth. Luke rubbed his eyes. God, he had to stop thinking about her breasts.

It was bad enough his gaze had continued its journey to her flat stomach, softly rounded hips, and down her long, long legs. By the time he'd gotten to her painted toenails, the elevator doors had opened and snapped him out of his trance. What he wouldn't give for that damn ding now, though he could've dealt without the room service attendant's arrival or Ezzie's sudden disappearance into the room somewhere.

True, it had been his only chance to escape her presence. Her lavender scent had already filled his nostrils and held him hostage, yet the knowledge of her brother downstairs pulled him out of the room. His only saving grace, he'd ensured room service had left too. He even gave the attendant a twenty-dollar tip with the promise he wouldn't come back to the room. God, what was wrong with him?

The good news of the day had been his ability to run himself numb this morning. Nate hadn't been in the room when he'd returned. He'd likely gone to get Ezzie, probably so she could start packing his stuff. Luke had showered and proceeded across campus to the auditorium. While he had to collect his own cap and gown, theoretically he should be able to get both of theirs. Studying the people at the table, he approached one of the women and charmingly smiled. "Lucas Jonnihan and Nathan Donovan."

"And you're which one? Because you can only get your cap and gown."

"I'm Lucas Jonnihan, but Nathan Donovan is my roommate. I'm sure you can make an exception." He leaned on the table and flashed the smile again. The girl stared at him like he was stupid. This normally always worked. How could it be possible his smile failed to work its magic? It couldn't be because of Ezzie? Could it? No. That was crazy.

"Luke, is that you?"

He glanced at the dark-skinned beauty heading his way. Who was she? Mary? Maggie? Had he slept with her? Yes? At least he thought he had. The way she sashayed toward him; he'd have to go with yes. But how long ago? The charming smile returned to his face. He wrapped his arms around her when she came in for the hug. She smelled like... vanilla. Nope, still couldn't place her. "Hey. How're you doing?"

"I'm better now. You look great. We should get together before you leave."

"Yeah. Maybe we can meet up at one of the parties tonight." Good thing he didn't intend to go to any of them. Dinner with his parents, Ezzie, Nate, Becca and her parents was enough. Then if he was lucky, Ezzie would go back to her hotel room, so he could hide in his dorm room all night.

She grinned as if accepting the invitation. Turning her attention to the girl at the table, the dark-skinned beauty squeezed Luke's bicep. "Gina, help out a friend. Go ahead and give him both sets."

"Sure thing, Maria." No longer holding the caps and gowns hostage, Gina placed two sets of a cap and gown on the table.

More good news; he had a name for the face. Bad news: he still couldn't remember sleeping with her. But by the way she'd felt him up, they'd definitely hooked up. Probably sometime before March. He hadn't been with anyone since Ezzie had shown up out of the blue to spend her last couple of days of spring break with him and Nate. What had she done to him? *Focus, jackass.* Luke collected the items laid out on the table. "Thanks, Maria."

"Anytime." She placed a chaste kiss on his lips and sauntered away.

Man, he had to get out of here. With the caps and gowns in his arms, he hurried off back to the dorm room. Even if Nate had already picked up Ezzie, at least he wouldn't be alone with her. Yeah, he'd told Nate he'd watch out for her, but he could keep his word and avoid her at the same time. Especially as he was the one person she really needed to be protected from. Being alone with her was bad for his health. Hers too. It would be best if he stayed away from her all together, but he couldn't bail on his best friend like that.

Determined to do the right thing, he opened the door to his and Nate's room without a second thought. There she stood: the girl running a marathon in his brain.

"Hey." Ezzie looked up from the box of things she'd started packing.

Damn she looked sexy. Barely-there shorts; small, tight tank top; and that damn tattoo. It mocked him as if it knew something he'd either decided to ignore or simply overlooked. *Shit!* It had known something. Luke surveyed the room. "Umm, hi. Where's, uh, where's Nate?"

"I sent him for some breakfast. Figured it was the least he could do since I'm up after practically no sleep."

"Oh? Anywhere in particular?" *Please say yes.* No, wait! Damn it. *Please say no.* If Nate had run to the cafeteria, no big deal. He'd been back in five, maybe ten minutes. Tops. But if she'd asked for something more specific, it could be a while. Either way, he couldn't stand in the doorway like an idiot. Luke glimpsed at the open door. Closing the door was a bad idea. Going inside was a bad idea. Swallowing, he tried to relax his nerves and shut the door.

"Yeah, he went to Panera. Told him to get a small pack of bagels and a couple of their soufflés."

Great. Fucking perfect. Being alone with her much longer was not an option. He gripped the back of his neck and crossed over to his side of the room in three long strides. Hardly glancing in her direction, he dropped the packages on his bed. The best thing he could do was leave. "Can you tell him I got his cap and gown?"

"Sure." She sighed and faced the box in front of her.

Hanging his head, he stared at the carpet for all of five seconds. That damn sea-green negligee popped into his head. *Fuck me.* Steeling himself up, Luke turned his head and focused on Ezzie. With her back to him, he could take his time studying her. Her brown locks had been pulled into a sloppy ponytail. The tank top wasn't anything special and the faded denim shorts had obviously worn over the years. Still, she looked perfect. Every inch of her was gorgeous.

"Thanks."

She glanced over her shoulder at him and caught him staring. *Shit!* Luke focused his eyes elsewhere. Inhaling deeply, her sweet lavender scent filled his nostrils. He had to get out of there. Otherwise, he might lose his sanity. Although he had no idea where he would go, he headed for the door.

"You're leaving?"

"I've, uh, got some things to do before, uh, before I pick up my parents." His answer was a cop out, but he couldn't really go into detail. Not without revealing way too much about his blatant attraction to her.

"Really? Or are you just avoiding me?"

Luke paused with his hand on the doorknob. Her question called him out on his lie and acknowledged the actions he'd taken when she'd been around in mid-March. And she'd be around for the next few days. He'd have to face the music sooner or later, but later seemed better. "I'm not avoiding you."

"Bullshit." Ezzie padded across the room and stopped behind him.

Maybe he couldn't see her, but he could sense how close she stood. Heat spread through his body like wild-fire. He ensured his hard-on couldn't be spotted, then spun around and faced her. "Will you please let this go?"

"No. You ignored me the last time I was here. I have a right to know what the hell is going on, especially after last night. You tossed my dresses and just disappeared."

"Ezzie, now is not the time for this conversation. Your brother could come through the door any minute." He dropped his hands to his waist. Whatever they needed to talk about or not talk about could be interrupted. The last thing he wanted was for her brother to find them in an awkward position. With the way she looked in those tiny-shorts and that way-too-tight-tank top, it could absolutely happen.

She moved closer to him. "All the more reason for me to be sure there will be time to have it."

"There will. I just, I need you to be a little patient right now." He could easily reach out, take a firm hold of her and press his lips to hers. One taste wouldn't be enough. If he tasted those full and pouty lips, he'd want more.

Resting one hand on his pectorals, she stepped into his body. His breath quickened. Using her other hand, she caressed the nape of his neck and lightly brushed his lips with her own.

The kiss was sweet and innocent, but he hungered for more. His arms locked around her shoulders and his lips crushed hers. Gently, he pried her mouth open with his tongue. The instant his tongue found hers, she moaned. Her sound was pure ecstasy. It got him harder than he'd been before their lips touched. Desire consumed him from the inside out. If he kissed her any longer, he wouldn't be able to stop himself. Slowly, he ended the kiss.

He pressed his forehead against hers. Inhaling deeply, he breathed in the shared air. He could still taste the kiss. Exactly why something had to be done with his mouth and quickly. Some things had to be honestly addressed. Example: their timing could've been better. Then again, it would've been best if he hadn't kissed her. And it would be so easy to do again. Space. He had to put some space between them, otherwise his dick was going to get him in a load of trouble.

Luke inched back and caressed her cheek. "I don't want to avoid you."

"That's not you saying you won't."

"Shit."

Of course, she'd heard the unspoken *but*. He navigated around her and paced the length of the room. His eyes remained glued to the carpeted floor as he stalked past both beds and stopped at the mini-fridge. Turning around, he faced the door. He lifted his gaze to her and stared into her eyes. They sparkled with longing and a little bit of frustration.

"Sums it up pretty well if you ask me."

Hanging his head, he dragged his hand down his face. "I'm sorry, Ezzie. I—"

"Luke, just stop. If you aren't going to give me any real answers then stop. I don't want excuses. To think ... you know what? Never mind." She snatched her purse off her brother's nightstand and stormed toward the door.

If he was smart, he'd stay put and let her go. But damn it, he couldn't stand there and do nothing. She had to understand what was going through his head. Luke grabbed a hold of Ezzie, spun her around and pushed her against the door. Her purse fell from her hands and landed on the floor. Lust flashed into her eyes and the entire room lit up. *Fuck!* He couldn't explain himself when she gawked at him like that. Instead of opening his mouth to say something, he leaned his muscled body into hers and pinned her against the door. The proximity of her mouth was too much. No way he could pass on another taste.

His lips crashed against hers. Wrapping an arm around her waist, he squeezed her low back. Her skin was so warm. He reached up and loosened her hair. He liked it better flowing around her shoulders. It also gave him range to fist a palm full of it. Her tresses were like the silk nightgown he'd seen her in last night. Arms came around his back and nails dug into his shoulder blades. Everything about Ezzie bloomed beneath his touch.

If he had half a brain, he'd end this before things went too far. The dorm room was no place for him to take her. Not to mention, the door wasn't locked and her brother could arrive any minute. Forcing his body into action, Luke released his hold and left the room.

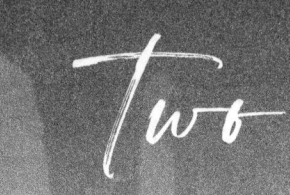

Two

BREATHING HEAVILY, EZZIE GAWKED AT the open door. What the hell just happened? One minute they were kissing and his hands were all over her, the next he's out the door. Crikey, she was so confused. It was like he wanted her, but he had an issue with how he felt. This was awful. She picked up her purse, closed the door and flopped back on Luke's bed. Boxes covered her brother's bed. Besides, if she had to be left hot and bothered, at least this way she could be close to the one who'd made her that way. She curled up to his pillow and caught a whiff of his fresh clean air scent.

So, what if he smelled good? Sighing, she rolled out of the bed and traipsed over to the other side of the room. One box of books had been all she'd managed to pack. Ezzie scanned her brother's side of the room and inwardly grumbled at all the packing that still had to be done. Why couldn't he complete one simple task? Unfortunately, the answer was her and their mother. The two of them had coddled Nate for far too long. Maybe they should've stopped years ago. Probably too late now.

Biting the inside of her lip, she stole a quick glance of Luke's side of the room. The man certainly had skill when it came to putting things together. He was also pretty skilled at kissing. Not something she'd likely forget anytime soon. Ezzie groaned. Why couldn't she get him out of her head? Hell, he'd even wiggled his way into her heart. Truly, she hated the attraction she felt for him and the butterflies that had settled in her stomach a few years ago when they'd met for the first time hadn't gone anywhere.

After four boyfriends, she'd assumed the butterflies for Luke would've disappeared. Instead, they grew stronger every time she visited him and her brother in Virginia Beach. March had been the first time she'd noticed he'd looked at her differently, almost as if she'd gone from Nate's baby sister to a woman he'd date. His kisses certainly proved how he saw her now. Still, he'd barged out the door, like he couldn't get away fast enough. Maybe she should too. Forget all about her plan to seduce him. It was a stupid idea anyhow.

The door opened again. Her heart fluttered at the possibility of Luke returning. She glanced over her shoulder and the smell of baked egg hit her nostrils. It was her brother. Shaking off her disappointment, Ezzie smiled. "Took you long enough."

"Sorry. I had to wait for the soufflé you wanted. Hey, you okay?" Nate raised an eyebrow quizzically.

"Yeah. Why?"

He gestured to the open, empty box in front of her. Shutting the door, he set the bags of breakfast on his nightstand and shuffled to her side. "You know you can talk to me about anything."

"It's not a big deal. I was just thinking about the past and how things have changed." When it came to her brother, he always expected her to answer. And unfortunately, he'd gotten good at being able to tell when she lied about something. Meant she had to learn the art of vague answers. She gave him truth without details. It worked for them. Most of the time.

Frowning at her, Nate moved the box of books off the end of the bed. He placed it on the floor and then yanked the empty box from her hands. "You aren't thinking about that douche ex-boyfriend of yours, are you?"

"God no." Ezzie grabbed the bags off the nightstand and sat on her brother's bed. She and Justin had broken up over spring break. He was the reason she'd spent the last two days of her vacation with her brother and Luke. Well, Justin and one of her friends. For the rest of the school year, her friend had been labeled a slut. Not that Kayla hadn't deserved it. After all, she had been caught hooking up with Justin. He'd been ostracized too, which was less than he deserved.

Nate removed two soufflés, two Asiago cheese bagels and two packages of cream cheese. "Good. Otherwise, I might be sorry I didn't kick his ass."

"No worries. I'm over Justin." Her brother and Luke had taken very good care of her that weekend. Even if Luke had spent most of the weekend away from the dorm, the time he had been there had been ... nice. His compassion had broken through the exterior player status he'd portrayed. It had certainly renewed her attraction for him.

Shaking her head, she smiled at Nate and reached over for her part of the food. She always ate the soufflé first and polished off the bagel second.

Scooping cream cheese onto part of the bagel, he eyed Ezzie and studied her carefully. "You should come out tonight with me and Becca after dinner."

"Yeah. No."

"Why not?" Nate shoved a piece of bagel and cream cheese in his mouth.

How civil should she be? Okay. Best if she left out his girlfriend's choice words at what would happen if she missed any alone time with Nate tonight. The horrible description that had come out of Becca's mouth had been scary enough. Ezzie shuddered. "Let's just say your girlfriend is adamant you two have alone time together. And I promised I would stay out of the way tonight."

"You're my sister. How could you..." He made a silent oh with his mouth. Obviously, he'd gotten the picture. With no other response, Nate stuck the last of one half of his bagel in his mouth.

"It's fine. I'll be okay by myself."

He frowned again. "No way. I'll talk to Luke. He can take you somewhere after dinner. I'm sure his parents won't mind."

"I'll be—"

"Nope. It's settled." Biting into the soufflé, he stared at her.

Arguing would get her nowhere. Her brother had already decided on a plan of action. It was best if she accepted his word as final, even if she intended to ignore it later. Ezzie smiled. "Fine."

"Good. Glad you see things my way."

Luke leaned his left hand against the wall and hung his head as cold water from the shower head trickled down his back. His gaze traveled down his body. He had one option left. It was the last thing he wanted to even consider. Except he couldn't spend the rest of the day like this. Either he manned up and followed on his instincts or he'd end up with an awful case of blue balls.

Bolting from the room and leaving Ezzie alone had been the hardest and best decision. Too bad it had left his hard-on with nowhere to go. At the time there had been at least a couple of hours before he had to pick-up his parents. Time to kill was bad. He'd done the only thing he could do: worked out. Over the last few months he'd gotten into the habit of keeping a spare set of gym clothes in the trunk of his car. The run hadn't accomplished much. He sweated his ass off, but he'd still been turned on.

Option two had been to go back to the dorm room and stand under a cold ass shower. Thankfully the room had been empty when he'd come back twenty minutes ago, but the cold water had proven useless. He had no choice. Giving into what his body demanded, Luke traced his hand down his pelvis and grabbed a hold of his dick. He moaned at the sensation and the memory of Ezzie beneath him flooded his brain, front and center.

Her skin had been softer than he'd dreamt. And those lips. So full and pouty. They'd been irresistible. He hadn't been able to control himself. Kissing her had been pure bliss. Then that exquisite sound escaped her mouth. It had taken every fiber within him not to take it further. She deserved more than that. At least this moment, here in the shower alone, he was safe. Luke held on to the images of Ezzie in his mind.

Not just the feel of her body beneath his or her lips against his own, but the image of her in that sea-green nightgown. He imagined closing the door after the room service attendant left and staying behind. In his mind it was safe to kiss Ezzie. Safe to slide the thin straps of that nightgown from her shoulders. Safe to nibble on her neck. Her collarbone. And slowly envelop her breast with his mouth.

Rubbing up and down his shaft, he used the memories and fantasy as fuel. The thought of how her nipples would taste. Would they be sweet? Like her lips. And god, what if he went further? The same way his eyes had. Just the image of her revved him up; several strokes and he was perilously close to orgasm. One more stroke to the head of his dick and he peaked. Fire burned through his core and a release grappled him. Before the first orgasm had a chance to settle, a second orgasm exploded from his body.

Luke stared at the shower stall wall as his body relaxed from the release. He was a dirty bastard. How could he have used memories of Ezzie like that without her knowledge? What the hell was wrong with him? He dragged his left hand down his face and shut the water off. Snapping the towel off the toilet, he dried off and yanked on a pair of jeans. He stepped into the dorm room and tossed his towel on the end of his bed. Stopping in front of his dresser, he plucked a t-shirt from a drawer and pulled it over his head.

It never bothered him before. He'd slept with countless women over the last four years. Forgotten so many names because their faces all blurred together. If he'd jacked off before, no one invaded his head space or left him feeling guilty over a bodily reaction. Ezzie shouldn't be different, but she was. She was very different. No one had ever taken hold of him like this. Whatever. He had to get her out of his head.

The dorm room door opened. Nate walked in alone. "Good, you're here. I need to talk to you."

"Can't. I need to go get my parents." Luke sat on the bed. He had to get going if he planned to make it on time to the airport.

"What're you talking about? I just dropped them off."

His head popped up and he stared at Nate. "How the hell did that happen?"

"Didn't you get their message? Their flight got in early. They tried to reach you, but you never answered. When they couldn't get a hold of me, your mom called Ezzie."

"What?" His mother had Ezzie's phone number? Since when had the two of them talked? Or spent any time together? Could it have been last summer? His family and Ezzie and Nate's family had all vacationed together. There had been a day Ezzie, her mother and his mother had all gone out shopping. Maybe they'd bonded then. If so, why hadn't he known about it?

Nate shrugged. "I guess they still had my old number. Anyway, I had to take Ezzie back to the hotel anyway, so no big deal."

"Wait. They're staying at the same hotel?" How could he have been this clueless? He hadn't given it a whole lot of thought when he and Nate dropped Ezzie off at the hotel last night. His parents even e-mailed him the information of the hotel they planned to stay at. The three of them at the same hotel. Great. Just great.

"Yeah. Makes it easier. Ezzie is going to catch a cab with your parents back to campus for the ceremony and we'll take both cars when we head to dinner. You think Ezzie could ride with you?"

Without giving it a second thought, Luke nodded. He almost asked why, but he already knew the answer. Becca's parents were joining them. In all likelihood, they'd ride with Nate and Becca. Which left an empty space in his car. Four people fit more comfortably than five. "Sure."

"Thanks. Oh, I think your parents planned to go somewhere after dinner. Check with your mom, but I heard her talking to Ezzie about a club or something. Whatever you end up doing, think Ezzie could go with you?"

"I figured she'd go off with you and Becca." It wasn't a good idea for him to spend any more time with her than necessary. The time alone they had earlier had been more than enough for one day.

"Yeah, I talked to Ezzie about that and she made a point to remind me my girlfriend would kill me if she and I don't get some time together tonight. Feel me?"

Right. He remembered something Becca mentioned once about time alone with Nate. A small smile tugged on the corners of Luke's mouth. "I'm sure my parents will be okay if Ezzie tags along."

"I think it'll just be you and Ezzie. I'm not certain, but I think your parents meant the two of them." Nate headed into the bathroom and shut the door.

Shit! Luke reached for his phone and texted his mother. The response he got back confirmed what Nate suggested. His parents planned to hit some club after dinner. They probably assumed he intended to celebrate with friends tonight. Damn. Meant he and Ezzie would be alone. The last thing he wanted and he was going to get it.

Nate stepped back into the room. "Avoid the parties though. Ezzie needs something to take her mind off things. She looked a little upset when I came in earlier. She denied it, but I think she was thinking about that ex-boyfriend of hers."

"The cheater?" He'd heard about what happened to bring her to Virginia Beach over spring break. He'd seen her for all of five seconds, maybe a minute. A day he'd never forget.

With his backpack slung over his shoulder, Luke opened the door and blinked. His roommate's younger sister stood on the other side with a suitcase at her feet. "Ezzie, what're you doing here?"

Sobbing, she threw her arms around his neck.

Shit! What the hell had happened to her? Hugging her tightly, he glanced across the dorm room to Nate.

Nate rushed over.

Luke shifted her from his arms to her brother's and headed off to class.

The only reason he knew anything about what had gone down was because of his roommate. Information had been shared not too long after her arrival. He and Nate worked hard that weekend to take care of Ezzie.

But he'd be surprised if that was what had been on Ezzie's mind that morning. Luke hung his head. Not as if he'd correct his best friend.

"Yeah. Really makes me want to kick his ass. I can save that for when we get back home. For now, Ezzie needs to be reminded there are better guys out there for her."

There were better guys for her. And he was certainly not one of them. That was something she had to know. He'd never be good enough for her. Luke rubbed his sternum. The thought hurt, but it was true. "Yeah. I'll, uh, make sure she gets the picture."

"Thanks, man. I knew I could count on you."

There hadn't been a whole lot of time for them to talk before or immediately after Nate and Luke's graduation ceremony. For once she was grateful not to have any time alone with Luke. That conversation could wait until, gee, never. It wasn't a discussion she looked forward to having. As if his walking out hadn't said all she needed to know. Ezzie glanced at the silver watch on her wrist. Ten more minutes and they'd arrive at the restaurant she'd chosen for Nate and Luke's graduation dinner.

She hadn't told anyone where they were going. An address had been all they'd received. Their reservations had been slightly altered, but only to eliminate two seats since her parents wouldn't be there to join them. The restaurant had been amenable to the change. Easier to take away two people than add two people. A lot of five-star restaurants despised last minute changes. Not as if she could help her parents had gotten food poisoning.

Her eyes successfully remained diverted for the first half of their drive toward the restaurant. Luke dressed appropriately for the graduation ceremony. She was almost positive the suit was Armani, but she sucked at designer stuff. Whatever it was, he looked gorgeous in it. Midnight blue suit, pale blue crisp button-up, and a star-speckled tie to match. His light olive skin tone offset the suit perfectly and the color made his brown hair darker. Talk about a man she'd kill to spend the night staring at. Naturally, Ezzie forced her eyes elsewhere. Otherwise, she might've drooled.

"Where are you guys planning to go after dinner?" Luke glimpsed in the rearview mirror at his parents.

"It's a jazz club Esmeralda recommended to us."

Her full first name. Luke's mother never liked to use her nickname. She shifted in the passenger seat and frowned. "Will you ever call me Ezzie, Mrs. Jonnihan?"

"Hush, child. Esmeralda is a beautiful name; one you should be proud to wear. Now, no more of this Ezzie nonsense." She had clearly passed her stubborn nature onto her son. Beverly Jonnihan was a force to be reckoned with. No one argued with her, ever. Something Ezzie learned over summer vacation last year. And now was not the time to test the waters to see if they'd changed.

"Yes ma'am."

"Good. Now, Lucas, I expect you to go out and have fun this evening. Esmeralda, I'm assigning you the duty of ensuring he does. He deserves to celebrate."

Okay. She agreed with only a small portion of that. Dinner with people surrounding them, one thing Ezzie could survive. Making sure Luke, who confused the hell out of her, had fun, whole other story. Regardless, his mother made a valid point. "You're right. He should be able to celebrate. His accomplishments are something to be proud of."

"I'll have fun tonight, Mom. I promise. But we should still do something as a family. Tomorrow?" Luke turned into the parking lot and easily located a space.

"It will have to be in the evening. Your father and I have a spa day planned."

He raised an eyebrow at his father, the man who'd given him his chocolate-brown eyes and jaw-line. "Spa day?"

"I expect it should be relaxing." Luke's father smiled in an achingly familiar charming way.

Covering her mouth Ezzie stifled a giggle. Best not to laugh at the shocked expression all over Luke's face at his father's lack of reaction. The hotel they were staying at had all kinds of amenities and those two mentioned earlier their intention to take advantage of them. Without further addressing the issue at hand, she unbuckled her seatbelt. "Shall we head inside?"

"Yes, but a lady always waits for a gentleman to open her door." Luke's mother rested a tender hand on Ezzie's arm and shifted her gaze to the two men in the car.

Right. Do not argue with her. It was absolutely pointless. Neither Luke, nor his father grumbled as they climbed out of the car first and ambled to the passenger side doors. Each held the door as appropriate. Ezzie swung her legs out together and lifted her gaze to the offered hand. It wasn't like she had no idea what to do with it; the gesture simply seemed out of sorts. Swallowing to wet her dry throat and silence her nerves, she slipped her hand into Luke's and got out of the car.

Standing on her own two feet, Ezzie slowly pulled her hand away and brushed the skirting of her dress down. Hopefully she'd hidden her reactions well. Plastering a smile on her face, she eyed his parents. Neither acted as if they'd noticed anything out of the ordinary. Good. Dinner. All she had to do was make it through dinner. The four of them approached the entrance to the restaurant. Her brother, his girlfriend, and Becca's parents stood outside.

Everyone took a collective moment and studied the inside. Appearing to float, lanterns hung from the ceiling. Zebra wood tables had been strategically spaced throughout the dining area. Glass and dark-wood stained panels separated the cooking and serving area from the patrons. Terrapin was quite beautiful. She couldn't wait to try to the food. Ezzie peered at those around her. "Shall we?"

"Absolutely."

"I'm starving."

"Yes." Their entire group echoed some form of an affirmative response. His father escorted his mother in first. Becca's parents followed second and Nate and Becca took up the caboose, which worked in Luke's favor.

He required a moment alone to speak with Ezzie. Terrapin was a five-star restaurant that delivered first class service. He'd eaten there once or twice in the past. Everything about the place catered to a certain clientele. It was the kind of restaurant his parents would've dined at without a second glance at the cost. Whether or not Becca's parents were along the same line, he had no idea. But Nate and Ezzie's parents, they would've celebrated at the local pizza parlor and been happy. Somehow, his best friend's sister managed a reservation at a restaurant that took his parents into account. At the least, Ezzie deserved his appreciation. Luke snagged her arm. "Can I talk to you for a second?"

"Um, yeah, I guess. Sure." She tucked a piece of mahogany hair behind her ear.

Probably should've thought this through more. Although he recognized the location, he hadn't put two and two together until they'd already arrived. Shoving one hand in the pocket of his slacks, Luke gripped the back of his neck. "Thank you for this. I know you probably went out of your way, but I mean it."

"Like I said. You deserve it."

"Not after the way I acted earlier." Bolting from the dorm room had been all about him. How could he tell her he wasn't good enough for her? Probably would help if he looked at her, but the dress she'd chosen did a number on him. A simple, sleek plum colored dress. It clung to her curves, but in a classy way. Then the heels that lengthened her already long legs. Those solid black pumps screamed *fuck me* in his ear, even if they hadn't to anyone else. The moment his gaze landed on her; she'd knocked him on his ass. And if he lifted his eyes to her now, he'd stare. No way to skirt around the truth.

"Just forget about it. We're here for dinner to celebrate. Can we focus on that?"

Forget about it? His eyes snapped to hers. Their beautiful sapphire-blue coloring had simmered. The sorrow in them had been caused by his hand. This was his fault and he'd do whatever was necessary to make it right. Without hesitation, Luke hugged Ezzie against his chest and wrapped his body around hers. He leaned close to her ear and whispered a heart-felt apology. "I'm sorry."

"I swear to God. If you make me cry Lucas Daniel Jonnihan, I will hit you."

"The full name, eh? I guess you mean business." He chuckled. The real smile he spotted on her face made the moment worth hanging up every fear he had about them. Stealing a quick peek through the window panes made it even better. No audience. He'd have to remember to thank his mother later.

Ezzie stepped out of his arms and quickly swiped at the corners of her eyes. "Come on. We should go inside before anyone pokes their head out."

"No worries. We've got all night. After all, it'll just be you and me tonight." Luke reached for the door and held it open. An unreadable expression crossed her delicate features as she brushed past him. What was that about? He'd make certain to ask later. His hand rested at the small of her back like it was second nature as he escorted her inside.

The door shut behind them and the maitre de stepped forward. With a slow bow, he presented an unlabeled envelope to Ezzie. "A message for you Miss Donovan."

"Thank you."

The polite smile returned to her face as she accepted the envelope. Not like she had to read the note inside. One other person beside her knew where she'd planned to take everyone and they'd helped her set it up.

Still, she'd read it because it was the right thing to do. Whatever. She had bigger fish to fry. Like, what the hell was up with Luke? He'd actually apologized. Truly apologized. What was she supposed to make of that? And that comment, about later? Then there was his hand on her back.

The maitre de nodded and gestured toward the dining area. "You're quite welcome. Now, if you will please follow me?"

"Of course." She glided across the floor. Surprisingly, the four-inch heels hadn't bothered her feet at all. The practice paid off. It had taken days for her feet to get accustomed to the damn things, but Matt had insisted. How many times had she strutted around the kitchen at his parents' house? The first few attempts had gone badly. She'd fallen on her ass and almost twisted her ankle.

Luke scooted past her and pulled a chair out for her right next to his mother. Ezzie scanned the table. No choice. Which meant she'd be seated beside Luke for the entire meal too. Great. Just freaking awesome. Keeping the polite smile on her face, she eased into the chair. She'd make them all think the seat suited her fine.

The rest of their group hardly acknowledged she and Luke had joined them. They'd all been so engrossed in conversation. Two could play that game. With her hands in her lap, she dug the note out of the envelope and quickly skimmed it. No reaction. She couldn't show any kind of reaction. Tucking the paper back in the envelope, she folded it and placed it under her leg.

Draping an arm on the back of her chair, Luke leaned in. "Who's it from?"

"My parents. They wanted me to tell everyone how much they wished they could be here and that tonight, dinner is on them."

Bold faced lie. Partly. The letter hadn't been from her parents. That part had been a lie. The rest had been true. Her friend and his parents had left the message and they were paying for dinner. She'd check with Matt later, but she suspected his reason for taking care of the bill had to do with her. She hated him and loved him for it too. Her credit card would've gotten hit pretty hard if she paid as she'd originally planned. Four hundred dollars was a stiff hit for anyone and that assumed no wine.

"That's nice of them."

Ezzie nodded. Thankfully the wait staff interrupted and relieved her of an unnecessary reply. One poured all but three of them a glass of wine. Another presented the first course. Four courses. She only had to survive four courses. For once, she wished she could drink. It might make the night go by easier.

Luke propped himself against the car. Cleaner than the building. Less likely he'd get dirt on his suit. He crossed one ankle over the other and folded his arms across his chest. A few feet away Ezzie and Nate had a semi-heated discussion. What the hell was it about? At no point had either of them gestured to him so it couldn't have had anything to do with what transpired that morning or before dinner. Their tones changed and Nate held his hand out. Ezzie handed her brother what he was pretty sure had to be the note she'd received on their way in.

Made sense. He'd figured it had been from someone other than whom she'd said. Dinner for eight at Terrapin had been way out of their parents' price range. That was before the wine had been served. Who could it have been from? Unfortunately, the two of them were too far away for him to hear what Nate uttered. Well, he had time alone with her. Talking about the letter would work as a good starting place. It could lead to a conversation about the kiss. Yeah, he had to not go there. Even thinking about it got him hard. Talking about it could be saved for another day. After all, his parents wouldn't be around and neither would Nate and Becca.

Ignoring Ezzie was out of the question. Being alone with her in any secluded room wasn't an option. He checked the front of his pants and reminded his dick it would stay put. There would be nowhere for it go this weekend. Given his current mood, he had one choice. Stay busy.

Where could they go tomorrow? Hmm. He hadn't been there in a while. And they had that food and wine of the world thing. She'd like that. Plus, roller-coasters. It could be fun. Something for both of them. Luke smiled as a plan formulated in his head.

Nate trekked across the parking lot in his direction. "Sorry about that. I just needed a few words with her."

"Sure thing, man. I understand. Don't worry. I'll take care of her tonight." He glimpsed at Ezzie. Yeah, she was a little teed off. Probably best he didn't take her straight back to the hotel. At least his parents had already jetted off for the jazz club.

"Thanks, I appreciate it."

Shoving his hands in his pockets, Luke nodded. "Go be with your girl. I got this covered."

"I owe you, big." The two of them exchanged a brief shake. Nate jogged to his car where his girlfriend and her parents waited. Quickly he climbed in, backed the car out, and took off.

Being alone with a pissed off—where the hell had she disappeared to? Hadn't she been standing on the other side of the lot? Damn it. Luke strode to the spot he'd last seen his best friend's sister. He scanned the immediate area. She'd marched down the sidewalk toward the boardwalk. Of course. Sighing, he chased after her. "Ezzie, wait up."

"Go away, Luke."

"Come on. Don't be like that." Though it really hadn't been necessary, Nate obviously chastised her. No reason for her to take her anger out on him. He hadn't done anything wrong.

Ezzie pivoted on her heel. "Like what? Exactly what am I being like?"

"I get it. You're upset with your brother, but that has nothing to do with me."

"That's what you think? Wow. And here I thought you couldn't be any more self-absorbed." She smirked, turned around and stormed off.

Frowning, he watched as she continued in her original direction. What the hell just happened? How had she managed to turn his choice of words back on him? Especially when all he referred to had been completely realistic. Her annoyance with her brother shouldn't have reflected or been used against him at all. Luke followed after her. "How am I self-absorbed?"

"Oh, I don't know. I mean, honestly, how could my frustration have anything to do with you? Right? It all has to be about my brother. Nate was being his normal over-bearing protective self, so it only makes sense my annoyance would be with him. Nothing to do with you."

"Okay. I might've been a little presumptuous. If that's not the case, mind clueing me in?"

"You apologized. For what? Kissing me or leaving?" Pausing mid-step, she spun on her heel and faced him.

His plan had just blown up in his face. What could he do now? Talk or run? Luke shoved one hand in his pocket and gripped the back of his neck with the other. Running sounded really good, but he was no coward. More time would've been preferred, but apparently that wasn't in the cards. "The last thing I want is for you to be unhappy. I'd be lying if I didn't say part of it was the kiss, but it was more because I hurt you. Leaving was best for both of us."

"Why?"

"Honestly, Nate would kick my ass if he'd caught us in that position." *And I'm no good for you.* Not that he'd admit it to her.

"That's not the entire truth. All of it or none of it."

What could he say? He had nothing. This had never happened before. In the last four years, he'd never once been speechless. Even if he'd lied his ass off, he'd always come up with something. That was the problem. He couldn't lie to her. She was different. Shaking her head, Ezzie stomped past him back toward the parking lot. It couldn't end like this. He had to say something, anything. But was honesty really best at the moment?

No, he wasn't going to say it. Was he?

Luke opened his mouth and the words flew out before he had a chance to swallow them. "You deserve better than me."

"What?"

She couldn't have heard him correctly. No way had he said she deserved better. No way had he thought that little of himself. Ezzie halted and glanced back at Luke. So much tension in his entire body, as if the words that had fallen from his lips had frozen him solid. How could he not know how great he was? How could he feel inadequate? Given all he'd accomplished in the last four years and the direction his life would go, it made no sense.

"I'm no good for you."

Shocked by his second statement, she gazed at his back in silence. He'd always seemed so collected to her, as if nothing in his world was out of sorts. He was a great guy; friendly, smart, sexy as hell. Plus, his parents were awesome. He had everything going for him. How could he think he wouldn't be good enough for her? Hesitantly, she closed the distance between them and navigated toward him. "I don't understand. How you can think that?"

"I told you the truth. Can we please just change the subject now?" His hands dropped to his waist and he peered out over the night sky.

From the brief glimpse she'd caught, there was shame in his dark-brown eyes. His refusal to look in her direction confirmed her thoughts; which confused her more than ever. She'd already tossed the seduction plan, but a new purpose filled her soul. For the next two days it would be her mission to prove to him how wonderful he was until he believed it. "Luke, please look at me."

"It's late. I should get you back." He moved to turn.

He easily had over a hundred pounds on her. And even if she planted her feet firmly on the ground, the heels would've resisted. She had to come up with something else and fast. Thinking quickly, she grabbed a hold of his hand and squeezed. "You always put others before yourself. Like tonight. Nate is out with his girlfriend and I bet you agreed to watch over me despite your own feelings. And your focus on school and the future is nothing to balk about. You're amazing. Maybe you don't see it, but I do."

"I also sleep around. I tell lies just to get women in bed. Is that the type of man you want?" Luke flipped his eyes to her.

His self-loathing went deeper than she suspected. But nothing could deter her. She'd been made aware of his reputation. It had been the one true thing Becca had really done for her. Ezzie frowned. "If you think telling me that is going to change my opinion of you, you're wrong. Maybe you lied to those women, but you've never lied to me."

"No. I haven't."

"Listen, we're obviously attracted to each other. Doesn't mean we can't be friends. We can do that, right? Hang out?" She hung out with Matt all the time. Okay, bad comparison. She had the wrong equipment for him to be intimately interested. There were other guys she'd spent time around. She could friend zone Luke. Letting go of his hand would be a good start. Forcing herself, Ezzie released her hold. An emotion of some kind flashed in his eyes. Disappointment? No. She had to be reading that wrong.

He half nodded. "Yeah, we can do that. But... you might have to lose some of your sex appeal."

"Umm, okay. I'm not exactly sure how I do that, but I can try. Hmm, let me think. I know. Maybe if I quack like a duck. Quack, quack, quack."

Shaking his head, Luke chuckled.

"No? Maybe if I cluck like a chicken. Brawwcckk. Brawwccckk." Ezzie tucked her hands in her armpits, jutted her chin forward and flapped her pretend wings. No one could see that as sexy, but that hadn't been her point. She wanted him to smile. Mission accomplished.

Busting out in a fit of laughter, he held onto his ribs and shook his head again. A slow grin crawled on his face. "Stop. You have to stop."

"You leave me with no alternative." Instead of cracking a joke, she navigated to the handrail and used it to steady herself. Lifting one foot, she proceeded to remove her heels.

Still grinning, he placed a hand on her arm and prevented her from losing a shoe. "I don't want you walking around here barefoot."

"That's good. I mean, it is a little too cold to run around without any shoes." A shiver crawled up her spine. Whether it was from his lingered touch or the slight breeze, she couldn't say for sure.

Hearing the word "cold" must've reminded him of where they stood. He reacted quickly. Being the gentleman, he was, Luke removed his jacket and draped it across her shoulders. "Oh, here."

"Thank you."

Ezzie wrapped his suit jacket around her body. She slipped her arms through the sleeves. Much better. The warmth felt good against her skin. Seriousness aside, she was glad they'd talked. She smiled at him.

He rubbed the back of his head. "You're welcome. Listen, I should probably get you back to your hotel."

"I wouldn't be a good friend if I let you drop me off knowing you weren't planning to go out and celebrate. Tell me you're going to a party after you take me back and we'll go." Not to mention she'd have to contend with his mother. Nope. No way she intended to deal with her wrath.

Sighing, he shoved his hands in his pockets. "I wasn't planning to go."

"Then I'm not ready to go back yet. Besides, I made a promise to your mother. And I always keep my word. Plus, we really should celebrate. So, how about a movie? I think *Insidious: Chapter 3* just came out. We can go see that?"

"You'd go see a horror movie?" Luke raised an eyebrow.

Ezzie canted her head and grinned. She headed toward the lot where the car awaited their company. "It's either that or *Ted* 2 and the first one sucked."

"What? You're insane. The first *Ted* was awesome." Luke hurried after her.

Three

"WE'VE GOT ABOUT AN HOUR before the movie starts. Let's see if we can find anything in the game room."

Luke stepped away from the ticket window and approached Ezzie. The game room had been the most logical place for them to kill time. They headed in together. Both surveyed the various games. Racing videogames, shooting videogames, ski ball. And? Their eyes landed on the pinball machines next to each other. He raised an eyebrow at her to see if she was up for it.

"It's been a while, but I'm certain I can still beat you."

Ha! She sounded rather confident she'd kick his ass. Pinball had been their go-to since the day they'd met. Maybe she'd won back then, but he'd been practicing. No way she'd beat him again. He smirked. "Only in your dreams."

"Then we must be in an alternate universe where reality and dreams are the same thing."

"Fine. Loser buys popcorn." Luke held out some change for Ezzie. He hadn't planned on making her pay, but she issued a challenge. And he happily accepted.

"You're on."

He eyed the machine's back-glass. Pirates and treasure. Not as if the story mattered much. The idea for every single pinball game was the same. Pull the plunger and control the ball for as many points as possible. Let the game begin. As soon as he let his ball go, he shifted his hands to the buttons on the sides. Bouncing the ball back and forth Luke quickly collected hundreds of points. Beside him Ezzie grunted a couple of times and muttered a few, "Yeahs," under her breath. How had she faired?

Stealing a sidelong glimpse, Luke checked out his competition. He intended to take a peek at her score. His eyes had other ideas in mind. Her mahogany, silky hair swung to and fro with each move she made. Wouldn't be hard to touch at this distance. The end of his jacket hung below her waist. It was so huge; it practically swallowed her. But the dark blue worked quite well with that plum dress of hers. He glanced back at the pinball machine in front of him. Ball one rolled down the middle and dropped into the hole at the bottom. *Shit!*

Distraction. She was a fucking distraction! He had to stay focused, otherwise he'd lose for sure. Determined to make a real go of it, Luke pulled the plunger and another ball flew into a maze of marks. Ready to garner some real points, he took hold of the buttons and worked through the second ball. The second ball dropped into the hole at the bottom. He chanced a glance at her points thus far. *Two hundred and fifty-six thousand! Fuck me!*

His points had barely jumped over a few thousand. *Damn.* One ball left. This had to count, though the likelihood of him catching up without some kind of bonus round or several was zilch. All because he had to look. If he paid enough attention to this ball, he could at least get something. He released the plunger and off the ball went.

"Come on, baby," Ezzie hollered at the machine.

What the hell? Ignore it. Ignore the curiosity. This was stupid. He shouldn't look, but he couldn't help himself. Luke stole another peek at Ezzie. His eyes picked up right where they'd left off and traveled past her waist. His coat hung below her ass, but he remembered how nicely that plum dress hugged her body. And those heels elongated her legs. Man, she was fucking hot. Tingles crawled up his spine. Afraid of getting caught, he forced his gaze back to the pinball machine and watched as the third ball dropped into the hole.

He hung his head. He'd been defeated. Even if she hadn't finished on her side, he had on his. No way this was over. As long as he kept his eyes on the prize. Not Ezzie. Why couldn't he stop looking at her? His attraction for her couldn't be stronger than he admitted. Friendship simply had to work with them. Luke peered at Ezzie as her game continued on. She'd earned a bonus round. Of course, she had. For tonight, he'd simply enjoy the movie and her company.

Tomorrow? Well tomorrow they'd spend part of the day in a place where no one knew him. A place where no one knew about his past. Where he could escape the man, he'd become. Where his past didn't define him. Where he could be someone else. He could be the man Ezzie deserved. Could he have a weekend like that? A weekend with her. Maybe. Just maybe. What would it be like if he tossed friendship out the window? Could they give it go? Could they pretend for a weekend?

"You can't be done already?"

With her by his side, yes, he could. He could even do so much more than lose a game quickly. No. He couldn't let it get physical. He could certainly be the man she deserved, but no way could he let it get physical. He'd have to keep his hands to himself. No problem. Provided she wore clothes that covered—everything, unlike the dress she had on. Absolutely had to get that out of his mind. Luke grinned. "Another round?"

"Only if you think you can handle losing again. Soda wager?"

"Flavor?"

"Of course." Ezzie laced her fingers behind her back and smiled.

For a smile like that, he'd do nearly anything, even if he only got to have her for the weekend. He could totally be unhinged for the weekend and be the man she deserved. "Game on."

Three games. She'd won every last one of them.

There hadn't really been anything to wager for the third pinball game or the zombie shooting game Luke insisted they play. Ezzie tossed a couple pieces of popcorn in her mouth to hide the smirk. That had been all about his pride. Wasn't hard to recognize. She beat him at that too. Strangely enough, he smiled the whole time she'd been kicking his ass, almost as if he enjoyed the losing streak.

She nearly asked why, several times, but they were having such a good time. After their serious talk on the boardwalk, all she wanted was for a little less weight on her shoulders. Not thinking about what waited on the other side of tonight, well, it helped. She'd hold off the questions for as long as possible. Ezzie pushed the inside button. The foot rest extended and she got comfortable in the luxury seating. The movie theaters at home certainly needed these things.

The previews started. Luke adjusted his seat and kicked back. She glimpsed at him out of the corner of her eye as he lounged in the chair. He looked good stretched out like that. Nice and relaxed. His suit had been chosen well. Even without the jacket, he was gorgeous. The whole friend's thing would be hard as hell, especially since they had half-acknowledged their mutual attraction for one another. Swallowing to wet her dry throat, Ezzie forced her eyes to the movie preview on the screen and dug into the bucket for more popcorn. A hand touched hers.

Oh shit! Cupping her hand around a couple pieces, she quickly yanked her hand back. They'd reached into the bucket simultaneously. Wasn't the damn thing supposed to be big enough for two hands without them getting in the way of each other? Crap. No way she'd successfully manage to friend zone him, not unless she avoided him. Strange turn of events. She hadn't expected to avoid Luke or that her plan of seduction would be officially out the window.

Finally, the movie came on the screen. If nothing else, it would distract her and keep her from staring at Luke too much. Exactly what she needed. "And cue scary music."

"Sshh." He tossed a couple pieces of popcorn at her.

Smirking, she threw popcorn back at him. Satisfied she got Luke back, Ezzie focused on the screen. Crows, really? A cliché right in the beginning. Oh, this was going to be good. Okay, a lady was heading inside. There are other people, yet nobody's talking. Keeping her voice low, Ezzie whispered. "They can't figure out who's supposed to speak next."

"Guess somebody forgot their line."

Ezzie giggled. Now, this would be fun if they both cracked jokes over the idiotic shit. There were only three other people in the theater besides them. Best way ever.

"She's hearing things. I think the old lady has lost her mind."

"Wait. I hear something too. I have to look." Ezzie snickered. Lay it all out. Be honest. But you know the only way the movie goes on—some dumbass has to ignore the warning. And then she climbs on shit? What the fuck? Really? Has this chick not ever seen a scary movie? Ezzie rolled her eyes. Of course not.

"Time for me to do something stupid."

Stupid? The epitome of a horror movie. Annoying brother? She understood that sentiment all too well. Except he wasn't younger. Still drove her insane. Scope the room; only way to learn anything about this girl. Dysfunctional family dynamic at work. Flock of birds? Twice in less than fifteen minutes. That's a new one. Elevator not functioning? Gee, shocker. Ezzie smirked. "Are we sure this is a scary movie?"

"I know; so many redundancies, one right after the other."

"If I don't see something freaky soon, I might have to protest." She stole a sidelong glimpse of Luke out of the corner of her eye. It was easy to crack jokes with him over the idiocy of a movie. Crikey, why was he so hell bent on this friend's thing?

Luke grabbed a handful of popcorn and raised an eyebrow. "Then you'd miss the insidious part."

"Lame." Really? He had cracked better zingers in the past. Ezzie snickered. He'd have to work to get back in her good graces.

"No?"

All she gave him in return was a silent glare. His response required as little acknowledgement as possible. Ezzie shifted her eyes to the screen. Somebody's waving. The chick is staring and ... she grabbed Luke's arm. "Oh shit."

"Death isn't an option here."

"Nope. Ladies and gents, I present to you our out-of-body experience. How else are we going to bring something bad back with us?" Ezzie grinned. The movie had finally begun to pick up.

"Remind me never to bring you to a horror movie again." A small smile played on Luke's lips. The words had come out of his mouth, but with no real sincerity.

She knew he'd absolutely enjoy another movie with her; horror or otherwise.

Man who can't breathe. Interesting. Ezzie peeked at her watch. About an eighth of the movie and they've discovered the freaky shit. Took long enough. Just in time to take five steps backward. "Come on, that's a total cliché."

"I'm watching you."

"Only because it's dark," Ezzie said.

Nothing good could happen unless all the lights had been out. Standard horror movie rule. Several applied to this movie, including a few things to make the main girl think she'd begun to lose her mind.

"She is trying to tell you something. You're stupid."

Ezzie covered her mouth and stifled a chuckle. Okay. She'd give him props. That was funny. Biting on her bottom lip, she glanced at Luke. His profile stood out against the light from the movie screen. He was more than a handsome face. He had a personality she liked. He'd been compassionate and sympathetic when she needed it most. Not to mention he genuinely cared about other people's happiness. How could he not see how great he was? Not wanting to get caught, she turned her gaze back to the movie. The psychic wasn't afraid of the villain? Ha! Challenge accepted. Where was he?

"I'm right above you."

"For once, I'd like to see them make a horror movie without clichés," Luke said.

"Don't think they can." Ezzie dug into the bucket of popcorn. Half way empty and they were about half way through the movie. Good. She hated when the bucket disappeared before the movie was over.

"They always have to look under the bed. Why?"

"Because stupidity is a requirement of a horror movie. At least now, it's bound to get freakier."

Just a matter of time. But what? Unanswered questions existed: the psychic, for example. Who had she been talking to in the beginning? The demon hadn't come into the picture yet. Something from her past. Maybe something dark from her past. She'd have to try again to help the girl. Hmm, still fifty some odd minutes left in the movie. Too soon for closure. Then what?

"You know what it is, don't you?" Luke asked.

"I may have an idea." Ezzie smiled.

Shaking his head, Luke lifted the soda they'd opted to share and sipped from his straw. "Never again."

"Should see me during a chick flick." Those were way more fun than a horror movie. Talk about unlimited puns. Especially a good one.

He sighed. "She's not going to help."

"Of course, she will, but first—bring on the amateurs."

"I'll admit it. The last forty minutes were the best part."

"I could tell. You grabbed my arm like five times."

Not as if he minded one bit. The feel of her fingers as they took a firm hold of him shot heat throughout his body. It made him grin every time it happened. Like winning the lottery. And he wanted more. More of her attention. More of her touch. More of her eyes on him. More of her smiles. More of her laughter. More of her words. More of her.

"But it took forever to get to the main part of the story."

"How else were they supposed to build it up?"

Ezzie rolled her eyes and groaned. "You're missing the point."

"Which is what? That the first hour of the movie provided the opportunity for several wisecrack remarks or that almost any movie has to shove a lot of information in a short amount of time?" Regardless of how she responded, he had a great time. He got a kick out of her jokes. Each certainly garnered a chuckle out of him. The night had been one he'd always remember. Had also been a great way to celebrate his graduation. He looked forward to more time of the two of them together over the weekend, starting with tomorrow morning.

"All of the above?"

Sounded like half an answer. Or a lack of one. Luke grinned widely. "Admit you had a good time and I'll say no more on the matter."

"Ugh! Fine! I had a good time. Happy?"

"Only because I know it's true."

They stopped outside the door to her hotel suite. Maybe his plan started this evening. He'd been a true gentleman and escorted Ezzie to her room, but he wouldn't stay. Hands off. At least he'd keep his hands to himself. Everything over the next two days had to be just them without adding the complication of sex. It wouldn't be easy, but it could be accomplished.

Removing the keycard from her evening bag, Ezzie beamed. "It is. But mostly because I kicked your ass."

"Rematch. Any day, any time."

"You're on. Now, as much as I'd love to revel in my glory a little longer, I'm exhausted. I shall bid you good night." She slid the keycard into the slot and pulled it out. A green light flashed on the door handle.

"Not so fast. Give me your phone."

"Excuse me?"

Holding out his hand, Luke offered no real response. His intentions would be revealed soon enough. At the moment, all she had to know was he required her cell phone. "Please."

"Care to explain why?" With a frustrated sigh, she dug her phone out of her purse and handed it over to him.

Accepting her phone into his hands, he accessed it. No lock code necessary. Unsafe. Who knew what kind of things she had stored on her cell? Left her wide open for anyone wanting to learn anything about her. He'd fret over it later. They had a whole hour in the morning to discuss the importance of a good lock feature. He typed out a quick text and shot it off. His phone dinged. Leaving the message out for her to see, Luke returned the phone to her. "Be ready to go at nine."

"You can't be serious." Ezzie's eyes widened.

Nine was pretty early. It was close to two in the morning. She wasn't going to like his reply, but they had to get a move on if they were going to get there when the place opened. His mind burped up a memory from last summer. Something about a punch from the gorgeous woman who stood before him. Luke backed up and stepped out of hitting range. "Read the message."

"Pain in my ass." Getting into her phone, she scanned the text and grinded her jaw.

"I promise it'll be worth it."

She opened the door and pointed a finger at his face. "Fine, but you owe me breakfast. And none of that skimpy egg white shit you eat. Real fucking carbs."

"Got it. Just make sure you're ready to go." He grinned, spun on his heel and waltzed down the hallway. The door slammed shut behind him. Nice. Stealing a quick peek, he ensured the door actually closed with her inside. It had. His phone dinged. Another message. He got his cell phone out of his pocket and entered his security code. Two text messages from an unknown number were front and center. Had to be from Ezzie's phone.

I'll have the following things ready in my backpack by 9am.

Change of clothes (including sneakers), sunscreen, sunglasses or hat, lip balm (with SPF), ID, & hair tie.

That had been the message he'd typed out.

Seriously!

Pain in my ass!

Luke busted out in laughter. Obviously that message had been issued from Ezzie herself. He pushed the button for the elevator and tapped out a reply. *Only in the best way possible.*

Had everything on the list been packed? Ezzie peered inside her backpack. T-shirt, shorts, socks, spare bra and panties, plus her tennis shoes. She only had one pair of sneakers and she was going to wear them. Sunscreen, check. Wallet with ID and credit card, check. Cell phone in her right back pocket. Sunglasses on the coffee table. Lip balm in her left front pocket. She'd already tossed her hair into a ponytail. Hmm; if he mentioned the hair tie, she may have to take it out at some point.

Poking her head around the corner, she snagged the hairbrush off the bathroom counter and threw it into the backpack. Now, she had it all put together. She zipped it up and traipsed into the living room. Her sneakers and socks had been left by the couch. Those would go on in a minute. Dropping her backpack on the floor, she trekked into the kitchen.

Based on his list, they'd likely be doing a lot of walking. Although he hadn't listed water amongst the items, it made sense to bring a couple of bottles along. If they never got used, then she could always return them to the refrigerator. She grabbed the bottles and set them on the kitchen counter. Fully prepared for their adventure, Ezzie headed toward the living room. Her stomach rumbled. Against her better judgment, she'd woken up an hour ago, but hadn't eaten a thing. Luke better arrive with food. The kind that had been suggested on his way to the elevator. Failure wasn't an option.

Knock! Knock! Knock!

Pausing mid-step, she pivoted on her heel and opened the door. A hint of a smile crept on Luke's lips. It was too early for him to be so damn chipper. Still her heart melted just a little at the sight of him and her eyes drank him up. How could he look so damn hot in a t-shirt and shorts? This really wasn't fair. Her gaze drifted down his chest to his abs to his... hands? Was that a Panera bag in his hands? Her stomach grumbled again. "I hope this means you're feeding me."

"Yep. You about ready?" He offered her the bag of goodies and entered the hotel suite.

Screw a vocal response. Food first. Pulling a freshly baked cheese soufflé out of the bag, she immediately took a bite and moaned. So good. To answer his question, she lifted her foot off the floor and wiggled her toes. Ezzie padded across the carpet into the living room and plopped down on the couch. "I just have to put my shoes on."

"Good. What about the checklist I sent you? Everything in your backpack ready to go?"

"All together."

She took another bite of the soufflé, picked up a piece of paper and handed it to him. The text had served its purpose, but she felt better having a transcribed copy of his list. It also gave her amicable room to add anything else she could think of. All she'd scribbled down had been the bottles of water. Seemed as if he'd covered everything else. At least without her knowing exactly where they were going. She tugged on a sneaker.

"Two bottles of water?"

Ezzie gestured to the bottles she'd left out on the kitchen counter. "I figured we'd need them."

"Why two?" His eyes lifted from the paper in his hand to the bottles on the counter and back to her.

What a strange question. There were two of them. Logically the response made sense, but had he not understood that? She glanced over her shoulder and stared at Luke. No playfulness in his eyes. Had he never had someone think of him before? Turning away, she tugged on her other sneaker. "One for each of us. Hydration is important."

"Good point." He gathered her backpack off the floor and slipped the strap over his shoulder.

No explanation would be given. Right. She'd give him this one. But it would be nice to break through some part of his exterior wall. One conversation at a time. At some point, they would get there. For now, she'd let it go. Sneakers in place, she hopped to her feet with the food bag in hand.

Ezzie waggled her eyebrows. "Does this mean you'll tell me where we're going?"

"It's a surprise."

"Aww, come on. Not even a hint?"

Lacing her fingers in one another, she batted her eyelashes at him. The trick had worked on nearly every guy she knew: her father, brother, and a couple of her ex-boyfriends. Only guy who'd never fallen for it—Matt.

"Nope. Now grab the waters and your key. We have to go."

And Luke made two. Ezzie smirked. She tucked her room key into the back pocket of her denim shorts, opposite from her cell phone. Holding tight to the bag with her bagel she collected both bottles of water and held them in the crook of her arm. "Ugh. Pain in my ass."

"So, you keep reminding me." Grinning like a Cheshire cat, he grabbed her hand and they walked out of the hotel suite together.

Busch Gardens had been the right choice. Ezzie's eyes had been glued to the window the moment the rollercoasters came into view. Her smile brightened the closer they got to the entrance. He'd prepared his own backpack, as well as downloaded the app to his phone earlier that morning. Although he'd decided to let her choose their initial direction, it never hurt to have access to a map of the place. Despite the fact he'd lived in Virginia Beach for four years now, he'd actually never driven the hour to Williamsburg and visited Busch Gardens. It would be a first for him too.

His timing had also been rather well planned. It was the last weekend of the Food and Wine Festival, an event Ezzie would surely love, given her talent to make a meal out of almost anything. She was quite gifted. She'd never cooked for him directly, but he'd tasted the artwork she'd created from the leftovers Nate had around the room on occasion. There had been last year on the vacation their families had taken together, but she'd made the meal and dessert for all of them. Still, she'd enjoy the various foods they'd get to try from other countries.

They pushed through the turnstiles and headed into the park. Shops to the right. Theater to the left. In the middle, a Big Ben replica towered over them. Ezzie rushed over to the clock and lifted her eyes all the way to the top. Luke stopped behind her. It was a rather amazing sight. Almost as if they were actually in England.

"Thank you! This is awesome!" Her entire face lit up. She threw her arms around his neck and hugged him tightly.

Caught off guard by her reaction, he hesitated to return the hug. He vowed to keep his hands off, but if he wrapped his arms around her waist, would it really be breaking that rule? His body responded before his mind actually realized a decision had been made. It wasn't sex, but it was just as dangerous. Way more intimate. Forcing his arms to break their hold, Luke cleared his throat. "You're welcome, but you haven't seen anything yet."

"Yeah, but I'll never forget this." She kissed him on the cheek. Releasing her hold, she dropped to her feet and gazed at him. Tearing her eyes away from his face, she bit on her bottom lip.

Heat licked up the back of his spine. God, she had to stop that. Otherwise, he'd never stick to his vow. Luke massaged the back of his neck to release some of the tension. *Focus, asshole. Focus.* "So, umm, what country should we start in?"

"Here, or we could go see Ireland. Or head to Scotland. Ooh, or what if we went to France? Or maybe..." Ezzie dug her cell phone out of her back pocket. A woman after his own heart. She'd spent the drive to the parking lot downloading the app too.

They had a lot of options, but only a certain amount of time to get all they could in. He glanced at the Rolex on his right wrist. Five hours, forty-seven minutes and counting. His mother had made reservations for the four of them. Not that she'd gone into details. All he knew was they had to be back to the hotel by five, which meant they had to leave Busch Gardens by four. Shifting his gaze back to Ezzie, Luke took in the sight of her.

She stared at her phone as if it were a lifeline. Her sapphire-blue eyes flitted back and forth across the map. The wheels in her brain obviously turned over every choice they had. A finger slid to the corner of her mouth. Was she even aware of the action? Such a small nuance, but it stood out, probably because after several seconds, the same finger danced across her bottom lip. It reminded him of how sweet her lips tasted, made him want to kiss her again.

Luke shoved his hands in the front pockets of his shorts and looked away. Now was not the time to think about that. He had to get that moment of weakness out of his head. It simply couldn't happen again. "Or?"

"I got it. We'll hit the shops in England. Candies are a must! Then we can head to Scotland, check out the Clydesdales and take a ride on the Loch Ness. After, we'll head off to France for some food tasting, then more rollercoasters in Germany."

"Sure you haven't been here before?"

"Positive. I'm just good at organization. Now, let's not waste any time."

"No arguments here." Luke grabbed her hand. His brain half registered the action, but her hand easily settled in his and they strolled together toward the land of sweets.

"Would you two like your picture taken?"

After the Clydesdales and a rollercoaster in Scotland, Ezzie and Luke had trekked over to France for another rollercoaster and some Creamery De Chocolat. Best ice-cream sundae she'd ever tried. Real coco made a huge difference. Then they'd popped into Trappers Smokehouse, Candle Carvers and hitched a ride on Le Scoot in New France. Followed by two more rollercoasters and shopping in Germany. They'd stopped for Pretzels and Beer. Well, Luke had the beer, she had the pretzels.

From there they'd taken the sky ride back over to England and walked to Italy. Their first ride had been a water ride, where they'd both gotten dutifully wet. Thus, the reason they waited on the bridge. Hopefully their clothes would dry a little. She hadn't purchased photographs at every single ride; just most of them, all of which were in her backpack in the locker she'd gotten prior to the water ride. Ezzie glanced at Luke. As far as she was concerned, they could never have too many pictures. Maybe he was tired of them.

"I'm game. You?"

"Sure, but we may want to wait a minute. I think the boat's about to—" His statement hadn't needed to be finished. The ride they'd gotten off of a few minutes ago made another huge splash. Water swooshed up and soaked them all over again.

The timing was impeccable. Ezzie laughed and shook water from her arms. "I'm beginning to think we were doomed to get drenched."

"What happened to a little water never hurt anyone?"

"I said a little!"

Nothing little about this. She'd convinced him to go on the ride. Hadn't water rides been the entire reason for a set of back-up clothes? If not, then they had to be doing something wrong. Her intention had been for them to hit another water ride too. At this rate, they'd never make it, not if they wanted to hit The Battering Ram and two other rollercoasters in Italy. Plus, they still had a few others to find gifts for.

No matter. They'd gotten wet enough from this ride to make up for the ones they'd miss. If they planned to hit at least the two rollercoasters, they'd both have to change. Ezzie rung out the bottom of her t-shirt and lifted her gaze to Luke. There was that look again. The one that warmed her up from the inside out. Fire replaced the butterflies in her stomach. Almost like a volcano burned with only one outlet for eruption. She swallowed. He had to stop eyeing her like a piece of meat, otherwise the whole friend zone thing would never happen.

Luke brushed her wet hair from her face and tucked it behind her ear. He caressed her cheek. His brown eyes darkened. Inching closer, he leaned down toward her. *Click. Click. Click.* Quickly straightening his spine, he eyeballed the cameraman he'd apparently forgotten had stopped.

The park employee smiled as if nothing happened. "You two make such a good-looking couple."

"We're not—"

"Thanks."

Before Luke could even finish his statement, Ezzie crossed over to the camera guy, accepted the paper card for their pictures and headed for the lockers. Changing clothes seemed like a good excuse to get the hell away from Luke for a few minutes. This back and forth from him was driving her nuts. One minute he's acting like a doting boyfriend, the next he's distancing himself from her. What the hell was going on with him?

Luke chased after her. "Ezzie, wait, I—"

"I'm fine. I'm going to change." Hopefully he accepted the first two words she'd muttered, even if she wasn't fine or even okay. There was still time left and she refused to spoil what remained of their day together.

"Ezzie, come on. I—"

She pivoted on her heel and smiled as sincerely at him as she could muster. Unfortunately, her fake smile didn't work on him last night, so it probably wouldn't work now. "I promise, I'm okay. I just want to get out of these wet clothes."

"Are you sure that's it?"

"Yes." She couldn't make it any clearer. Even if she wasn't okay, the subject was off limits. This way they could go back to enjoying their time at the park.

He sighed. "Okay."

"Umm..."

After their last picture incident, part of him wanted to say no. Even if he liked the idea. Caricature artists always made their subjects look cartoony. He peered at the beautiful woman standing next to him. Ezzie had the best smile and didn't care if it was goofy. Maybe he shouldn't either. And if he agreed to her request, he could have a moment of them together provided she wouldn't push him away. And he'd be less likely to attempt to kiss her this time.

Taking encouragement in her smile, Luke nodded. He laced his fingers through hers and they trekked the short distance to the artist. One stool. Hmm. Okay, maybe he wouldn't kiss her, but he certainly wanted a picture of them together. They set their bags down and he handed two twenties over to the attendant. Nodding to the artist, he hopped up in the chair and wrapped his arms around Ezzie's waist. "Two pictures. Nothing silly."

"Oh, come on. It's no fun if it isn't silly." Ezzie shifted in his arms and peered over her shoulder at him.

He wanted something iconic. A piece to represent what could be. Man, he enjoyed being the man she deserved way too much. How many times had he almost kissed her? A few. In front of the water ride. The store where her face lit up as her eyes landed on a handmade tiger lily pendant necklace. Again, when he'd draped the necklace around her neck. Then the cannoli they'd shared not five minutes ago.

Luke lowered his lids and dropped his gaze from the sparkle in her eyes to her lips. Tingles trickled down his spine. Damn it. The desire to kiss her again burned through his belly and stopped in his pelvis. This had to stop. Lifting his chin a little, he swallowed. He had to keep his mouth to himself. All he had to do was focus. "One playful, but serious. One goofy.

Acceptable?"

"Yes, but only if I get to pick the second pose."

"Are you always this difficult?"

"Only to those I like." Ezzie smirked.

The comment shouldn't have pleased him the way it had, but it touched him in places he didn't expect. Tightening his grip around her waist, Luke nuzzled Ezzie's neck. "Then I'm glad I'm one of them."

"Me too."

four

"WE'LL MEET DOWNSTAIRS IN AN hour."

"An hour."

With a quick nod, Ezzie unlocked the door to her hotel suite and disappeared inside. Luke's mother texted her on their way back from Busch Gardens and mentioned something about attire delivered to her room. What had Luke's mother sent up? And where the hell were the four of them going in an hour? Neither Luke nor his mother would tell her anything. His mother's response she'd expected, but not his. Then again, he hadn't told her where he'd intended to take her that morning either. What was with the Jonnihan family and surprises?

Scanning the room, she set her bags down on the kitchen counter. Her eyes landed on the two boxes stacked on the coffee table. The bottom box was big and long, maybe the size of a dress? The top box was small and wide. About the size of shoes? Oh boy. Ezzie swallowed and inched toward the boxes. It wasn't like they'd explode or anything, but whatever lay inside could be just as risky.

She wrung her fingers together and eased forward. The boxes were within arm's reach. If she stayed right where she stood, then she'd never have to open them. Her back pocket vibrated and she jumped. *Shit.* It was just her phone. Ezzie dug it out and peeked at the screen.

Downstairs. One hour.

Squinting her eyes at the door, she scowled. Luke had probably left, but in case he hadn't, he deserved to know how much of an ass he'd been for shooting her that text. "Oh, for crying out loud. Go away."

Tightening her grip on her cell phone, she closed the distance between her and the boxes. Best to get it over with, especially as it appeared there'd be no backing out. Damn him. And his mother. She was making way too big a deal out of this. She wasn't one to run scared. Groaning, Ezzie set her cell on the coffee table beside the boxes and lifted the lid to the smaller box. "Holy shit."

Her knowledge of fashion was practically non-existent. She'd never shared her best friend's talent for recognizing a designer on the spot. But when a gorgeous pair of sparkly, silver, four-inch heels stared you in the face with LouBoutin clearly signed in the sole of the shoe, no way to deny the truth. Amazing. If the shoes were spot on designer, then what the hell had Luke's mother sent for clothes? And how much had been spent on everything? Shaking the outrageous amount of money out of her head, she set the shoe box aside and hesitantly lifted the lid for the larger box.

"Oh my." Certainly explained the shoes. Her jaw slackened and she openly gawked at the beauty laid out before her: a perfectly exquisite halter style blue dress with leaf embellishments around the neck and along the sides. Wow. Talk about designer. She had to take a picture, otherwise Matt might not believe her. Ezzie snagged her cell and accessed the camera application. She snapped a quick photograph and texted it to her best friend.

Not a minute later her cell phone belted out *"Born This Way."* She didn't need to check the ID to see who called. Matt and Lady Gaga went together like peanut butter and jelly. A response wasn't required. Besides, he should've been busy scoping out the local hangouts. Ezzie answered the call. She opened her mouth and Matt spoke right over her.

"You have a Cavalli. I'm dying right now. How do you have a Roberto

Cavalli gown?"

Greetings were highly overrated anyway. Not as if they had to say hi. It was the luxury of knowing one another for as long as they had. Any form of "hi" was no longer a necessity. All he cared about was the damn dress. She smirked. "Luke's mom. They're taking me ... well, I have no idea where they're taking me."

"A surprise outing? And his parents are going? How did that happen?"

"Fuck if I know." The harsh words were uncalled for, but they'd come out before she had the chance to stop them. Maybe she shouldn't go this evening. Even though the dress was absolutely stunning, she'd be awful company.

Matt hissed. "Put the cat claws away. Why are you so grumpy? I thought getting laid was supposed to relax you."

"We haven't slept together. We just ... we agreed to be friends."

And therein laid the problem. Yeah, she'd mumbled the words and made the statement, but she hated every single part of it. Then Luke goes and does something nice like Busch Gardens. Not only had he taken her to some place she'd wanted to go, but he'd acted like the world's greatest boyfriend all day long.

"Wait, wait, wait. Has he seen you in the dress?"

"No. We talked after dinner last night and I kind of nixed the plan. I told him we could be friends, but he took me to Busch Gardens today. It was amazing! The most fun I've had in forever. And it was almost as if we were a real couple. He almost kissed me again nearly four times, but he kept stopping. I thought the friend's thing would be an opening or maybe I could figure out how to not be attracted to him, but then he does something wonderful. I don't know what to do, Matt."

Silence. Absolute silence. Great. She actually asked for some advice and he had nothing. No, wait; his heavy breaths tickled her ear. He had something. Annoyance. "I'm not exactly sure where to start." He paused. "Wait. What do you mean 'kissed again'? And Busch Gardens? Are you shitting me?"

"We might've kissed yesterday in the dorm room."

Whoops. Right, she hadn't mentioned that little incident to him. Fact was, she hadn't spoken with Matt in over twenty-four hours. Okay. He had every right to be a little upset with her. They told each other everything. Hell, he knew when she'd lost her virginity. Not a road of memories she wanted to travel down.

"We'll discuss this. Not right now because you have an evening to get ready for. Here's what you're going to do. You're going to shimmy your little ass in that dress and ... shoes, I'm assuming there's shoes."

"Yeah. LouBoutin."

Matt's cell phone protested in her ear with several loud bleeps. He must've hit some buttons. Sounded like the bleeps producers used when trying to cover up cuss words. A few tap, tap, taps replaced the noise. What was he texting her? "I truly hate you right now. I sent you a picture. The updo Kristen Stewart has will be adorbs on you."

"I'm not sure which is worse. That you used the word adorbs or that you combined it with Kristen Stewart." She ignored the comment about hating her. He didn't mean it. Ezzie eyed the dress and shoes. Then again, maybe he really did. Nah.

"Shut up. You know you belong to the fandom."

"In whose dreams?" She let Matt ramble on for a minute about the fandom crap. Not as if she actually listened to anything he muttered. Carefully, she removed the dress from the box. Time was rapidly ticking away. Ten minutes had been killed with her best friend, but she was glad she'd texted him the picture. Walking toward the bedroom, she turned the dress around and her jaw dropped open. The grip on her phone loosened and it nearly fell from her hand. Two straps from the halter crisscrossed in the back. "Holy shit! There's no back to this dress!"

"Just use the bra we got to go with the black number."

"Ugh. I hate that thing." It wasn't even a bra. It was two black cups that taped to the sides of her breasts. If she'd picked up on more of the girly things, maybe she could've selected her own dress.

"Yeah, but honey you're too busty to go without one."

Damn D cups. Not only had she gotten her mother's round hips, but she'd inherited her chest too. Stupid genes. Maybe in this case she could blame Luke's mother. She had been the one who'd decided on this dress.

"You'd think Luke's mom would've taken that into account when choosing this dress."

"She probably thought you were a girl and would know these things."

"Except I'm not! I don't know jack about designer shit. Even girly crap. It's what I have you for."

Not as if any of that mattered now. She had the dress and the shoes and everything else, well, she'd suck it up. Ezzie draped the dress across the bed and shucked her tennis shoes.

"Don't I know it. Remind me, how are we friends again?" he joked. And that was a good thing.

Neither of them could forget the day she'd rescued him. "Because I'm your knight in shining armor."

"Right. About that?"

"Are you telling me I've been replaced?" Ezzie gasped in mock horror.

Matt had met *the one* seven times since freshman year. His longest relationship lasted three months. She'd held out hope for his last boyfriend. He could've turned out to be the one, until shit hit the fan and the relationship blew up.

"Possibly."

One-word answer. Nope. Not the one. Still, it felt good to jest with her best friend about the possibility of a relationship. "It's official. I think I might hate Los Angeles."

"Whatever. Go get in the shower. You need to get dressed. And wear a thong."

"I'm really beginning to despise you." Ezzie groaned and against her better judgment retrieved the items she required for the monstrosity on her bed. First, the backless bra with minimal support. Now the piece of floss to ride up her ass. What was next? Right. The hair. Shit! The hair. She shifted the phone from her ear, put it on speaker and checked the picture Matt had texted her.

"No, you don't. You love me. Now go."

Wisps of hair around the face. Easy enough. Braid around the crown. A little more difficult, but manageable. No, wait. It went around to the back of the head and meshed into a bun. No way! "Fine. Umm, you're going to walk me through this updo? Right?"

"Okay, but you'll have to FaceTime me. And promise me no more ass shots."

"FaceTime, yes. Ass shots, no promises. I mean, come on, it's a nice ass." She giggled. The memory of their last FaceTime attempt flooded her brain. He'd told her to wear a thong then too. And he'd seen more of her ass than her face. That had been fun.

"Doesn't mean I want to see it."

Smiling, she headed into the bathroom and got the shower running. How much time left? Forty-five minutes. She could get ready to go in that time frame. "Yeah, yeah, yeah. Wrong tree and shit."

"And don't you forget it."

"Whatever. I'm getting in the shower now."

His fingers laced at the small of his back, Luke paced in front of the elevator. He'd given her a full hour. It should've been enough time. He glanced at the Rolex on his wrist. Ten minutes past six. Where the hell was she? What could be taking so long? The dress couldn't have been that difficult. Yes, she wasn't very girly, but it was one of the things he found attractive about her. Damn it! He had to stop that.

This was his problem. His mother had sworn the dress she'd selected was suitable for the evening's festivities, but elegant. Really all she had to tell him was the dress covered everything. Her perfectly round ass. The swell of her breasts. Her exquisite back. How many times had he almost kissed her during the day? Too many. Way more close calls than he planned. If she showed up in some dazzling number, he was done for.

Two more minutes. Ezzie had two more minutes and he'd go upstairs to check on her. Then he'd at least get to see what kind of night he was going to have. Luke tugged on the cuffs of his tuxedo.

"Stop fidgeting. She'll be down shortly." His mother squeezed his arm.

His mother had always been able to see right through him. Too bad she had no clue what caused those little ticks at that very moment. He opened his mouth to inquire once again about the attire chosen and the elevator dinged. The doors parted. Ho-ly shit. He was in trouble. Deep, deep uncontrollable trouble. Luke swallowed to wet his parched throat.

Holding a silver studded clutch, Ezzie stepped out of the elevator. "Hope I'm not too late."

"Not at all my dear. You look absolutely gorgeous." His mother grabbed a hold of Ezzie's hands and placed a tender kiss on her cheek.

"Thank you, but I owe it to you. This dress; I mean, wow."

"Oh posh. It was obviously meant for you. Now, shall we go? I do believe our car awaits."

Luke's father offered his arm to his mother and the two glided toward the doors. Left alone with Ezzie, he adjusted his bow tie. It was all he could do not to stare. Talk about a masterpiece. The blue in the dress matched the color of her eyes perfectly. As his mother had commented, it was almost as if the dress had been designed specifically for her. Straps crisscrossed in the back and hung just above the top of her hips. It clung to her body splendidly and revealed every natural curve as if it had been intended.

Although he couldn't see the tattoo, it wouldn't be hard to find. He'd only have to slide the straps to the sides and watch the dress pool at her feet. Not the place or time to think about what little she had on underneath.

He offered his arm to Ezzie. "You're stunning."

"Thank you." Her lips formed a bright smile and she hooked her arm into his.

"No sarcastic response? Or witty comeback?"

"What? I can't accept a genuine compliment without one?"

A broad grin crossed his lips and he raised an eyebrow. "Who said it was genuine?"

"The look on your face gave you away. No way to hide it." Her cheeks tinged a touch of pink. The color complimented what little make-up she'd put on her face for the night's festivities. Not as if she ever needed a whole lot of anything. It simply made her natural beauty stand out.

"You two make a beautiful couple. Would you like a picture for the evening?"

Pretend or not? The word snapped him back to reality. Luke regarded the member of the hotel staff who'd paused in front of them. "We're not—"

"Thank you, but no." Ezzie interrupted the truth he'd been prepared to admit.

"Of course." The staff member nodded and walked away.

The same fake smile Ezzie plastered the night before at dinner appeared on her face once again; she returned the nod and slid her arm from Luke's elbow. Sometimes all one had to go out on was pretend, but she hadn't been required to be lady-like enough to stay hooked to his side. Date or not. She brushed the skirting of her dress down, not as if it had been necessary. But she didn't need to see another empty apology spread across his face. "Come on. Your parents are waiting. We should go."

"Hey. You okay?"

"Perfectly fine." Why wouldn't she be? It hadn't been like he'd reminded her every time she'd turned around; they weren't a couple. Or every time somebody accidentally mistook the two of them for a couple. It had been two days and she'd grown tired fairly quickly of his innate ability to defend their lack of a relationship. He'd painted the picture quite clearly. She strode forward. They had to get a move on.

Luke grabbed the crook of her elbow and prevented her from getting further than a few steps. "That's bullshit and you know it. Now, what gives?"

"Next time, just say no thank you."

"Excuse me?"

"You don't have to advertise you and I aren't together. Just say no to the picture. Satisfied?"

There. She'd explained it all. It hadn't exactly covered her frustrations for the day, but the energy required for that conversation had already diminished. Never had one man gone back and forth so much over an attraction to her. He fought his feelings more than anyone she'd ever met. And she couldn't keep up.

"Listen, I'm—"

"Can we just not? Your parents are waiting. Really, I'd just like to go."

Dropping his gaze to the floor, he shoved his hands in the pockets of his tuxedo pants. "Yeah."

"Thank you." The same two words that had started their conversation. Funny how things always returned where you least expected. For a moment, a brief moment, she almost believed the night would be special. Then she got reminded of the position he'd branded on the two of them. Friends. Man, she loathed that word.

Putting on a happy face, Ezzie headed for whatever event awaited them for the evening. Just a couple more days to survive and then she'd be going home. A town where Luke wouldn't be.

A place she'd give anything to be close to at that moment.

Shoving his hands in the pockets of his slacks, Luke stared at Ezzie's back. Part of him wanted to go up and wrap his arms around her waist and the other part wanted to drape his jacket over her shoulders. His mother had picked up one hell of a dress. He loved and hated it at the same time. How long did it take to pull a limo around front? Dinner had taken less time than this.

God, he wished he'd pressed his mother for more details over the night's outings. Then maybe he could forget all about dinner.

Their dinner reservation had been at one of the most exclusive restaurants in town. His mother had a knack for swinging last minute tables where no one else could.

A massive chandelier hung center stage from a high-top ceiling. Beautiful paintings covered the ceiling from the top of the walls and converged into one complete piece of work at the tip of the chandelier. Large white candles had been placed atop lace table-clothes at each table. The romantic restaurant hadn't been on his radar. Probably why, even though it suited his mother's taste, he'd avoided the more high-end eateries in town. His mother had gone so far as to order a bottle of Marilyn Monroe Merlot 1987 for the table.

Luke stretched out slightly in the leather-bound chair. Light from the candle's flames danced beautifully along Ezzie's cheekbone and highlighted the natural hues of pink he'd spotted earlier. It had been so unusual for her to blush, but it had been perfect.

"Esmeralda, I understand you were accepted into the University of Southern California. I believe congratulations are in order." His mother lifted her glass of wine.

Ezzie's cheeks tinged a soft pink. "Yes, thank you, I was. I start in the fall, but I'll probably head up a few weeks before classes begin. Get settled and everything."

"Wait. What?" He shot up ramrod straight and knocked over the glass of untouched red wine in front of him.

"Lucas!" His mother chastised.

It hadn't been one of his better moments. Luke eyed the time on his Rolex. Hopefully whatever the second half of the night entailed didn't require their presence at a specific time. Though maybe this was the perfect opportunity to discuss the whole college thing. In fact, it was the perfect time. He saddled up beside Ezzie. "I need to speak with you privately."

"What do we have to talk about?"

"Southern California." It crossed his mind to wait until they had privacy later, but his lack of self-control had to be considered. Luke snagged a hold of Ezzie's elbow and escorted her out of immediate earshot of his parents.

Keeping her voice low, she yanked her arm from his grip. "Are you freaking kidding me?"

"Not about this."

"Then exactly what is there to discuss? SoCal happens to be a good school."

"I'm not saying it isn't."

His reaction had nothing to do with the school and everything to do with the location. She'd be two states further away from him, at least another five hundred miles in distance. She'd be there alone. Luke shoved one hand in the pocket of his pants and gripped the back of his neck with the other. Not like he could explain his feelings to her. He'd demanded friendship. She'd already given him the cold shoulder on the way to the restaurant. If he opened his mouth, would he only make things worse? "I just don't like the idea of you there by yourself in an unsafe area."

Ezzie narrowed her eyes at him and glowered. She folded her arms across her chest. "Number one, not that it's any of your business, but I won't be by myself. A friend of mine got accepted too and we'll be living together. Number two, I'm a grown ass woman and I can do what I want."

"Yeah, and two women is better than one." Luke snickered. Damn it. He didn't intend to sound misogynistic. If he'd been any other guy and he'd heard those words uttered, he'd have kicked their ass. There'd never been a reason for him to not trust Ezzie or her judgment. But he'd been unprepared for her to be so far out of reach.

Not nearly as close as she stood right then. Draped in an exquisite gown that hugged every curve. His mother may have selected the number because the blue matched the sparkle in Ezzie's eyes, but he enjoyed it for other reasons. Even angry, she was sexy as hell, especially with her arms across her chest and her breasts at full attention. Luke swallowed. He had to focus. Too bad his eyes had other plans and wandered down the full length of her body.

"You're damn lucky because if your parents weren't around the corner, I'd slap you for a comment like that. And not that it makes a difference, but it's a man, not a woman."

Another man? Oh, because that's so much fucking better. Shut up, nimrod. Biting his tongue, Luke kept his mouth closed and swallowed the words he desperately wanted to scream from the top of his lungs. He hated the entire situation. Every single thing about it. From the asshole she planned to live with to the school she intended to go to. All these decisions and not once had she bothered to consult his opinion. Not as if he'd ever given her a reason. His gaze shifted from the glare in her blue eyes and paused on her collarbone. His eyes lingered on the slight hitch in her chest and continued their trail to her hips, then ended on the floor. Flashes of her and another man cracking jokes about a lame horror movie popped into his head. Nope, he couldn't let it go. A low growl rumbled from deep within. "I like that even less."

"You don't get a say in the matter. As you've pointed out repeatedly, you *aren't* my boyfriend." Ezzie pivoted on her heel and stormed off in the direction of the door.

Her words socked him in the gut like someone sucker-punched him and knocked all the wind out of his lungs. The clicks of her high-heels against the wooden floor resonated in his heart and widened the wound she'd inflicted upon him—even if she'd only used his words against him. To hear her throw the comment out there suggested nothing more than a common cold. An annoyance. Luke rubbed the center of his chest. His day of pretend hadn't gone so well.

And the night had only begun.

The entire day had to be a dream—or an endless nightmare. Ezzie couldn't quite figure out which. A culmination of everything she couldn't have. Throughout the day, Luke almost acted like a real boyfriend. Even after dinner, he'd gotten upset with her over not consulting him about school and her choice of roommate. Though his assumption about her future roommate's sexual orientation hadn't been accurate, she didn't correct him either. Not to mention the theater and how helpful he'd been when they took their seats, or the conversation at the play's intermission. The closest thing she'd gotten to a Broadway musical and he acted genuinely interested in her thoughts.

As the last scene concluded, Ezzie peeked at the man who'd sat beside her during the play. *How could he play the part of a boyfriend, but not want to be my boyfriend?* Nothing about his actions made any sense. Returning her attention to the front, she clapped along with everyone else. The lights in the theatre came up as the last of the cast executed their bows. Ezzie stood. Luke's hand landed on her arm to help her to her feet. Without waiting, she yanked her arm from his grip and glided past the empty seats. Maybe she couldn't leave the theatre entirely, but she could escape her pretend suitor.

She could use the bathroom to compose herself for the quiet trip home. Love stories never played out in the real world like they always had in fiction. Ezzie slipped into the ladies' room and paused in front of one of the mirrors. Staring at her reflection, she surveyed the blue dress and the way it hung on her body. She didn't really notice it before they'd left. How could she have missed the part she played all night? Was she supposed to have been the doting girlfriend? Or had the dress merely been a device that failed in its purpose? She'd rip the thing off if she had something else besides a bra and thong on beneath it.

"Is all well, my dear?"

Dropping her gaze from her reflection, she glanced out of her periphery at Luke's mother. Of course, she'd been followed. Ezzie stepped away from the mirror and sat on one of the tiny couches. "Why'd you bring me here tonight?"

"Have you not enjoyed yourself?" Luke's mother settled on the couch beside her and crossed one leg over the other.

"Everything has been wonderful. I just don't understand why you brought me here tonight."

"You believe I had an ulterior motive other than ensuring you had a good time."

Although she didn't indicate the statement as a question, Ezzie nodded. It was the truth. Nothing else made sense. They'd been shopping together in the past. Luke's mother had seen the clothes she tended to wear. The dress. The shoes. The restaurant. The play. None of it had been selected by pure accident.

"You're a smart young woman. I've always liked you. The way you've grown and matured, you're correct. There is an ulterior motive. I tried to be patient and see if the two of you would come together on your own, but that doesn't seem to be in the cards."

"Please, please tell me I'm not hearing this." Her one hope for the weekend had been for her and Luke to have been given a chance, for him to see her as more than Nate's little sister. Now that she decided to give him up, it turned out his mother hoped for the same thing.

"I've seen the way you look at Lucas and the way he looks at you. I'd be lying if I told you I hadn't hoped the two of you would come together."

Ezzie lifted a hand and stopped Luke's mother before she could say another word. She stood and walked back over to the mirror. "It's not going to happen. Even if he looks at me a certain way, he doesn't think he's good enough. And I'm tired of trying to change his mind. It's breaking my heart, but ... I need to let him go."

"My dear Esmeralda, please do not give up on him. I'm certain if anyone could make him see the truth, it would be you."

"And what's that? Because I don't even know anymore."

"That you and my son belong together." Luke's mother rose to her feet and emphasized each word as if it were her last, a point that simply had to be made.

Leaning on the sink, Ezzie hung her head. She'd laugh if she thought it to be a joke or even amusing, except she believed in her heart it was true.

But it would never be reality. Shaking her head, she spun on the ball of her foot and peered at Luke's mother. "Last night we agreed to just be friends. Things have been different with him today. For a moment I think maybe we can, then he corrects some stranger on the status of our relationship. I can't be with someone who is constantly second guessing themselves. I won't put myself through that kind of pain."

"Listen to me, dear. Don't make any rash decisions. We can discuss this more thoroughly tomorrow while we shop. It'll just be you and me. The boys will be out playing golf."

"I don't think you understand me. I've already made up my mind. I'm letting him go—completely. No friendship, no nothing."

Aside from their argument after dinner, she'd ignored him practically the entire evening. Ezzie had even been quiet the whole limo ride back to the hotel. Despite the number of times he'd attempted to engage her in conversation, she hadn't uttered a word. The elevator dinged and the doors opened to her floor. Luke shoved his hands in the pockets of his tuxedo slacks. This had been the longest they'd gone without speaking. Something had to give, even if he had to open the lines of communication first.

"Come on Ez, don't you think enough is enough with the cold shoulder. What's going on?"

"I'm eighteen. Despite what my brother has said to you, I don't require a babysitter."

"That's not why I'm here." Yeah, her brother asked him to watch out for her. But he'd spent the day with her because he'd yearned to be around her. Normally her smile could make his day brighter, but she hadn't smiled at him in hours.

"Really? Then why *are* you here?"

Her question hadn't been sarcastic, though it had dripped with annoyance ... frustration ... possibly even a little bit of anger. And still, it had been a real question that required an honest answer, one he'd been unprepared to deliver. How could he admit the truth to her? She deserved better than his truth. Luke opened his mouth and closed it. Nothing. He had nothing. No line; no way to break the wall she'd placed between them.

Luke frowned. "I..."

"You know what, I'm done." Ezzie threw her hands down in a defeated attitude and proceeded toward her room away from him.

"Done? What do you mean done?"

No answer. In silence, she continued down the hallway and dug the plastic room key out of her clutch. Ezzie blatantly ignored his question.

No. This isn't happening! She can't mean... Friendship, he'd readily accepted what she'd offered the day before. In no way had he ever expected she'd completely walk away from him. He couldn't lose her. Luke jogged after the girl who'd meant more than he'd wanted to admit. Catching up to her, he grabbed her arm and forced her to face him. Tears welled up in the corner of her eyes. Clearly it had taken every ounce of her power for them not to roll down her cheeks. Again. He'd hurt her again.

"I'm sorry Ez—"

"For what? Do you even know what you're apologizing for?" She folded her arms across her chest.

Hurting her seemed the most logical explanation. Too bad he had no idea what he'd done to cause her pain. No response he could come up with made sense. Though she'd commented about his consistent corrections earlier, he'd been certain they'd dealt with that. Hadn't they? And okay, yeah, he'd gotten a tad jealous earlier. They'd kind of discussed the inappropriateness of his reaction. Hadn't they? Had there been something else? Another reason she'd have to be upset with him. None came to mind.

"No? I didn't think so. Like I said, I'm done."

"Please don't give up on me." Had that plea really come out of his mouth? It had. Too late to take it back. Not that he wanted to. He needed her in his life.

Shaking her head, Ezzie dropped her gaze and uncrossed her arms. "I'm not. I'm just ... I thought I could do a friend thing. But you make it damn near impossible."

"I don't understand. What're you talking about?"

"I'm talking about you acting like a boyfriend, but keeping me at arm's length. I don't do in between. So, you know what, you have a choice. All or nothing." Room key in hand, Ezzie flipped her eyes up to him. The expectation of an actual valid reply from him settled in her gaze.

Her brother would kill him if he acted on his emotions. With an ultimatum like that, he may not have much of a choice. Either he responded the way he desired since the airport the other night or he walked out of her life—for good. Talk about a rock and hard place. "That isn't fair."

"No. Denying our attraction to each other isn't fair. Pretending I'm not hurt every time you correct some stranger about our relationship isn't fair. Having you ask me to just be your friend after the kiss we shared isn't fair. Acting like you don't look at me in a manner not befitting a friend isn't fair. I'm tired of the whiplash. So, make a choice. All or nothing."

"Ezzie..."

"So be it." She turned around and used the plastic key to unlock the door. The light flashed green and the door opened.

In a matter of seconds, she'd be out of his life forever. There had to be some sentence, some line, something he could come up with before that happened, before she disappeared into her hotel room and refused to see him again. Nothing popped in his head. No lie entered his mind. Later he could inspect his inability to open his mouth and say something that could've prevented her from leaving him. Right now, he had to act. Despite all the reasons he'd spouted off yesterday for them not being together, not a single one offered him comfort at the idea of losing her.

His heart raced and his pulse quickened. He'd sworn to keep his hands to himself and not to follow through on his desires. But the determination had been in her eyes. If he stood there without acting, she'd walk away for good, and he just couldn't lose her. Stepping forward, Luke shoved the door open with one hand and with the other he gripped the back of Ezzie's neck. Leaning his body against hers, he pushed her into the doorframe and lowered his lips to hers. His tongue plunged between her lips and he kissed her deeply. He hungered for every part of her beneath him.

She dropped the clutch and wrapped her arms around his back. Her pert breasts pressed into his chest.

Holy fuck. If he let her get any closer, he'd take her right there. And no one else needed to see her exquisite body. A low growl rumbled in his throat. True he'd only imagined what she'd looked like under that dress. He was on the verge of inching those little straps down each shoulder, but she still had all the control. One *no* and he'd walk away with the biggest case of blue balls he'd ever faced.

Panting, Ezzie stared at him with those sparkling sapphire blue orbs of hers.

Luke swallowed. As much as he wanted to learn every curve of her body and feel her writhe beneath him, he had to explain himself first. She deserved no less. Hell, if he had half a brain, he would've let her go. Too bad his body and heart had other plans. He leaned in, brushed a tender kiss across her lips and pressed his forehead against hers.

"Please don't give up on me."

five

HAD THOSE WORDS TRULY COME out of his mouth again? He had never pleaded with anyone before, let alone asked someone not to give up on him. Not as if he ever stayed with any of woman long enough to remember their name. There had only been one before Ezzie—no, he couldn't go there. She was in the past and Ezzie, well, shit ... he had no idea what she was to him. But god he wanted her future.

Luke looked down at the beautiful woman in his arms. Ezzie felt so right in his arms, like it was exactly where she belonged. Not that he deserved to have her there. If she ever found out the truth about him ... she'd never see him the same. Her eyes would burn with hate, not desire. That was part of the problem. As much as it scared him to be with her, it terrified him more to be without her.

What he needed was time. Time to find a happy medium. A place where they could both be content. Yeah. Content. A fucked-up emotion people got stuck in when it was the only option available. While it might be okay for him, it would never be good enough for Ezzie. She deserved the best life had to offer. Luke drank in the shine in her bright blue orbs as her eyes fluttered open.

Lowering a hand to the small of her back, Luke tightened his grip. He longed to kiss her again. Hell, if he had his way, he'd throw her over his shoulder, close the door and carry her sweet ass into the bedroom. After stripping her of the dress, he'd spend the next few hours showing her exactly how he felt. As great as that plan sounded, he had to explain himself first. Not that he had a clue how to go about doing that.

Ezzie bit on her bottom lip. "Give me one good reason why."

Definitely nixed the caveman crap. They had to talk. Meant he had to let her go. Luke instructed his arms to release their hold. His body had other ideas. *Damn it! Don't screw this up. Step back.* Luke told his libido. Getting with the program, his arms eased from around Ezzie's waist and backed up. "Okay, but can we at least talk in your room?"

"Yeah, we can do that." Inhaling a deep breath and blowing it out, Ezzie brushed the skirting of her dress out and crouched down to collect her clutch. She grabbed the key card to her room, stood up and faced the door. Unlocking the door for the second time, she pushed open the door and walked in. Setting the key card and her clutch on the kitchen counter, Ezzie glanced over her shoulder as Luke sauntered into the room and shut the door.

The last thing he should be doing was closing them in together, but a serious conversation required privacy. Not as if he was certain he could give a reason. At least a valid one. Luke watched as Ezzie disappeared into the kitchen. Had she purposely put some distance between them? Of course, she had. He'd practically ravaged her in the doorway. It was all he could do to stop her from pushing him away for good. Now ... now he had to do what she asked.

He stopped in the kitchen entrance and stared as Ezzie leaned into the refrigerator. The hardly there dress teased him with her bare back. Her skin had been so smooth and soft underneath his fingers. He was nowhere near close enough to caress her body again, but man he craved the sensation of her beneath him. To keep himself in check, Luke shoved his hands in the pockets of his slacks.

Letting the door swing shut behind her, Ezzie held out one of two bottles of water to him. "Here."

"Thanks." Luke accepted the bottle, popped the cap and took a couple of swigs. It had definitely gotten hot in there. He swallowed more from the bottle of water to wet his parched throat. It was a delaying tactic. Yeah, he agreed to talk. But he had no idea what to say.

Ezzie leaned against the kitchen counter and returned the top to the bottle. She glimpsed at the floor and frowned. Lifting her eyes back to him, she opened her mouth—

No. It wasn't her place to get the conversation started. It was his. Luke spouted the first thing that popped into his head. "I don't want to lose you, Ezzie. I know that isn't much of a reason or really a reason at all, but I'm not sure how else to explain it. I just ... I can't imagine my life without you in it."

"I feel the same way, but I need more than that. You've been back and forth so much over the last couple of days, I don't know what you want anymore. And I can't keep doing it."

His self-control lacked when it came to her. He hungered for her like bears hungered for honey. Not that it prevented him from fighting his urges. Because it was the right thing to do. Yeah. The right thing.

Luke dragged a hand down his face and sighed. "You're right and I'm really sorry about that."

"Stop apologizing. It doesn't do any good if you have no idea what you're apologizing for. Or if you just can't admit it. I don't know. You'd think I presented you with pie and cake, but you can't or won't decide which one is right. I'm not sure. All I know is you need to figure it out."

He knew exactly why he kept apologizing. He just couldn't get the words out to explain himself. Luke shifted his eyes to the bottle of water in his hands. She had constantly put him first, hadn't she? He looked back up. He used to know how to do that, but it had been so long, he'd forgotten how to do it. Only left him with one thing. "I feel like all I have are apologies and I wish I could give you more. You deserve that."

Ezzie eyed Luke and shook her head. "Just go."

"I ..." He grabbed the back of his neck and squeezed. "Please don't do this. Please give me a chance."

"To what? Apologize some more? I'm tired of apologies. I want real answers and you can't seem to do that. So please ... just go." Ezzie hung her head as tears prickled the corners of her eyes.

Luke opened his mouth and snapped it shut. She was in pain. And it was all his fault. He caused those tears. For all the anger he had toward the guys who'd hurt her before and there he stood joining their ranks. This was wrong. He cared about her too much to put her through anymore heartache. She deserved more.

Backing out of the kitchen, Luke crossed the hotel room to the door. The only way he could give her better was to walk out her life. He lingered at the door with his hand on the handle. As much as it pained him, he had to leave her alone. But she should know the truth. After the grief he caused, it was the least he could do.

"For a moment, I thought I could pretend I was the man you deserve."

"What?"

Ezzie lifted her gaze to Luke. Had she heard him correctly? Why would he have to pretend? She pushed off the kitchen counter and took a few steps forward. His self-loathing had become more obvious over the last few days, but she didn't think he hated himself so much he had to pretend he was someone else.

"That's why I kept," Luke paused, "why I keep pushing you away. I told myself I could be that man, but I couldn't touch you. It's one thing for me to pretend to be that deserving, it's another to deserve it all."

Why couldn't he see he deserved everything? And what girl had convinced him otherwise? Because she needed to go kick the bitch's ass. No one should ever have their self-esteem so demolished they don't believe they deserve love. Unless his line of thinking had to do with whom she was, or rather her family? It couldn't, right? Ezzie closed more space between them. "Is this because of my parents? I know we aren't as well off as your family, but that doesn't mean I can't hold my own."

Luke's head snapped up and his hand fell from the door handle. "What? God no. Your family is some of the best people I know. I'm the problem. I know you think I'm this great guy, but I swear I'm not the man you think I am. If I was that guy... " His words trailed off. Dropping his hands to his waist, he regarded the door.

It didn't take a genius to see what had gone through his mind. He'd leave. And the thought of him walking out the door and out of her life put a hole in her heart. This connection they shared was nothing she'd experienced before. Giving herself to him scared the shit out of her. Not the physical part, but the emotional. Yet the idea of never taking a leap with him terrified her more. Ezzie stepped out of the kitchen.

She chewed the inside of her cheek. The emotional, womanly side of her wanted to reach out to him. The intellectual side told her to let him walk out the door. But she couldn't do either. Although she despised the idea of him being with anyone other than her, if it was what he truly desired, she'd let him go. She cared too much to hold him back. Ezzie stopped in front of Luke and finished the sentence he'd left dangling in the air. "You'd leave, wouldn't you?"

"Yeah, I would." Luke looked back at her and sighed. "But I need you in my life. As much as I should walk out that door, I don't know that I have the strength to do what's right."

"So, don't."

Where would the right thing get them? Alone and hurt? Aching for the other? His pretend option hadn't been any better. The right thing didn't exactly feel right for them. Maybe the only way to figure out the right thing would be to do the wrong one. Ezzie focused on the swirls of hazel in Luke's brown eyes. His chocolate-brown irises flared with heat and stirred an ache in her lower abdomen. If he kept staring at her with that carnivorous look in his eyes, he might burn her from the inside out.

Luke swallowed and his grip tightened around the water bottle still in his hand. "You can't mean that."

Oh yes. Yes, she did. Two words and they were the truest she had spoken in the last few days. What could she say to make him understand that? Maybe words weren't enough. Ezzie placed a hand on Luke's forearm. She slowly ran her hand up along his arm and maintained eye contact as the hazel in his eyes darkened.

"We're attracted to each other. I could tell you that's the bottom line, but you and I both know that would be a lie. There's something more to it. More than your average sexual attraction. And I wish I could explain it, but I can't. Not anymore than you can. It just is. We can either fight it and pretend we're okay while secretly hurting on the inside or we can embrace it and figure the rest out along the ride."

Embrace it? Was Ezzie out of her mind? Yeah, this attraction between them was anything, but normal. And no, he couldn't explain it. Didn't mean he deserved it either. Fighting it seemed logical. Maybe even right. He could deal with the pain, at least on his end. Seeing the hurt in her beautiful face, that he couldn't handle. It nearly broke him in two. The fact that it was his fault made it worse. But giving in? Was that the right answer?

Luke gulped. The gentle movement of her hand making its way up his arm and over his pectoral muscles lit up every synapse in his body. With one hand resting tenderly against his chest, Ezzie's other hand followed the same path on the other side of his body. His grip tightened again around the plastic bottle. At this rate the bottle might explode and spew water everywhere. Either that or he'd toss the damn thing aside and relinquish all control.

Even if it felt good for a little while, could it last? Could he keep her from finding out the truth about his past? What if she did? What would happen then? Would he lose her forever? Luke stared into Ezzie's bright blue eyes. They sparkled with hunger like he was exactly what she craved. God help him. He longed to do as she asked. While he'd never tell her the truth, he had one last card to play. One he hoped would push her away, for her sake.

"Your brother—"

"Isn't here. Last I checked he doesn't make my decisions for me." Ezzie wrapped a hand around the back of Luke's neck and brushed a soft kiss upon his lips.

Fuck me. She tasted good. As starved as he was, one gentle kiss was not enough. Luke dropped the plastic water bottle, grabbed Ezzie by the waist and captured her lips with his own. His tongue danced with hers as her hands tangled in his hair. That was it. He was done for. Right thing be damned.

With one hand, Luke played with the hem of the dress at the small of her back. With the other, he trailed his fingers up along her spine. The velvety texture of her skin set his body ablaze and nearly made him combust right then and there. Ezzie in the blue dress alone was enough to wake his cock up. The smooth feeling of her skin beneath his hands made the fucker salute.

His fingers trickled over the nape of her neck and Ezzie moaned into his mouth.

Fuck, he needed to see more of her. But not too much too fast. He planned to enjoy every second of the evening. And most of it would be spent with him buried deep inside of her. Luke pressed kisses along her jaw-line as one hand curled around her shoulder and the other traced the length of her spine.

Another sultry sound escaped Ezzie's mouth encouraging him onward.

Placing more kisses down her neck, Luke unzipped the back of the dress and the straps loosened as if they had been waiting to come undone. He slid the hand around her shoulder under one strap and slipped the halter down over her collarbone. Her skin tasted so sweet, like pure cane sugar.

Dragging his hand over her shoulder blade, he tugged the other side of the halter down. The top of the dress hovered just at the curve of her breasts. "Fuck, you're beautiful."

Luke paused and lifted his gaze back to her eyes.

Panting, Ezzie bit her bottom lip and stared at him with those wide blue eyes of hers radiating pleasure and desire.

They were both too far gone to turn back now. And he needed her too much. He needed to feel her ... all of her. Luke crashed his lips against hers and enveloped Ezzie in his arms. Switching positions, he spun her around and pushed her up against the wall. Pulling her dress down further, he revealed some kind of black bra-like thing over her pert breasts.

The dress hung between them until he lowered his head and licked the top of her breasts. As if the silky material had a mind of its own, it drifted all the way down Ezzie's body and pooled at her feet. Luke felt more than saw the shift between them. For a moment he had to step back and admire the breathtaking woman before him. His imagination didn't do her justice.

Not. At. All.

His eyes and hands traveled over the bra to her soft belly over the arc of her hips and around to her plump ass. Luke pulled his jacket off and threw it to the side. He leaned into her body, tucked a loose piece of hair behind her ear and caressed her neck with a tender kiss. "Absolutely exquisite."

Ezzie 's hands roamed over the contours of his forearms and knocked the undone bowtie from the collar of his shirt on their way up his bulging biceps. Inching her way to his broad shoulders, she nuzzled his neck and nibbled on his earlobe.

He trembled beneath her touch. Fuck. Her hands were so warm and delicate as they moved along his arms and shoulders. Luke smashed his lips against hers again and sucked on her bottom lip. A husky moan from Ezzie vibrated through him.

The sounds she made were pure bliss, like a shot of orgasm down the back of his throat. Luke tugged on one side of the bra. Screw the bedroom. He had to have her right there. But first he had to see all of her. He had to feel all of her.

Ezzie unbuttoned his shirt with great precision and yanked the tails free from the pants. Her back arched as one of Luke's hands cupped the now exposed breast.

He dipped his head, suckled one nipple into his mouth and wrenched the shirt off his arms. Tossing the damn thing aside, Luke peeled the other side of the bra off and threw it on the floor. A low growl rumbled in his chest as his eyes fell to the fullest and most gorgeous breasts he'd ever seen.

And they deserved special attention. Dropping his mouth to one breast, he sucked on one of her nipples. He brushed his thumb against the other nipple and kneaded the breast itself.

With a gasped moan, Ezzie curled her fingers in his hair and urged him closer to her breasts.

Fuck! Moving his mouth to the other breast, he ran a hand over her hip and squeezed. Her half naked body pressed against his. Luke kicked his shoes off and brushed kisses along her breast bone up to her neck and hovered over her lips. Pinning his lips against hers, their tongues entwined.

As much as he longed to explore every inch of her curves, there'd be plenty of time to learn all she had to offer later. His cock hardened more with each touch and sound that passed her lips. His desire to be inside of her overrode anything else. Luke took off his belt, undid his pants, let them fall to the floor and booted them aside. He gripped her waist and drew her breasts against his chest.

He groaned at the skin to skin contact as she moaned into the kiss. Ezzie's arms wrapped around his back and her nails dug into his shoulders.

Luke ran a hand down one long smooth leg. Hooking his fingers behind her knee, he lifted it up against his hip. God, she felt so good. Giving her tongue one quick suck, he covered a breast with his mouth again. With the other hand he trailed his fingers along her belly and lingered over her lace thong. He had to slow things down slightly, enough that he could make sure she was completely ready for him.

Ezzie's fingernails gently scraped down his back until they reached the top of his boxers. One hand continued over his ass, while the other outlined the contour of each of his abdominal muscles.

Another growl rumbled in his chest as Luke switched to the other breast. He tugged on the thin material of the thong and rubbed it against her slit.

Tossing her head back, Ezzie squeezed his ass with one hand, and then with the other she broke the barrier of his boxers and wrapped her hand around his rigid length.

He moaned against her breast. Sliding the lace thong aside, Luke thrust a finger inside Ezzie's slick folds and licked the tip of her nipple. Fuck! She was so wet.

"Oh god!" Ezzie threw one hand against the wall. Tightening the grip around his waist with her leg, she fondled the skin around the head of his cock.

Luke nipped her neck and caressed her clit with his thumb as he slipped another finger inside of her. He sucked on her earlobe and whispered, "You need to stop or I'm going to come."

Lowering hooded eyes at him, she bit on her bottom lip. "What if I want you to?"

"I'm not saying I don't want to. I just want to be inside you when I do," Luke purred. He longed to be inside of her. And they would get there. Soon. She wasn't quite where he wanted her. Not yet.

Ezzie gave his hard length one last squeeze, then gripped the back of his neck and covered his mouth with hers. Her tongue dove past his lips and licked the inside of his mouth.

His tongue entangled hers as he stroked the inside of her slippery folds. Luke re-adjusted her leg on his hip and pressed his rock-hard erection into her thigh. He dipped his fingers inside her inner lips and rubbed circles around her clit. Her head tossed back and Ezzie propped both hands against the wall behind her. Her back arched and the walls of her core tightened as she cried out another moan.

"That's it. Come for me." Luke lowered his head and closed his mouth around a nipple. Sucking her breast into his mouth, he groaned as the floodgates opened and cream drizzled over his fingers. If he'd been more patient, he would've lapped at every ounce she had to offer with his tongue. For now, he'd accept a small taste. Lifting his head, he eased his fingers out and brushed a tender kiss upon her lips.

Setting her leg down, Luke licked the remnants of her orgasm from his fingers.

Panting, Ezzie hooked her thumbs into the sides of the thong and inched it down her long, smooth legs. Tossing the lace thong aside, she reached for one of the heels.

"Leave them on. Please."

In response to his request, Ezzie let her hands fall to her sides and leaned against the wall. Luke drank in the sight of her with nothing on save the fuck-me high heels. His favorite kind. He yanked his boxers off and dug a condom out of the pocket of his slacks.

Ezzie shoved her breasts out.

"Fuck."

No more waiting, Luke ripped the packet open and rolled the condom onto his erection. He gripped her hips and dropped his hands to her ass. Cupping her round cheeks, he hoisted her off the ground and her legs wrapped around his waist.

Her ankles crisscrossed at the small of his back as he lowered her and thrust his cock inside her core. With the heels digging slightly into his ass, he pressed her against the wall. Luke covered her mouth with his and kissed her deeply. Damn, she felt good. He wouldn't last long if he moved too—

Her arms snaked around his shoulders. Ezzie held on tight and rocked her hips up and down.

Neither one of them would take long if she kept going. Squeezing her ass, Luke retreated and slammed back in again. Her fingernails dug into his back as he grinded into her deeper. This time he didn't stop. Still he relished the sensation of her inner muscles clenching around him as he pumped in and out of her core. He had no idea anyone could feel like this. He had no idea sex could be this perfect. That a connection with someone could be this strong. This ... powerful.

They found a steady rhythm as her hips bucked against his thrusts. Luke deepened the kiss between them and tightened his grip on her ass. He couldn't hold out much longer, but he'd be damned if he released before her. Luke pulled out, adjusted his hold, and drove himself deep inside her core.

Ezzie cried out and grabbed the wall behind her with one hand and held onto him with other. "Oh god! Luke ... I'm..."

"Fuck, Ezzie!" He buried his head in her neck. Her heat contracted around him as he thrusted in and out again and again. Her inner walls clamped and released one final time as his body peaked into an explosion. Luke moaned into the soft skin beneath her jaw as they each rode out their own massive orgasm.

Breathing hard, her head dropped against his and she ran her fingers through his hair caressing the nape of his neck.

Taking a second to gather his own breath, he eased his face from the curve of her neck. Luke tucked a loose strand of hair behind her ears. He could fret over all the reasons he didn't deserve her in the morning. For tonight and tonight only, they would enjoy one another's company.

He brushed a soft kiss over her lips. "That was amazing."

"Right back at you."

Luke smiled. *One night*, he reminded himself. "Keep your ankles locked."

"Okay?" Ezzie raised an eyebrow.

No need to explain. His movements would do that in about thirty seconds. Luke glanced to the floor. He had precious cargo in his arms and the last thing he wanted was to trip over the clothes they'd strewn everywhere. Careful to maneuver around her dress and his tux, he strode toward the bedroom.

"Uh, why are we heading into the bedroom now?"

Because he was greedy. And he wanted more. Much more. Yeah, they both had to be up in the morning, but he was nowhere near finished exploring her body. "Because we're not done."

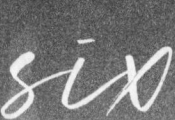

six

USING THE SPATULA, EZZIE FOLDED one side of the omelet over the middle, then the other. She beamed at how well it had come together. Scooping it up she set it on a plate with a fork. Turning the stove off, she placed the frying pan on one of the unused back burners. She'd give it a few minutes to cool off and then put it in the sink to soak. Wiping her hands on the kitchen towel, she turned around as Luke stepped out of the bedroom in only his boxers. "Good morning sunshine."

"Morning. What time is it?" Luke rubbed the back of his head.

Ezzie eyed the watch on her wrist. Shit! Was it really that late? She snagged the plate off the kitchen counter and set it on the breakfast bar. "Eight-thirty. You hungry?"

"Famished."

"Good. Sit and eat. Don't worry, it's perfectly healthy. Egg-white omelet with spinach, peppers, onions, mushrooms, and ham sprinkled with mozzarella cheese." She meandered out of the kitchen into the living room, snatched her purse and slung it over her shoulder.

Luke sat on one of the bar stools, picked up a fork, cut off a bite and shoved it in his mouth. "Oh my god. Ezzie, this is amazing."

"That's nothing. Wait until you try my apple turnovers."

"I—wait, where are you going? Aren't you going to eat?"

"I already did. And I have to go. I'm meeting your mom in five minutes." Striding back into the kitchen, she moved the frying pan into the sink and turned on the faucet.

"I thought you guys weren't getting together until ten."

"We were, then she texted me an hour and a half ago and asked to meet earlier. I couldn't exactly say no."

Not that anyone said no to his mother. Ezzie shut off the water. She traipsed out of the kitchen and stopped beside Luke. Even first thing in the morning the man was sexy as hell. Half-naked with the most gorgeous head of bed-hair. She ran her fingers through his locks, gripped the nape of his neck and brushed a tender kiss over his lips.

"Ezzie—"

"I have to go." She interrupted before he could say something they'd both regret. "And don't worry about your tux. I bagged it so it can be cleaned. Plus, I brought your gym bag up from your car. It's on the dresser. But I didn't think gym clothes would be appropriate for golf, so I swung by the shop downstairs and picked up a pair of shorts, polo, and shoes. You've got about forty-five minutes before you need to meet your dad."

Scrubbing the back of his head, Luke shifted on the bar stool and turned toward her. "Ezzie—"

"Look, whatever you're going to say, don't. Whatever you're thinking, stop. Last night was amazing. Nothing can change my mind about that. Now, I'm gonna go, but I'll see you later." She kissed Luke one last time and dashed out the door. If she didn't leave, he'd say something to ruin all that happened between them. And it had been more than she could've ever expected. More than she dared to dream.

No relationship was perfect, although sometimes it felt as if they all started out perfect. The truth was in the beginning of every relationship people were still figuring each other out. Her and Luke—yeah there were things neither knew about the other, but she knew it was far from perfect.

Just perfect for them. Ezzie sighed. If only he could see it that way.

She pressed the down button for the elevator. Man, she truly hoped he figured things out quickly. They could keep their relationship a secret from her family for now. But Luke would eventually have to get to the point where they could tell her brother, especially since Luke and her brother planned to room together at graduate school. Ezzie chewed on the inside of her cheek.

Not to mention she and Luke fit so well together. It was a stupid cliché, but last night showed her they were the perfect lock and key. Not that she had any idea which was which. The elevator doors dinged and opened. Ezzie strode in and pushed the button for the first floor. Crikey, she had to get this shit out of her head. Spacing out while shopping with Luke's mom would be a great way to tell her more than she ever needed to know.

Ezzie cracked her neck, shook out her whole body and plastered the fakest smile she could muster. *Concentrate on shopping, not Luke and his issues.* Something they'd probably have to talk about at some point, just not anytime soon. Or so she hoped.

Hopping to his feet, Luke followed after Ezzie until the door closed. He stood there in the empty hotel room and stared at the door as if he could will her to walk back through it. One part of him wanted to chase after her down the hall, drag her back inside the hotel room and spend all day in bed. The other part of him understood it was her way of shutting down anything he had to say about the night before.

Folding his arms across his chest, he glanced back to the half-eaten plate of food on the breakfast bar. Luke looked over to the unoccupied carpet by the living room wall. Dragging a hand down his face, he grabbed the plate and shoved another bite of the omelet in his mouth as he strolled into the bedroom. Stopping in the doorway, he turned his attention to the dresser.

She'd made him breakfast, addressed the mess of clothes they'd left all over the living floor, and gotten him fresh clothes to wear for the day. Nearly everything Ezzie had done that morning had taken him into complete consideration. He'd already known she was an incredible person, but the last twenty-four hours had added to his opinion. She was not only breathtaking, but she was also magnificent in bed. And beyond thoughtful.

Fuck! He did not deserve her, not any part of everything she had to offer a man. He had screwed over one woman in his life and he didn't plan to add to that number. After the way he'd treated his ex-girlfriend, he swore he'd never get that close to another woman. And what did he do? The complete opposite. He'd done things with Ezzie last night that he hadn't done with anyone in years. Hell, the last few months he'd become celibate. Sex certainly hadn't interested him. No, that wasn't right. Sex with random women hadn't interested him.

His mind had turned sex into a dream since Ezzie's last visit. Then he goes and sleeps with her. Luke regarded the crumpled sheets and comforter on the bed. No. That wasn't true. They'd shared more than just mind-blowing sex. They'd connected on a deeper level. Therein laid the problem. She wanted more and so did he, but he wasn't worthy of any of it.

Lowering the plate in his hand, Luke sat on the edge of the bed and eyed the remnants of the carefully constructed omelet in front of him. Ezzie was too good for him. Despite his feelings, she should have the kind of man who warranted her love. Maybe he couldn't have walked away last night, but he could now.

She'd hate him for what he had to do, but it was better this way. Inhaling deeply, he eyeballed the clock on the nightstand. Thirty minutes to accomplish all he needed to do to leave Ezzie the way he should've last night. Fuck. He wished he had more time, but it would have to suffice. Luke stood and finished the last few bites of the omelet on his way to the kitchen.

Ezzie eyed the skinny jeans on the rack. They were more her style, but not amongst any of the items currently slung over her arm. Her gaze shifted to the mix of blouses and tight pants she held and sighed. She had no clue what she even had a hold of. Matt would know. He'd prattle off the designer labels like they were the ingredients to her raspberry chocolate cake.

With a silent groan, she walked away from the rack and over to the designer bags where Luke's mother scanned the store's merchandise. She insisted Ezzie try on everything she had stacked in her arms, plus the items that had already been placed in a dressing room. Even with all this shopping, her mind continuously looped back to Luke.

She'd walked out of her hotel room nearly three hours ago and the change in him still tumbled around her brain. How had he gone from *I need you* to *I'm not good enough for you* in less than twenty-four hours? Hell, it hadn't even been twelve. They'd gotten back to her hotel room last night close to eleven and she'd left a little after eight-thirty that morning. That had been what, nine hours? Ezzie chewed on the inside of her cheek.

"May I take those to the dressing room for you miss?"

"Hmm? Oh, yes." Ezzie shuffled the clothes from her arms to the store attendant's arms. At least she didn't have to hold onto that load any longer.

"Which do you think will work best with the dress I bought? The Saint Laurent Kate or the Prada Daino Crossbody?" Luke's mother glanced at Ezzie.

Her gaze shifted from one purse to the other. What was the difference? They were both black. Not that Luke's mother would accept that kind of answer. If she was asking, there had to be some kind of obvious difference, aside from the designer label, right? Inhaling and exhaling a slow deep breath, Ezzie focused on one, then the other again. Well, one had a gold insignia and the other didn't. Crikey, she was awful at this. Okay, think. What would Matt say if he were there? Oh! Her eyes widened as a response popped in her head. "Neither. That dress is all black. So, you want a purse with a little color. Something that pops."

Luke's mother smiled. "You're right. You know, I think Gucci has a beautiful red Dionysus bag that will go perfect with it. I'll have an attendant check while you try on clothes. Come. Let me see how everything looks on you."

"Okay."

Relieved Luke's mother accepted her answer, Ezzie started for the dressing room. Good thing she actually listened to her best friend once in a while. Of course, if he had been there, his response would've been more detailed and a suggestion would've followed. If she had to offer another option, she probably would've gone by color alone.

She paused outside the dressing room ready and waiting for her presence and peered over her shoulder. As promised, Luke's mom had stopped an attendant and inquired about the purse previously mentioned. Ezzie tilted her head and stared at Luke's mother. Would she know about who convinced Luke he was unworthy? It was possible. She and her mother knew a lot about her brother's love life, probably more than either of them cared to know.

Only one way to find out. As Luke's mother approached the dressing room, Ezzie stepped inside the stall and surveyed the items neatly hung up. So many options. Where to start? Given what she intended to do, perhaps something demure would work best. She quickly stripped out of her shorts and t-shirt and plucked the navy-blue and white dress from its satin hanger.

Unzipping the dress, she stepped into it and slid her arms through the short sleeves. Getting everything situated, Ezzie looked over herself in the mirror. The embroidery on the dress was decadent. With the neckline close to her collarbone, the intricate lace design and the semi-fluffy skirt, she was gorgeous. She could understand why Luke's mother had selected this dress. Collecting herself, she waltzed out of the dressing stall into the staging area.

"Oh my. That dress is absolutely beautiful on you. Turn around, let me see the back."

As requested, Ezzie spun in a slow circle and smiled when she returned to her initial position. The way Luke's mother's face beamed said it all. Hopefully her questions wouldn't kill the vibe. She brushed her hands down the dress's skirting and swallowed. There was no easy way to begin. Then again, they did have that conversation last night in the bathroom. Maybe that was her way in.

"Umm, Mrs. Jonnihan, last night you asked me not to give up on Luke. Do you mind if I ask you about that?"

"You can ask me anything, my dear. I will do my best to answer any of your questions."

Good. This was good. But what did she ask? She couldn't blurt out the one thing she really wanted to know. Maybe she didn't have to. Maybe all she had to do was ask questions around the subject. Ezzie nodded. "Has Luke ever introduced any girlfriends to you and Mr. Jonnihan?"

"Only one."

Not what she expected. Yeah, Nate's girlfriend had warned her Luke was a bit of a player, but she thought that had been recent. Had he not seriously dated more than one woman? Ezzie frowned. That didn't seem right. Maybe he had and just never introduced them to his parents. That seemed more likely. But one was a place to start. "Oh? May I ask who?"

"Jessica Carlisle. Now go try on another outfit."

Either Luke's mother had an excellent memory or whatever break-up he'd gone through had been just as recent as his player status. Ezzie spun on her heel and stepped back into the dressing stall. She closed the door and proceeded to remove the dress as she selected another item. Something closer to her style.

"How long ago did he introduce you to her?"

"Well, it would have been a little over four years ago. They dated when he was in high school."

High school? Ezzie blinked as she tugged the simple blue, sleeveless-dress over her head. Luke had to have dated someone since then. Right? He wasn't the type of guy just interested in sex. Shaking the thought out of her head, she stepped out of the stall and back into the staging area.

"What happened between them?"

Luke's mother studied Ezzie from head to toe for a moment, then finally shook her head. "That dress does nothing for your figure. Try something else."

Hiding the frown, she turned around and re-entered the stall. Hopefully that wasn't all the information she would get about Luke's past. Ezzie looked over the remaining outfits and decided to step it up a notch. Maybe if she opted for something sexier, Luke's mother would give her the information she sought. Taking the blue number off, she hung it up and removed a red-dress with a slit up the right side and a single shoulder-strap. "Do you know why they broke up?"

"I presume they split up because they chose not to pursue a long-distance relationship. Though I'm not positive my line of thinking is accurate."

Unzipping the dress, she eased into it. The dress hugged every curve of hers perfectly. Definitely the sexiest thing she'd tried on since their shopping trip began. Ezzie exited the stall once again. "What makes you say that?"

"Just a feeling I had about the girl." Luke's mother gestured for Ezzie to spin.

"What feeling?" Ezzie inquired as she turned around in a slow and deliberate circle. She really liked the feeling of this dress against her body. It almost felt like a second skin.

"I got the impression she was manipulative. I cannot say I was heartbroken or unsurprised when we stopped hearing about her." A smile pulled at the corners of her mouth. "Now this is a dress."

"I kind of like this one too." Ezzie grinned. The two of them hadn't agreed on much in the way of outfits that day. But it was nice when they did.

Luke's mother stepped forward and gripped both of Ezzie's shoulders. Knowledge filled her eyes as if she knew exactly what Ezzie had been up to with the questions. "Listen to me; you are a beautiful and intelligent young woman. Do not compare yourself to the women from his past. I know Lucas has changed in the last few years. Whether or not Jessica is the reason, I cannot say with certainty. I can only tell you that I believe in all of my heart that you are the woman he is meant to be with. And I just ask that you be patient with him. I know one day he'll see how truly special you are. Now, why don't you try on something else and we'll keep looking for outfits to help my son see that sooner, rather than later."

"Whiskey neat," Luke told the bartender as he climbed onto the bar stool. Great thing about country clubs, they all had bars. After a few hours of golfing, he could use the drink. Ah, hell. Golf had nothing to do with it. A certain brunette had danced around in his head all morning and thrown him completely off his game.

It was the first time his father had beaten him in years. For an eighteen-hole course with a par of seventy-two, his average score was ninety. Today, he might as well have been worse than a beginner at one hundred twenty. Everywhere he turned something reminded him of Ezzie. Made him think about last night and how quickly it all ended. Or at least how it would end. Luke dragged a hand down his face.

The bartender set a glass half-filled with bright gold liquid down in front of Luke.

Sitting on the bar stool to Luke's right, his father nodded at the bartender and set a credit card on the bar. "An Old-Fashioned, please."

"Of course, sir."

Glancing at his father out of his periphery, Luke picked up the glass and took a sip of the whiskey. It was a sweet, slow burn down the back of his throat. He didn't want to drink it all at once, even if it would help lighten the load on his shoulders a little. Maybe he should get a bottle on his way back to the dorm. He didn't have any other plans and getting knock out drunk sounded pretty good right about then. Yeah, he'd probably have a hangover in the morning, but it was what he deserved.

"Is everything all right with you, son?"

"I'm fine, Dad."

At least as *fine* as he could be. Sometime within the next couple of hours, Ezzie would return to her suite and discover the note he'd left behind. He hadn't been cruel, just honest. Hell, with the way things had been left between them that morning, it shouldn't have anything other than *thank you*. It did say that. It just didn't end with that. God, he was a real asshole. Maybe he could get it back before she saw it. Luke peeked at the watch on his wrist. There was still time.

The bartender returned with his father's drink, set it down on the bar, and moved onto another patron. "I hope you don't think that answer is going to fly. I know something is bothering you. How about you tell me what's wrong?"

Luke knocked back the remainder of the whiskey in his glass and pinched the bridge of his nose. Rubbing his face, he eyed the empty glass and debated on another. Though taking off and doing what he could to get back in his girl's—shit! She wasn't his girl. She was his best friend's sister. Fuck. He should've never slept with her. Not that he could take it back now. A gift a major part of him was grateful for and absolutely wanted to do again. Setting the glass on the bar, he nodded to the bartender and tapped the glass for a refill. Shifting toward his father, Luke sighed. "You ever have a time in your life when what you want to do and what you believe is the right thing don't coincide?"

His father lowered the glass from his mouth. "I think we all have those moments. What you have to ask yourself is what is truly the right thing? And who is it right for? Is it right because that is what the law says or is it right because it's the option with the least risk? Every decision we make in our lives has some risk associated with it, but that doesn't mean that one path isn't safer than the other. In those situations, you simply need to trust your heart will lead you in the right direction."

That certainly hadn't been the answer he expected. While he'd always considered his father wise, Luke didn't expect a real response of any kind. Definitely not a life lesson. And that was exactly what he'd gotten. If only he was positive, he could trust his heart again. He turned to his fresh glass of whiskey. At least getting pass out drunk sounded less appealing. Now if he could make a decision about Ezzie, he'd be set.

Luke lifted the glass to his lips and grinned. "Thanks, Dad."

Shifting all the bags to one arm, Ezzie dug the key card out from her back pocket and opened the door. Heading over to the couch, she dropped the bags on the floor and flopped backwards. It felt so good to be off her feet. That shopping trip had gone on way longer than she anticipated and she wound up with way more clothes than she imagined possible. It almost seemed as if Luke's mother had transformed into a professional shopper since the last time they'd gone shopping together.

Not something she ever wanted to do again. How many bags had she come back with? Six? Seven? Most of the bags were brimming with clothes by designers whose names she couldn't pronounce. Ezzie rubbed her eyes. She had no idea how she allowed Luke's mother to talk her into so many outfits. Never mind the fact that she insisted she pay for everything, even for a graduation gift it had all been a little much. Yeah, her credit card limit didn't even scratch the surface of the Jonnihan limit, but she wasn't incapable of paying her own way. For anything.

The muffled sound of Lady Gaga's *"Born This Way"* filled the room. Ezzie groaned as she shifted on the couch, pulled her cell phone out of the back pocket of her denim shorts, and brought it to her ear. "Hey, Matt."

"You sound awful. Oh my god, please do not tell me this is an indication of how last night went."

"Gee thanks. And no. I've been out shopping all day with Luke's mom."

And it could not compare to last night. A soft smile crawled on her face as the events from the night before replayed in her mind. Last night had been amazing. Ezzie peered around the room. Not that any evidence remained. Her suite was spotless. And neither her dress nor Luke's tux would be returned prior to tomorrow.

"Explains why I haven't heard from you—wait a minute. Did you say you were shopping? As in for clothes? Real clothes?"

Rolling her eyes, Ezzie slowly sat up. Her clothes were real. So, what if they weren't designer? They were all made the same way. "Yes, we went shopping. For clothes."

"Your style or her style?"

"You've never even met the woman. How do you know her style isn't like mine?" Stretching, she smirked.

"Never mind, don't answer that." Crikey, she was tired. Even she heard the idiocy in her own question. She'd sent a picture of the dress Luke's mother had picked out for last night to him. Of course, he knew their styles were completely different.

"I'm so glad you understand how ridiculous that question is, which means I can assume you went shopping in her style. Correct?"

"Let's just say we could play dress-up with ninety-five percent of what I have."

Ezzie stifled a giggle at the excited clap that resounded through the phone. Sometimes her best friend was easy to please. She kicked off her tennis shoes, stood and stretched one last time. Stepping around the bags she left lying on the floor, she strode into the kitchen and got a bottle of water out of the refrigerator.

"While I'm dying to know everything you bought, we can discuss that later. For now, tell me about last night. Did his jaw drop when he saw you?"

She chugged some of the water back and turned around. "There are no words to describe last night."

"Does that mean?"

"Yeah, we..." Her statement trailed off as her gaze fell to the handwritten note on the breakfast bar. Ezzie strode closer and picked up the small, single sheet of paper. She read over it once, then a second time.

Ezzie,

I'm sorry, but we can't spend any more time together. Last night was more than I could've ever asked for and more than I deserve. I hope one day you can forgive me for leaving like this. I never wanted to hurt you, but you are worth more than I have to offer.

Luke

"You what?"

What the hell? Had she read that right? No. She had to be seeing things. Ezzie scanned the note one last time. Lowering the phone from her ear, she walked out of the kitchen and headed into the bedroom. The bed had been made up and looked untouched. The black bag of his she'd left on the dresser earlier that morning was gone. She couldn't even tell that Luke had been there. As if his presence had been erased while she was out. Tears prickled the corners of her eyes.

Ezzie swallowed. No. She would not cry. She had to be strong. She had to ... she had to talk to Luke. Her cell phone. Where was her cell phone?

"Hellllooooo?" Matt screamed.

Right. It was in her hand. She lifted the phone back to her ear. "Sorry, Matt. I ... uh ... can I umm, can I call you back in a few minutes?"

"As long as you promise to tell me what the hell happened. You just disappeared."

"I know. I'm sorry. I swear I'll call you back in a few." Her heart was breaking. Of course, she planned to talk to her best friend about it, but she absolutely had to call Luke first. The note could've been written in a moment of panic. He'd been freaking out a little that morning. And she'd texted him a couple of times throughout the day. Not that he'd responded, but she figured he might've still been playing golf.

"Pinky?"

"Pinky."

"Okay. Do what you need to do. We'll talk soon."

"Thanks, Matt." Ezzie disconnected the call. He had been through more than just a few boyfriends and bad breakups with her. Matt had been there for one of the most trying times in her life. One, no one in her family knew about. Her brother would've freaked out more over that than he had the tattoo.

Inhaling and exhaling a deep breath, Ezzie collected herself, pulled up Luke's information from her contacts and dialed his number. It rang three times and went to voicemail. She chewed on the inside of her cheek and waited for the beep. "Hey Luke, it's Ezzie. Would you please call me? We need to talk about this note."

Disconnecting the line, she shuffled out of the bedroom and into the living room. Had she done something wrong? Maybe she shouldn't have kissed him before she left that morning. Or made breakfast? Had she come on too strong? It just didn't make any sense. Tears trickled down her cheeks as she dropped onto the couch. Ezzie called Matt back up.

He would know what to do.

He always knew how to help.

No matter what she needed him for.

His cell phone rang for the fifth or sixth time in the last couple of hours. Luke glimpsed at the caller information and let it go to voicemail.

Again.

He hadn't answered any of Ezzie's phone calls, or any of the dozens of text messages she'd sent. Folding his arms behind his head, he stared up at the ceiling. He'd given everything his father said a lot of thought. When it came down to it, he'd never be able to offer Ezzie all that she was worth.

The phone dinged signifying another voicemail. He hadn't listened to a single one. Eventually he'd muster up the strength to delete them. For now, all he could do was let them go. Sitting up in his bed, Luke rubbed his face. He had to get out of this dorm. Do something. Otherwise he was likely to do something stupid like drive over to Ezzie's hotel suite and beg for forgiveness and a second chance.

Yeah. That would be really stupid. Luke brushed the back of his head. Whatever he did, he couldn't do it alone. He'd spend time with his parents, but they (a) had plans and (b) were staying in the same hotel as Ezzie. Too close to temptation. And he refused to hit any of the parties still going on across campus. Maybe he could go to a movie or something. But who could he go with?

Nate walked through the door with his cell phone pressed against his ear. "Yeah. I'll be there in about forty minutes. I'm just grabbing my keys now. All right, see you soon."

Nixed that idea. Unless he could tag along. Then again, if Nate planned to go off with Becca it would be a different story. While he liked Nate's girlfriend, he didn't relish the idea of being a third wheel. Luke frowned. No good solutions there.

"Hey man, you okay?"

"Uh, yeah. Just a long day."

"You sure?" Nate raised an eyebrow.

Had he always been this easy to read? His dad had figured out there was a problem too. Of course, this was his dad and best friend. Hiding things from them had never been easy. And he absolutely wanted to keep this from Nate. He'd kick his ass if he ever found out about the situation with Ezzie. Although sometimes he thought he could burn the dorm down by accident and Nate, if hyper-focused or with Becca, wouldn't even notice. Luke forced a smile. "Yeah. I probably just need to eat."

"Oh. Well, why don't you join us? I'm sure my parents wouldn't mind."

"Your parents?"

When had they arrived? Weren't they still sick? Why hadn't he been told? Not that it was necessary for him to know, unless Ezzie had shared the news in one of her several voicemails. Luke glanced down at the cell phone on his bed. Shit.

"Yeah. They called from the airplane. The food poisoning finally passed, so I'm on my way to get Ezzie and then we'll pick up our parents at the airport. Figured we'd get dinner before heading back to the hotel."

Made perfect sense. And Nate probably hadn't planned any of it. Not that it mattered. He absolutely did not need to be around Ezzie right then. Luke looked back to his best friend. "I appreciate the invite, man, but you guys go spend some time with your parents. I'm sure we'll get together before we leave in a few days."

"Of course, we are. We're all going to the museum tomorrow. Remember?"

Fuck. Ezzie had mentioned something about that a couple of days ago, hadn't she? Great. The one person he intended to avoid and he couldn't. Just perfect. Luke nodded. "How could I forget?"

Nate crossed his arms and narrowed his eyes as he studied Luke. "You hook up with someone last night?"

"What? No."

Hook-up was not the term he'd use to describe what he did last night. The meaning of that word was too derogatory. And what he'd done last night was nothing short of a trip to paradise. Luke cracked his neck to keep the memories at bay.

"You sure? The only time you ever act this spastic is when you've had a good piece of ass."

His fists balled up at the reference to Ezzie as nothing more than a "piece of ass." Inhaling a deep breath, Luke exhaled and uncurled his fingers. If Nate had any idea that he'd spoken about his own sister, those words would've never been used to describe her. Not that he had any room to talk. Fuck, he had to remind himself he left Ezzie a note. Luke frowned. "Again, no."

"No reason to be ashamed if you did. You deserve it, man. It's been what, three months? Hell of a dry spell if you ask me. And if that's what has got you all tied up, then maybe you should go see her again. You look like you could..." Nate's words trailed off and he checked out something on his cell phone. "Shit. I gotta go." He practically jogged out the door.

Luke's nostrils flared. It was a good thing his roommate left. He was ready to pummel him for speaking about Ezzie that way, even if Nate had no clue who he'd been talking about. Maybe he needed to learn how to speak about women period. Closing his eyes, Luke inhaled and exhaled another deep breath. Not that he had any room to judge. Fuck, he was a hypocritical idiot. He sat back down on his bed and hung his head.

How the hell was he going to get through the museum tomorrow? Sure, they'd be surrounded by their families and Nate would be there. But they may not be much of a buffer, unless Ezzie refused to talk to him.

Luke eyed his cell phone. Only one way to find out.

He reached for his cell phone and dialed into his voicemail.

seven

LUKE'S FEET POUNDED AGAINST THE rotating rubber. He stared out the window as he ran on the treadmill going as hard as his body could handle. He'd been at the gym for a couple of hours now and this was last on his usual routine. Although he typically didn't run this long or this hard. But he deserved nothing less.

Hey Luke, it's Ezzie. Would you please call me? We need to talk about this note.

Luke, it's me again. I really need you to call me. I don't know what this note is about, but we need to talk about it.

Luke, you need to call me. You can't just ignore this note. It won't go away.

Why won't you answer me? You had the balls to write this damn thing. Don't you think you owe me at least an explanation?

Luke, this is some serious bullshit. You leave me this note and don't have the decency to answer a single phone call or text? That's fucked up.

I thought you were better than this. But I guess you only know how to take the coward's way out. Don't worry, Luke. I get the picture. I hope you're happy.

All six of Ezzie's voicemails played in a loop in his mind. He couldn't get a single one out of his head. All night long her words danced on his brain like a never-ending chant reminding him of how much of an asshole he was. Each voicemail, hell each text had been progressively worse than the last. The only good news, in no way could he misinterpret her feelings.

Not. One. Bit.

Still, he held out hope that he could sweat out her words or at least exhaust himself enough that he'd be able to keep his trap shut while they were all out together. His family. Her family. Her brother. Fuck. How was he going to get through this day?

Slowing the treadmill down, he brought it to a walking pace and focused on steadying his breaths. Luke yanked the small towel off the handrail and mopped up the sweat from his face. Placing each foot on the side-rail, he shut the treadmill off and hung his head.

He wiped the back of his neck and stepped off the machine. Most of her voicemails were harsh, but it was the last one that stung the most. Ezzie rightfully called him out as a coward. His phone had gone silent after that. It emphasized the burn he felt down to his core, like a scorpion sting that hadn't healed. And he was clueless on how to properly treat the wound.

Tossing the towel into the bin, Luke snagged a bottle of water and eyeballed the time. Chugging half the bottle down, he exited the gym and meandered back to his dorm room. He walked through the door just as his roommate stepped out of the bathroom.

"Where the hell have you been?" Nate asked.

"At the gym. I was getting a workout in." Not that the workout served its purpose. His muscles were sore, but he'd failed in shoving Ezzie and everything she'd said out of his mind. Luke gulped down the rest of the bottle of water.

"Seriously? It's a good thing you shower quickly."

What the hell was he talking about? They had plenty of time before they were supposed to meet everyone. Luke threw away the empty water bottle and headed over to his bed. "Why does that matter?"

"We have to leave in fifteen minutes. Didn't your parents get a hold of you last night? We're gathering at the hotel for breakfast and then leaving for the museum."

"I thought the museum didn't open until ten." Which was another two hours away. And no one said a damn thing about breakfast. Luke frowned. Really, he needed to spend as little time as possible with Ezzie until he figured out what to do about everything.

"It does, but it's in Williamsburg."

Luke dragged a hand down his face. Of course, it was. Another hour and a half with Ezzie. Could this day get any worse? No time to think about it now. He strode over to his closet and dresser and selected clothes. "Shit. Alright. Give me ten and I'll be ready."

Normally she would've cooked her own breakfast, but it had been nice to laze about and not get up right away. Not as if she felt like eating anyway, except if she didn't her parents or her brother would say something. Fine, she could get a few small items off the open-style buffet and graze. It wouldn't cause reason for them to question her lack of appetite. Ezzie picked up a plate at the end of the buffet line and half noticed Luke and her brother enter the dining room.

Her parents and Luke's parents had already retrieved their food and chosen a table for them all to sit at. She'd opted to go last. It had been a last-ditch effort to get some kind of appetite. The hairs on the nape of her neck stood at attention. She didn't have to look to know who'd gotten behind her in line.

"Ezzie, can we talk?" Luke requested.

Refusing to acknowledge his presence, she moved further down the line and collected some fruit, scrambled eggs and bacon. Oh, they had French toast slices too. Ezzie grabbed the tongs and picked up two slices, then paused to pour a bit of syrup.

"You have every right to be pissed at me, but would you please let me explain?"

She bit her tongue. It took every ounce of power not to open her mouth and tear into him. Then again, maybe she should. She could tell him where to shove whatever excuse he drummed up. No. Because she had no desire to cause a scene. And she wanted to slap him. And kiss him.

Ugh! No! She didn't. Even she didn't believe that. Not that it changed how angry and hurt she felt. That stupid note of his. Then he ignored her on top of it. She might be able to find it in herself to hear him out, but not right then. Ezzie grabbed a glass of orange juice and turned toward the table the rest of their party sat around.

Luke managed to put himself in her path. "Please talk to me."

Her eyes narrowed and her nostrils flared. He had a lot of fucking nerve. Crikey, this was going to be a trying day. Three hours total travel time. Plus the couple of hours it would take them to get through the museum. Was she really prepared to be around him for the next five hours? Ezzie inhaled and exhaled deeply.

Remember the mantra Matt had you say over and over again last night, she thought. *I am a calm cool wind on a stormy night. Like the eye of the hurricane, nothing can stop me. Nothing can stand in my way.* Inside her head, Ezzie repeated the mantra two more times. It wasn't the time or place to give Luke a piece of her mind. But she could say whatever was necessary to get him to move.

"No. Now, get out of my way or I swear to God, I will dump this plate of food all over you and then you can explain it all to our families."

With a heavy sigh, Luke gripped the back of his neck and stepped out of the way.

Guess he did have half a brain. Tightening her grip on her plate and glass, Ezzie continued on and joined the rest of their party. She sat down as Luke walked up with his own plate of food and juice. Of the two empty seats to her left, he took the one directly beside her. Either he was glutton for punishment or he thought he could wear her anger down.

Nate approached a second or two later and slid in the last available chair. "Hey sis, I meant to ask you, how much of this museum has been planned out?"

Attempting to look past Luke, she plastered a smile on her face. "Not a whole lot really. I mean, Ripley's has a couple of extra things we can tack on if we like. I figured we'd buy tickets on the way there once we decided."

"Are you talking about the place that has the laser-race?" Luke chimed in.

She'd give him credit. He was determined to engage her. Despite her intention to ignore him all day, he'd succeeded in getting her to say something to him almost twice in the last five minutes. Two could play that game. Ezzie shoved a piece of French toast in her mouth and nodded.

"That sounds like fun," Nate said. "Does it have anything else?"

"Um, yeah. A 4D theater and mini-golf." She turned her attention back to the small pile of food on her plate. Ezzie stabbed a single piece of cantaloupe with her fork and popped it in her mouth as everyone proceeded to discuss their options.

After twenty minutes or so, they all agreed to a round of mini-golf. And somehow, she'd gotten roped into a round of laser-race with her brother and Luke. That probably wouldn't be so bad. At least she'd be riding with her brother. Cut down her exposure to Luke by a lot. She could do this.

Ezzie replayed Matt's mantra in her head. She could survive a couple of hours. Plus, they'd all be distracted by whatever weirdness they crossed at Ripley's. Strange and unusual was the whole point. Once it was over, she could spend the rest of the night hiding in her hotel room. The perfect plan.

Luke eyed the historical information on display in front of him and attempted to read it for the fifth time. After Ripley's, they'd all returned to the city and opted to hit one of the smaller historical museums. Even though he knew this particular museum like he knew Ezzie's body—Fuck! He seriously had to stop thinking about that. Massaging the back of his neck, he sighed.

Despite their confrontation that morning at breakfast, the day had gone fairly smooth. Probably because he hadn't made any further attempts to speak with her about their ... situation. Even if she had agreed to speak with him, he still hadn't decided exactly what he'd say, though he didn't care much for her being angry with him, so he had to come up with something.

With the way he'd left their relationship, he should've expected nothing less. At least he'd been able to see the smile he adored so much on her face, not to mention the eyeful he'd gotten when she crawled, shimmied, and slid around the laser beams in the laser-race. Needless to say, he lost.

As for mini-golf, Luke tried his hardest not to stare whenever Ezzie had gone up. That was only slightly easier given the number of people who surrounded them. The game would've been improved if he'd been able to congratulate her or joined in on her celebration anytime she scored a hole-in-one. Instead he had to stand aside in a perpetual world of non-existence.

Now he'd give anything for her to hear him out or agree to meet later. The latter worked better, then they'd have less of an audience. Although they had all gone off in their own direction, he couldn't take the risk one of them would interrupt what needed to be said.

Luke shook his head. There was no point in trying to read anything. He had Ezzie on the brain. Best he just wait for everyone by the gift shop. He took the shortest route possible and ignored the rest of the self-guided tour he'd done a million times. His pace slowed upon his approach to the exit and he stopped a few feet from the store's entrance.

His gaze landed on Ezzie who stood at the register laughing at some joke the male cashier cracked. Luke's eyes narrowed and green flashed behind his irises. What the hell? They hadn't spoken in less than twenty-four hours and already she was flirting with someone else? His blood boiled at the thought of her with anyone, but him. He stormed through the door and grabbed the crook of Ezzie's elbow. "I need to speak to you."

Clutching a bag against her chest, she glared at him. "Excuse me?"

"Now."

Luke didn't wait for a response. He ushered her out the door. His body had gone into beast mode. He didn't notice if Ezzie fought against him as they left the museum and made their way around to the side of the building.

"What the hell is wrong with you?"

"What's wrong with me? What's wrong with you? I saw you in there flirting with him." Luke pointed back in the direction of the shop. Like Ezzie needed clarification of her actions. He knew she knew exactly what she had done wrong. Maybe he'd been an asshole when it came to his feelings, but he sure as hell hadn't flirted with another girl.

Ezzie crossed her arms. "Flirting? I wasn't flirting with anyone. And even if I was, last I checked *you* are *not* my boyfriend. In fact, you walked away from any chance for us! Or have you forgotten all about the note already?"

Her emphasis on him not being her "boyfriend" stung in a way he'd never experienced. He felt it more now than the first time she'd said that. Since then, he'd given little thought on the importance of the term. Was this how she felt whenever he told someone they weren't together? It couldn't be. There was a difference. He focused on her worth and the fear ... the fear ... he would tarnish it. Crap. He hadn't written that note because she deserved better. He wrote it because he was afraid. Not that it changed what had happened earlier that day.

Luke frowned. "Of course not, but apparently it slipped your mind that I did try to talk to you this morning."

"Are you kidding me? I called you six times last night. Sent a dozen text messages and you have the nerve to think I'm going to jump the second you actually grow balls and respond?"

Yeah, that sounded bad. He hadn't really gotten the nerve to talk to her, other than earlier that day. He had pulled her aside because he'd witnessed her flirting. Wait a second. How had they gone from her flirtatious rendezvous with the cashier to him growing a set?

"I didn't expect you'd outright forgive me, but I did expect you'd hear me out. At the very least, I never figured you'd flirt with someone else. At least not so soon after."

"For god sakes, I wasn't flirting!"

"Then what would you call it?" From where he stood, a woman laughing at something a man said was considered flirting. Any kind of real eye contact constituted flirting. Spending any time more than required was flirting. Luke had witnessed her do all of the above. Therefore, according to his standards, she had flirted.

"Picking up your graduation present!" Ezzie shoved the bag in her hands into Luke's arms and stomped off.

Had he heard her correctly? No. Absolutely not. No way had he mistaken the exchange he'd seen. No way he'd made a bigger ass of himself. Luke peeked inside the bag and removed a book. One he swore was out of print. He blinked and stared at the title—*Lost Virginia: Vanished Architecture of the Old Dominion*. How many museum shops had he searched for this beauty? And she had found it? How? When?

Luke groaned. He couldn't be holding something this thoughtful. To be sure he wasn't seeing things, he opened the front cover and swallowed. A message had been neatly penned. *Congratulations, Luke! I'm so proud of you. And I know you'll make an amazing lawyer someday soon. Ezzie.* If he hadn't felt like a dickhead before, he certainly did now. She was thinking about him and he'd gone off the deep end and accused her of shamelessly flirting with another person.

Damn it! Luke shut the book and returned it to the plastic bag. He shifted his gaze toward the street in time to see Ezzie crawl into a taxi cab. He dug his cell phone out of his pocket and called her phone. It rang twice and went to voicemail. "Shit."

Tucking his cell phone back in the pocket of his jeans, Luke growled.

He'd really put his foot in it this time. He rubbed his eyes and pinched the bridge of his nose. Okay. She'd probably head back to the hotel. Not a problem. He had to take his parents back there anyway. All he had to do was delay his departure from the hotel for a bit. Then he could pop by Ezzie's room and beg her to hear him out.

Sounds like a great plan, he thought. Luke shook his head and blew out a deep breath. He'd figure something out. He walked around the corner and stepped back into the museum. He spotted his parents and Nate's and Ezzie's parents hovering near the shop.

Nate exited the gift store and approached both of their parents. "She's not in there. I don't know where she's at."

"Who?" Luke asked although he already knew the answer. The only person missing from their party. What would he tell them? He had to lie. No way he dared to utter the truth.

"Ezzie. You haven't seen her, have you?" Nate responded as they all turned toward Luke.

"Uh, yeah. She said something about not feeling well and caught a taxi back to the hotel." The lie came out quicker than he anticipated and most of them appeared to believe it. His best friend might have been the only exception.

Nate raised an eyebrow. "I wonder why she didn't say anything."

Luke opened his mouth to offer up another lie when his best friend's cell phone beeped. He let out a slow breath at the interruption. It was a brief interlude, but it gave him a second to figure out an answer.

"That must be her now." Nate checked his cell phone. Clearing his throat, he tapped out a quick response. With a smirk, he turned back to Luke. "You know, I liked your answer better."

"Oh?"

Oh shit. Ezzie had told her brother the truth. *Here it comes,* Luke thought. Nate would kick his ass. Adjusting his footing, Luke set his stance and prepared for an oncoming punch that never came. He studied his best friend who stood there looking a little pale. What the hell had

Ezzie said?

"Yeah. Then I wouldn't have images of my sister and womanly things flooding my brain." Nate shuddered.

"Womanly things?" What the hell had Ezzie told her brother? Luke glanced to his mother for some sort of explanation.

"Yeah, you know ... you know I can't even say it. This is my sister," Nate said.

"She got her period," his and Nate's mother said simultaneously.

"Gah! Don't say that. I'm not hearing this." Nate covered his ears and waltzed out the door.

Luke chuckled. Ezzie had gone with that. Made sense now why Nate insisted his answer was better. And her response played right along with his. With that settled, he could concentrate on more important things, like how to get Ezzie to give him another chance.

Arrogant son-of-a-bitch. Who the hell made him king for the fucking day? All that money must have finally gone to his head. Ezzie leaned back against the taxi seat and got as comfortable as she could given the circumstances. So, what if he tried to talk to her once in the last twenty-four hours. She had made multiple attempts and at one point contemplated taking a taxi up to the campus. Then her mother had called and plans changed.

For all the tossing and turning she'd done last night, his one attempt to converse with her was utter bullshit. If Lucas Jonnihan expected her to forgive him, then he had to do something big to make up for his enormous fuck-up. It wasn't like a forgotten phone call. Or a missed date. He had practically ended their relationship before it had even begun. He had turned their magical night into a one-night stand, something she didn't even think was possible if you knew the other person.

Her cell phone vibrated in her back pocket. Prepared to send him to voicemail for a second time, Ezzie yanked her phone out and paused. Wait a second. It wasn't Luke's name that populated across the screen. It was her seatmate from her flight. Answering her cell, Ezzie pressed the phone to her ear. "Hello?"

"Hey Ezzie, it's Tasha. I didn't catch you at a bad time, did I?"

"Nope. What's up?"

The two of them had exchanged numbers, but she didn't think she'd hear from her so soon. Hell, she had no idea if they'd ever talk again. Yeah, they'd had a fairly decent conversation on life plans, but that was par for the norm for her ... at least with Matt. Maybe not so common with perfect strangers.

"Um, well, I got the job! I'm sorry to just call like this, but I'm so excited and I just had to share it with someone. I mean, I told my mom and I thought that would be enough. Then I realized I wanted to go out and celebrate, but I don't want to go by myself. And you're the only one I know here."

Ezzie stifled a giggle. Something she discovered she had in common with her best friend. Both Tasha and Matt had a tendency to throw up words. It all came out in one breath. At least she had found another pea to their pod. "Okay, a couple of things. One, breathe. Good. Two, that is awesome news! I'm happy for you. I know how badly you wanted this job. As for going out and celebrating—"

"Oh, please say yes. This is some of the best news I've gotten in a couple of years and I'd really like to take full advantage of my time here. Please?"

Given her current mood, she probably shouldn't be around people. But how could she say no to a response like that? *Maybe Luke should take notes,* Ezzie thought and smirked. Off topic. Shaking her head, she freed herself from the Luke web developing in her brain. What had Tasha asked? Oh yeah. Go out. Be around people.

"All right. I'm in. What would you like to do?"

"Oh my gosh! You're awesome, Ezzie! Thank you so much!"

"Tasha, focus please. Have you thought about what you'd be interested in doing?"

The taxi pulled up alongside the front entrance to her hotel. Ezzie glanced at the meter and handed the driver a twenty-dollar bill. She gestured for him to keep the change as the back-passenger door swung open. Yeah, it was a fifty percent tip, but he did as he'd been asked without any questions. She climbed out of the taxi, nodded at the doorman holding the car door open and headed inside the hotel.

"Oh, right. Um, I heard about this little bistro on the strip downtown. And there's supposed to be a really hip club within walking distance from it."

A club? Which meant dancing. None of the new clothes she got were club material. And she'd worn—no, she hadn't. She still had one number that worked for dancing. Ezzie snickered. Looked like she'd get to wear that little black dress after all. "All right. Give me about an hour to shower and change and I'll meet you at the bistro. Text me the address?"

"I can do that," Tasha paused. "Thank you for doing this Ezzie. I know we only met a few days ago, but I already feel like we're going to be good friends."

"Me too. Besides, I'm happy to help you celebrate. I'll see you soon."

eight

DING! THE NOISE OF THE elevator doors parting snapped him out of his thoughts of Ezzie's long legs. With a groan, Luke dragged a hand down his face. He really had to get their one night together out of his head. Long enough they could talk. As much as he longed to be physical with her again, the emotional was more important.

She hadn't answered her door. That wasn't necessarily a bad sign. Maybe she'd gone downstairs for food or gone to her parents' room to spend some time with them. He had no clue which room they'd been given. Still, she had to be somewhere in the hotel. Where else would she have gone? She didn't know anyone else in town aside from him and her brother.

Luke stepped off the elevator and stopped as he caught a glimpse of an ass he knew pretty well shimmy out the front entrance of the hotel. Wait a second. Where the hell was Ezzie going?

And in that dress nonetheless.

Or lack thereof.

Snapping to attention, he strode across the hotel lobby and practically ran out the front entrance. He exited as a taxi drove off and headed toward the main street. Focusing on the taxi, he quickly confirmed Ezzie as its passenger. He shifted his gaze to one of two taxi cabs lined up along the sidewalk. Luke ran over to one and hopped in. "Hundred bucks if you catch that cab!"

"Yes, sir." The tires squealed as the driver forewent the meter, threw the taxi into drive, and peeled out of the hotel parking lot.

The movement flung Luke against the seat. At the rate the driver was going, they'd overtake Ezzie with no problem. As long as he survived the trip, he'd get his chance to talk to her. Starting with an apology. Plus, an explanation on why. Though she'd pointed out the reason quite succinctly, Ezzie deserved to know the truth. Most of it anyway. He wasn't prepared to go into details.

Not yet.

Maybe it would be quicker if he knew her destination. The car's tires shrieked as the driver made a hard-right turn. Luke grabbed onto the front passenger seat's headrest and held on tight. It would be *safer* if he knew her destination. Tightening his grip on the headrest, he dug his cell phone out of his pocket and attempted to tap out a text to Ezzie. Unfortunately, with the way the driver drove, his words came out garbled and mixed up.

The taxi screeched to a halt and Luke nearly lost hold of his cell phone as he bumped into the back of the front passenger seat. He lifted his eyes and groaned at the sea of taxis in front of them. *Shit!* Which one carried his woman?

"I'm sorry, sir. I did my best," the taxi driver said.

Luke scanned the taxis, but there were too many. He sighed and glanced around.

They were about five blocks or so from downtown. It wasn't huge, but it could take him a while if he had to check all the different restaurants, cafes, bars, even the clubs.

All right, new plan.

Shoving his phone back in his pocket, he plucked out his wallet and handed the driver a hundred-dollar bill. "I appreciate you trying."

"But, sir, I didn't catch the other taxi."

"It's okay. You got me far enough. I'll take it from here."

Tucking his wallet away, Luke climbed out of the taxi and headed for downtown. It wasn't much of a plan, but anything was better than nothing at this junction.

Bottom line, he had to do whatever it took to find his woman.

Ezzie's cell phone vibrated against the table for the tenth time in the last hour. She picked it up long enough to see who it was that time, though she had a pretty good guess. Luke had been texting her non-stop. Not that she intended to read any of the messages.

"Are you going to tell me who keeps interrupting our celebration?" Tasha asked.

Setting the phone face down, Ezzie stabbed a pasta shell and shoved it in her mouth. Great way to avoid the question. Too bad it couldn't last forever. "If I tell you, will you quit asking?"

"That depends. Will he stop texting?"

"I have no clue." She might if she bothered to read any of her messages. But she was still upset with him. Luke had pulled a whirlwind in less than twenty-four hours. Dropping her fork onto the plate, Ezzie leaned back in the booth.

Tasha shrugged. "Tell me anyway."

"It's this guy I like," Ezzie paused. She hadn't anticipated those words to come out. The "like" part anyway. Her anger at Luke didn't alter her feelings any. She didn't expect it to, but maybe some of her hurt had dissipated since their earlier altercation.

"Let me guess. He did something stupid."

More than one something, but no need to get into semantics. Either way, Luke had screwed up a couple of times. First with the note, then with the accusation. At the museum's shop she'd been uncertain about giving him the gift she'd ordered weeks ago. Then he'd gone off the deep end and acted like a jealous boyfriend. Before she'd realized it, she'd thrust the damn book in his hands and stormed off. Perfect way to end the fight.

Ezzie smirked. "Whatever gave you that idea."

"Because it's what they all do. Most of the time they're sweet and romantic, then bam! Out of nowhere they do something idiotic. At which point you're either forced to forgive them or walk away."

"So how do you decide?" Only one of her previous boyfriends had screwed up bad enough to not be forgiven. All of her other relationships ended amicably. For the most part. But Luke ... he was different. She wanted to forgive him. She just wasn't sure she could.

"Well, did he mess up so bad that you can imagine your life without him?"

That was a good question. Ezzie frowned. Could she imagine her life without Luke? Yeah, they'd known one another for a few years, but until recently they hadn't really spent any time together alone. They had always been around her brother or their respective families. But they had talked before. Plus, the way he cared about her brother. And how he treated his parents. Hell, the worry he showed over her. Even if he didn't accept it, Luke was kind-hearted, loving and he had an incredible soul. It was part of what attracted her to him in the first place.

She bit her bottom lip and sighed. "No."

Her cell phone vibrated again and Tasha snapped it up. "Then you need to give this poor fool a chance."

"What are you doing?" Ezzie's eyes widened and she bolted upright in the booth as she watched Tasha tap something out on her cell phone.

"Telling him where we're going."

Luke exited another restaurant empty-handed. He paused outside the entrance and inhaled the crisp summer air. Despite the number of bodies walking up and down the sidewalk, he noticed the gentle breeze that had settled throughout downtown. His long-sleeve shirt allowed him to remain comfortable as he headed in and out of restaurant after restaurant praying, he managed to find Ezzie at one of them.

He'd sent several texts, but all of them had gone—his phone vibrated in his back pocket. Had she finally answered? Luke dug the thing out and unlocked his cell. What? That couldn't be right. He blinked and read the message a second time.

I'm with a friend and we're heading to Club Jive. Feel free to join us.

Ezzie didn't hate dancing that he knew of, but Club Jive was known for one thing. Definitely not someplace she needed to be ... without him. Tucking his cell in the back pocket of his jeans, Luke surveyed his surroundings. If memory served, the club was two blocks across the street and the entrance down an alley. Shouldn't be hard to find.

He pushed through the throng of people and headed for the end of the block to the crosswalk. Waiting for some light to change was a hassle he didn't want to deal with, but people drove through downtown like it was a racetrack. Being with his girl was better than winding up dead in the middle of the road. He liked the sound of that. His girl. Luke's leg bounced impatiently as he stood there staring at a red stop light.

How would Ezzie feel about the title? How would Nate feel? The light flashed green and Luke jogged across the street. One issue at a time. First and foremost, he had to fix things with Ezzie. Then he could fret over her brother.

Between the crowd, the crosswalks, and the line to get in, it took him longer than he anticipated. From the Thai restaurant he figured ten minutes tops. It was closer to twenty by the time he got inside the club. Luke perused the bar area up front, but didn't spot Ezzie at all. There were two other bars, one in the back and one upstairs. Not likely she would hang out at either. She couldn't legally drink. Left only one other place.

He nudged his way through the mass to the edge of the dance floor and stopped. If her deep mahogany hair didn't stand out to him, the dress would. He had only caught a glimpse of the tiny black number she'd had on, but he'd seen enough. Luke searched the writhing bodies and his eyes landed on the one he'd been looking for.

Ezzie quit dancing and spun around on a man who had been all over her backside.

From this distance, he couldn't catch what she said, but her face scrunched up and her eyes narrowed at the man who stood there in a stupor. Luke balled up his fists and splayed his fingers out. Cracking his neck, he elbowed bodies out of his way and strode across the dance floor.

Crossing her arms, Ezzie glared at the dickhead that had been grinding up against her. "My ass isn't a tree. Stop trying to climb it."

The words had hardly left her mouth when Luke stepped in between her and the douche-bag, wrapped an arm around her waist and dropped his lips to hers. She felt the warmth of his lips from the top of her head all the way to the tips of her toes. Luke's tongue entangled with hers and he deepened the kiss as if she was the oxygen to his lungs.

Ezzie didn't intend to respond to Luke's kiss, but her body betrayed her. Of their own volition, her hands traveled the length of his arms. She grabbed a hold of his shoulders and pulled him closer. Oh, how she had missed him. They hadn't even been apart for twenty-four hours and already she couldn't imagine spending the rest of her life without him? Crikey. Stick a thermometer in her, she was done.

Releasing the kiss, Luke brushed his nose against hers and looked her straight in the eyes. "Sorry I'm late."

"You must be the guy," Tasha yelled over the din.

The comment reminded Ezzie they weren't alone. They were in public. Luke had kissed her in the middle of the dance floor as music blared around them. She blinked at the realization as he shifted around and kept one arm draped around her waist. Wait a second? He had never kissed her in public. True, it had only happened a few times, but they had always been alone. What changed? Had he kissed her for their benefit? Ezzie glanced over her shoulder. Or had it been for the benefit of the man who had already moved on to some other girl?

"You must be the friend," Luke said.

"That I am. Natasha Stovyck, but my friends call me Tasha."

"Luke Jonnihan. Ezzie's boyfriend."

Her eyes flipped back to Luke and Tasha, both of who were shaking hands as if the introduction were perfectly natural. Ezzie shifted her gaze to Luke. Had they entered an alternate reality or some shit? Traveled back in time? It had to be something freaky because last she checked she didn't have a boyfriend. And he certainly hadn't asked for the title.

"Nice to meet you."

"Yeah, you too. Mind if I borrow my girl for a few?" Luke asked.

"Feel free."

Luke nodded to Tasha and escorted Ezzie off the dance floor. They stopped and she watched as his head moved back and forth. He was searching for something ... or someone, but she couldn't tell what. Just as she was about to question him about it, Luke peered back at her and laced their fingers together. "Come with me, please."

He hadn't commanded or asked her to join him. He politely requested her presence. It wasn't unusual, but it was definitely out of place. Despite that, he probably knew she wouldn't refuse him. Not because she didn't have the capability to say no, but because she had to know what the hell was going on with him. The last twenty-four hours had been a funhouse she'd entered without full preparation of the outcome.

Even with all that, she'd still been able to speak, unlike the last five minutes which had completely stunned her to silence. It wasn't the first time she'd been clueless on how to react or what to say, but it had never been done so quickly before either. Hopefully it would be the last time that would happen tonight. In her life would be better, but tonight was more realistic.

Ezzie cleared her throat and found her voice. "Okay."

Seeming to accept her answer, Luke started forward and tugged her along. They walked around the outside of the dance floor toward the back bar, then surpassed it and headed down a long, dark hallway. Where the hell were they going? She didn't even know there was anything back there. Not like she'd been to the club before. Had he?

He led her by a couple of unmarked doors and stopped outside the next to last door. Luke opened it and gestured for her to go inside.

Ezzie surveyed the room. It wasn't that big. Bigger than a broom closet that was for sure, but not nearly as a big as an office. It was softly lit with a small bench, which was too high to sit on. What kind of room was this? She raised an eyebrow at him. "You want me to go in there?"

"Yes." Luke paused. "Do you trust me?"

Talk about a double-edged question. She had always trusted him. Always believed in him. The note had damaged part of that trust. His reaction afterwards broke it a little more. His jealously at the museum ... it didn't repair the damage, but it had led them to this moment. And that was more than just some peroxide on a wound.

"I trust you."

Without questioning the room any further, Ezzie stepped inside. It was larger than it appeared from the outside. She could easily move around without obstruction. On one side was a high-rise bench. Looked sturdy. Did it have a cushion? Opposite the bench was an armless, low-sitting red chair. Was that leather? Hmm. Interesting. Of course, the only way she could imagine being comfortable in the kind of chair was if she—Holy shit! This was a sex room!

Ezzie turned around and faced Luke as he flipped the lock in place. "Why'd you bring me in here?"

The question stopped him in his tracks. With the door locked, Luke drank in the sight of his girl. Wide midnight blue eyes glared back at him. Guess she figured out the true purpose of the room. He swallowed as he took Ezzie in from head to toe. The glimpse he caught of her earlier didn't do her justice. She looked delectable.

Her mahogany hair hung down in cascading waves. The black dress she wore tied off in a halter style around her neck and dipped to a "V" offering a beautiful view of her plump cleavage. From there the dress hugged every remaining delicious curve and ended a few inches past her oh-so-creamy thighs. And those matching fuck-me heels elongated her legs. If he had the chance, he'd devour her tonight.

Luke swallowed the lump in his throat. His intentions were pure and he had to remind himself of that. "Not for sex if that's what you're thinking."

Her shoulders slumped a touch. Ezzie crossed her arms. "Then why?"

Had that been disappointment that flashed in her eyes? It didn't last long, but certainly had been completely unexpected. He had to get that out of his head. Dropping a hand to his waist, Luke rubbed the top of his brow with his thumb. They were here for an important reason.

"I wanted to talk and this was the quietest place I could think of. I considered trying to convince you to leave with me, but I didn't think you'd go for that."

"You're right. I wouldn't." Ezzie glanced from the bench to the chair.

Great idea, dumbass, he thought. No real place for her to sit. The room didn't reek of sex, but it didn't have to smell to know what it was utilized for. What a way to make her feel secure. Luke sighed. "I'm sorry. I feel like I should've found another way to do this."

"This is fine. You said you wanted to talk. So, talk." Ezzie propped herself up against the wall.

Right. The reason he brought her in there to begin with. Where did he start? Why he kissed her in the first place? The reason behind his first apology? His last apology? God, how many times had he apologized to her? Luke frowned. A lot. But they had each come from the heart. Did she understand that? Even if she did and had previously accepted his words before, would they be enough now?

Lifting his gaze to Ezzie, he focused on the glisten in the iris of her blue eyes. "I'm sorry. I know I've said that a lot these last few days, but I swear to you each and every time I've apologized, I've meant it. So, before you say anything, please just hear me out. I messed up. I should've never left that note or walked out the door. As much as I'd like to believe an apology can make up for my idiocy, I don't think it goes far enough to show you how much I regret leaving you like that. I couldn't stop thinking about what I'd done all day yesterday. I know I only made it worse by not answering your texts or calls and I'm sorry for that. I should've talked it out with you."

Luke massaged the back of his neck. There was only one way he could mend the gap he'd created between them. It was something he'd decided on back at the museum. He had to open up to Ezzie, one of the many things she deserved. His past wasn't pretty, but that didn't mean he couldn't drop the wall he'd built to protect himself from feeling anything. She had already proven to be worth dropping his guard for and it was time he showed her.

"The truth is ... I got scared. You're the first woman I've been seriously attracted to in a long time. I guess I've avoided relationships for so long, I didn't really know how to handle that."

He could've sworn her hand lifted in his direction. That she had reached out to him. Whatever flitted across his girl's face didn't last long. With his admission hanging in the air, Luke desperately wanted to cross the room and wrap his arms around Ezzie. Just to hold her close, even if it was for one final time. But the decision was hers and hers alone. He stayed put.

"And now?" Ezzie pushed off the wall.

His heart fluttered at the question. He didn't dare draw too much hope from that or her actions. She could simply be re-adjusting. She had stood there in those fuck-me heels for a good ten minutes or so—perhaps longer. Inhaling and exhaling a soft deep breath, Luke rolled his shoulders. *Keep it together and be honest*, he reminded himself. "Now ... I don't know that I won't do something stupid again. I'm not perfect and I still believe you can do better. But I also don't want to live in a world that you're not with me. I don't want to go another day not talking to you. And I sure as hell don't want to see you with another man."

"Is that why you introduced yourself as my boyfriend? Because you saw that shithead dancing up on me?"

"I'm not going to pretend I liked it, but no." Luke grinned. The term had slipped off his tongue. Not that he had any desire to take it back. Thinking of her as his girl had been a hell of a lot better than pretending to be the man she deserved. Made him realize maybe one day he could be that man.

Stepping away from the wall, Ezzie closed some of the distance between the two of them. "Then why?"

"Because I'd like the title, if you'll give me the chance."

Movement was good. Fuck that! It was encouraging. He had no idea if he'd be able to come back from the last twenty-four hours. Maybe he had no clue what tomorrow would bring, but he loved where they were right then. Luke strode forward and met her halfway.

"Are you sure?"

He could think of a dozen different ways to answer that and they all boiled down to *yes*. Nothing could go wrong with her by his side. Luke caressed her cheek. "I've never wanted anything more."

"Then it's yours." She wrapped a hand around the nape of his neck and brushed a tender kiss against his lips.

His body hummed beneath the minor touch. So small and yet it solidified what they both desired from one another. Not just sex, but a relationship. There was so much to figure out, but he'd save all that for tomorrow. For now, he just wanted to be in the moment with his girlfriend. His girlfriend. Oh! He really liked the sound of that. Enveloping Ezzie in his arms, Luke pulled her body close. He stroked the inside of her mouth with his tongue and his lips crashed down on hers.

The uncontrollable need and desperation in the kiss they shared got him hard. He was dying to be inside of her, but that wasn't in the cards at the moment. Ezzie moaned, intensifying the growth behind the fly of his jeans. He'd have the biggest case of blue balls by the time they got back to the hotel, but he'd deal. He didn't have any other choice. He hadn't replenished from the other night.

Ezzie fisted Luke's thick, chestnut brown hair and thrust her breasts against his chest. The three times they'd been together the other night hadn't nearly been enough, especially with how the last twenty-four hours had played out. She needed him. Needed confirmation that all that had gone down in the past thirty minutes was real and not a dream.

Panting heavily, she released the kiss. Luke's deep chocolate brown eyes glazed with desire. Biting on her bottom lip, Ezzie eyed the red chair beside them. They were in a room made for sex and the walls had to be soundproof. She hadn't heard any noise the entire time they'd been in there.

Luke shook his head and leaned his forehead against hers. "We can't."

"I don't see why not," Ezzie teased. She could tell he wanted her as much as she wanted him. Unless he had a flashlight in his pocket, it was a rather hard part of him poking her in her belly. She nipped at his bottom lip.

Balling some of the fabric of the dress in his hand at the small of her back, he groaned. "Ezzie ... you've got to stop. I want you so bad right now, but if you keep this up, I'm going to lose control. And I don't ... I don't have any condoms with me."

Her mouth formed a silent *oh*. His reasoning was sound. She had the same rule. She had never slept with anyone without a condom. She didn't completely trust the guys she'd been with before. People lied about their number all the time. It was safest for both parties involved if sex occurred with protection.

None of that mattered with Luke. Yeah, he'd been a player, but she trusted he kept himself clean. She believed he had been tested regularly and she was on birth control. Hadn't they been apart long enough? Her body ached with desire and he was the only one who could quench that hunger. Her rule had been implemented for anyone, but Luke. She knew that in her heart. In her soul. She trusted him with her life.

Ezzie caressed his chin. "I'm on the pill."

"Fuck, this is a bad idea, but I need you too much." Fusing his lips with hers, Luke backed them up to the chair. He dropped in the seat and tugged Ezzie down with him.

The hem of her short dress automatically hiked up as she straddled Luke's hips. It was like the dress had welcomed their connection with open arms. Her knees pressed into the chair as she gyrated against his long, hard shaft through his jeans. That and the thin material of her thong created the perfect amount of friction.

Not that she could keep this up for long. Her body flushed with heat from head to toe. Using her hand, Ezzie slipped off her heels. Hell, if she could, she'd shuck the whole damn dress. Except it clung to her body. The only way she'd get out of it was if Luke peeled her out. Once it came off, it wasn't going back on. Something for later.

Luke's hands lowered to her ass and kneaded both cheeks. He growled, dropped his mouth to the curve of her collarbone and sucked on her neck. It was almost as if he was marking her, which turned her on more.

She rolled her head back and gave him better access to her neck. The coolness of his tongue counteracted the warmth of his mouth as he suckled. Whimpering at the touch, she dug her nails into his shoulder blades. God, she needed more of him. More of his tongue, all over her body. Not as if that was possible at the moment. Oh! But there was something she could have his tongue all over. Ezzie reached up to the nape of her neck and unhooked the small strap holding the top half of the dress in place.

Moving his hands, he massaged her hips and lifted his head as the halter part of the dress slid down and revealed her round breasts. Luke covered one pert nipple with his mouth and stroked the other with his thumb.

Arching her back, Ezzie moaned. She had never been so grateful for having decided to forego a bra tonight. Her core throbbed. This was going be quicker than she would like, but she couldn't hold out much more. Her hands roamed along Luke's arms and squeezed his biceps. His muscles strained and flexed under her nimble fingers.

Taking the other nipple in his mouth, his hand skimmed down her belly and skated over her thigh. Rubbing his hand against the lace material of her thong, he groaned against her breast. "Fuck, you're wet."

Tingling all over, she pressed into his hand and captured his lips again. Ezzie reached between them and undid the button and zipper of his jeans. She was done waiting. They could go on exploring one another later. She nibbled on his earlobe and huskily whispered. "I need you inside me now."

"Sit up."

Following his instructions, she hoisted her hips off of him and spread her legs a bit more. Luke yanked part of his jeans and boxers down. His cock popped out and stood fully erect.

Ezzie didn't wait for any further invitation. She pulled the thong aside and sank back taking in his thick length. They both moaned. A tremble passed through her body as he filled her to the hilt. Locking his lips with hers, she relished the taste of him as their tongues entangled and she fell into a steady rhythm rocking her hips back and forth. She was already so close.

He released the passionate kiss and repositioned their connected bodies. Luke slid further down the chair, grabbed her hips and thrust deep inside of her. Burying his face in her breasts, he nipped at a nipple and drove into her slick folds faster and faster.

She cried out as his shaft hit her G-spot over and over again. Increasing the pace, she rode him harder. Hooking her arms under his, Ezzie crushed their bodies together. With electricity searing through her body, she raked her nails down his back. It sent them both over the top and neither could hold it in any longer.

Her core lit up like Christmas in July as every synapse exploded and set off a chain reaction. Ezzie and Luke came together. Both shuddered and loud shrieks of ecstasy resounded throughout the room. Dropping her head onto his shoulder, she stayed linked to him until they both managed to catch their breath.

Luke pressed a feather kiss to her forehead. "This might sound weird, but since we're here, at the club, I mean, how would you feel about a dance?"

Sitting up, she smiled. "You'd do that?"

"For you I would."

"You do know I'm not the steadiest dancer, right? So, you may just have to hold on to me." Her dance moves consisted of shaking her ass and nothing more. The dance floor and her didn't get along all that well. Though if Luke were holding onto her, then she'd be in her favorite place. The rest wouldn't matter.

"That's even better. Means I never have to let go." Luke grinned.

nine

ROLLING ONTO HIS SIDE, LUKE patted the empty space next to him in bed. It couldn't be that late, could it? He cracked an eye open and glanced at the clock on the nightstand. Shit! Was it really just after eight in the morning? Sitting upright, he stretched and hopped out of the king size bed he'd spent the night in cozied up to Ezzie, at least when he hadn't been buried deep inside of his girlfriend.

Two words he never thought would go together: Ezzie and girlfriend. Talk about something that had a beautiful ring. Luke tugged on a pair of boxers and stepped out of the bedroom. Music drifted softly from the kitchen. Rubbing the back of his head, he followed the sound and paused in the kitchen doorway. He beamed as he took in the sight before him.

In nothing save his t-shirt, Ezzie swayed to a Maroon Five song as she danced between the kitchen counter and the stove.

He watched on as her feet tapped along to the beat. His eyes continued all the way up her long slightly tanned legs. The hem of his t-shirt fell just below her plump ass. It did nothing to hide her deliciously curvy hips, perfectly muscular waist and voluptuous breasts. He leaned against the doorframe as he drank in her slender neck, strong jaw, and silky mahogany locks. His body tingled as his gaze roamed the generous contours of her body. The idea of burying himself inside her for breakfast woke his cock up.

Ezzie spun on her heel and faced him. With a gasp, her eyes widened. "Crikey! How long have you been standing there?"

"Long enough." Luke closed the distance between them. Firmly gripping her hips, he pressed his erection into her belly and stroked her bottom lip with his tongue.

Fusing her lips to his, she deepened the kiss and sucked on his tongue. Moaning into his mouth, she released the kiss. "Good morning."

"Mmm, it would be an even better morning if you turned the stove off."

"I would, but we need to eat and leave." Ezzie slipped out of his arms and turned back to the crumbled sausage she was frying up.

Leave? Luke frowned. They hadn't made any plans with her family or his. Last he checked they could spend all day in bed together. Given they were all returning home tomorrow it sounded like heaven. Who the hell would ruin that?

"Says who?"

"My mom and I have to finish packing up my brother and I'm meeting Tasha for lunch."

"I thought Becca was helping Nate."

God, Nate. Luke ran a hand through his hair. He still had to tell Nate the good news. Maybe he could do that while Ezzie and her mother packed Nate's room. Witnesses seemed like a good idea, though maybe not her parents. Or maybe he should talk to them first.

"She was going to, but from what Nate said they ended up having to leave this morning." Ezzie shut the stove off and carried the frying pan to the sink. Using a partially cut water bottle, she drained the remaining grease and returned to the kitchen counter.

"And when are you supposed to meet Tasha?"

Mixing together two bowls of grits, eggs, sausage, cheese, onions and peppers, she glanced at him. "Noon. She's got a three o'clock flight, so we decided to have lunch before she heads home."

Hmm, maybe it would make better sense to sit her parents and Nate down together. Tell them all at once. That would be the right thing to do. Then at least any protests could all be made at the same time. "Okay. I guess I can pick you up after and we can talk to your parents and Nate then. Probably here in ... the ... hotel."

Halfway through the mixing process, Ezzie stopped and narrowed her eyes at him.

"What? What's that look?"

Setting the bowl of scrambled eggs aside, she twisted in Luke's direction. She had been thinking about that all morning. They had just gotten together and while she was positive her parents would be happy; her brother would probably be less than thrilled.

Ezzie sighed. "What if we kept this between us?"

"What?"

"I'm not saying forever, just a few weeks. Luke, you're going to Massachusetts in two months and I'm heading to California. The distance between our homes now is only three hours, but what's it going to be like when we're thousands of miles apart?"

She truly believed they would find a way to work the long-distance thing out. But what if they couldn't? What if it proved too much of a strain on their relationship? They'd been together a few days, if that. If they didn't work, then the last thing she wanted was for him to lose his best friend too.

Propping himself up against the kitchen counter, Luke crossed his arms. "I don't know, but we'd manage it."

"And if we can't handle the three hours apart, would you think the same thing?"

It had been a hard decision, but she'd weighed out all the possibilities. It would kill her to keep this secret from her family, not as if it would be the first and not likely the last, but it was the most logical.

"I don't know."

Ezzie reached up and swept her fingers through his chestnut locks that spiked everywhere. He had bed-head in the worst way. She caressed his cheek. "I like you. A lot. More than anything, I want this to work, but if it doesn't, the last thing I would want is for you to be in a new place with nobody there to support you."

"You really think Nate would turn his back on me? On our friendship?"

"Not permanently. I think he'll be pissed. He'd eventually forgive you, but I don't want to chance him ignoring you unnecessarily."

Her brother had forgiven people for worse. Hell, he'd given second and third chances to people she believed he was an idiot for trusting. She was the only exception. Anyone who hurt her might as well be dead. Ezzie loved her brother, but Nate was a stubborn fool sometimes and entirely overbearing when it came to her.

Luke brushed a loving kiss to Ezzie's lips and enveloped her in his arms. "Okay. So, what's the plan?"

"We give it four weeks. As long as we're still going strong, we'll sit down with him and my parents together. That'll give him another four weeks to get used to the idea of us as a couple." Ezzie rested her head against Luke's chest. His heart beat steady. She could fall asleep to that sound every night. Being even one night apart from him was going to be tough. She hated that they lived so far away from one another.

"Four weeks. When does that mean we'll get to see one another next?"

An unexpected rumble replaced the rhythm she had focused on. Grinning wide, she uncurled from his arms and finished putting their breakfast bowls together. Ezzie held one out to him. "Probably sometime later this week or next weekend."

"Guess I should make the most of the time we have together now then." He grabbed her waist and tugged her flush against his body. Crashing his lips to hers, Luke shoved his tongue in her mouth.

Wrapping her arms around his neck, Ezzie stroked his tongue with her own and moaned into the kiss. Electricity pulsated through her body and shot straight to her core. She could feel Luke's rock-hard length pressed into her belly. If they kept going like this, they'd never eat. With a ragged breath, she released her hold of Luke and held the bowls between them. "Food."

Waggling his brows, he collected both bowls and set them on the counter. "Food can wait. I can't."

Luke tossed her over his shoulder and smacked her ass. She squealed. "But it'll get cold!"

"That's what microwaves are for."

Sealing up another box of books, Ezzie turned to her mother. "Do you ever think we've spoiled Nate by doing all of this for him?"

"Oh, I'm sure of it. He's almost twenty-two and he still can't pack his own belongings, but if we wait on him to do it, it'll either be half-ass thrown together or halfway done."

With a shake of her head, Ezzie laughed and set the box on the floor. She surveyed the dorm room. Between the two of them, nearly everything had been packed. The only thing that remained was whatever was in her brother's closet. "Meaning we'd have to come behind him and fix it or finish it anyway."

"Exactly." Her mother closed the dresser drawer and set the final pair of jeans in Nate's suitcase.

Crossing the room, Ezzie paused in front of the closet and reached for a couple of shoe boxes from the top shelf. "Have you and Dad decided how you're going to move both of us at the same time?"

"Oh, that's easy. We're going to escort your brother to Massachusetts a day or two before you leave for California. You've got Matt's family. Plus, I figure it'll give you a little more time with Luke."

"What?" Dropping the shoebox in her hands, her wide eyes snapped in her mother's direction. Ezzie blinked. She had *not* heard her mother correctly. Nope. No way. Did not happen. Her mother had not uttered a single word that involved Luke.

"I'm not blind. I've seen the way he looks at you."

Ezzie swallowed. She and Luke had agreed not to say anything to their respective families. How had her mother figured anything out? Okay. She could handle this. She kneeled down and collected the mess of cards from the floor. "I have no idea what you're talking about, Mom."

"Maybe you're right. Of course, that would also mean it was some other man I saw you kissing in the hotel lobby this morning."

"Mom!"

Holding tight to the shoebox, Ezzie jumped to her feet and marched to the bed where her mother taped up another box. Oh shit! Shit, shit, shit. She had walked him down to the lobby earlier and hadn't thought twice about kissing him on the lips before they parted ways for the day. How in the hell had she missed spotting her mother in the same lobby? Or temporarily forgotten her parents were staying in the same hotel?

Her mother dropped her hands to her hips and smirked. "Esmeralda. You don't really expect me to believe that bull-honky you just tried to deliver, do you?"

Well, yes, she thought. Or she hoped. Who was she kidding? Her mother probably believed her clueless statement about as much as she believed the line about her period the day before. Ezzie placed the shoeboxes on the bed and sighed. "Okay, fine. Yes, you saw us together. Can you just keep it to yourself for now? We want to see if it's going anywhere before we say anything to Nate."

"I don't like it, but I get it. Your brother can be a little hot-headed at times, something he gets from your father." Her mother waved it off and packed up the items Ezzie had laid out on the bed.

"Does Dad know?" Her eyes widened for a second time. If her father knew, there'd be no keeping it a secret from her brother. They'd have to come clean and deal with the consequences.

"No. I was the only one downstairs and I haven't said anything to him.

I wanted to talk to you about it first."

Ezzie released a breath of relief. She and Luke would have to be careful until they got home. They were all on the same plane. They wouldn't officially go their separate ways until they reached the airport in Salt Lake City. Okay. No big deal. The two of them could handle this. She had secrets only Matt knew about. Compared to that this would be nothing more than a town bake-off. "Thanks, Mom."

"Listen, I know your father will be happy for you both. As long as your happy. As for Nate, he'll come around."

"I know. I just want to hold off. At least for a month. Please, please keep this to yourself," she begged. There had been little she'd ever asked her mother for. This was one of those decisions she needed her mother to trust was the right one.

"All right. You're an adult and I trust you know what you're doing."

Her cell phone in the back pocket of her denim shorts vibrated. Ezzie dug her phone out and checked it. Tucking it away in her back pocket, she gave her mother a quick hug. "That's my taxi. I'm off to meet my friend for lunch. You got the rest of this?"

The dorm room door opened and Nate walked in. "Are you guys done?"

Her mother squeezed her hands. "Yeah. I'll do the unthinkable and put your brother to work. Now, go have fun."

"Thanks Mom. I'll see you later. Later bro." Ezzie grinned as she raced out the door.

Whistling, Luke strode down the hall and headed toward his dorm room. Ezzie had texted him a few minutes ago that she was done with lunch with her friend. They planned to meet at the movie theater in an hour and then they'd head back to the hotel. Sounded like a great way to spend their last night in town together. Then they could figure out when they could see each other again.

Luke opened the door to his and Nate's dorm room and stepped inside. He paused in the doorway and cracked a grin. For the first time ever, he spotted his best friend packing up his own things with no one else around. "Did your mom entrust you to finish by yourself?"

"Seriously? No. She went to get a couple more boxes. Thought I had enough."

"That makes sense. Wait, why didn't you go down and get the boxes?" Luke frowned. Sure, their mothers weren't weak, but even still, Nate should've made the run. Not his mom.

Nate shrugged. "She offered? Actually, I think it's some kind of conspiracy between her and my sister. When I came in, I could tell they'd been talking about something."

Crossing over to his side of the room he grabbed his suitcase from the end of the bed. Shaking his head, he smirked. "Doesn't mean it was about you."

"Never know," Nate paused. "You already take all your stuff down?"

"Yeah. I packed everything up in my car earlier. Figured I'd crash at the hotel tonight with my parents."

Lingering at the end of the bed, Luke stared at his best friend. Would Nate really blow up like Ezzie suggested? Nah. She had to be overreacting. Yeah, they agreed to wait before saying anything, but he hated the idea of keeping a secret like this from his best friend.

"I should probably do the same thing. Make it easier on leaving. Plus, Ezzie's got the room."

Gripping the back of his neck, Luke set his suitcase back on the floor and opened his mouth. Then his friend's last comment registered. "Ezzie?"

"Sure. I wouldn't crash with my parents. Besides, I need to make sure no guy tries to pick her up our last night here."

"Don't you think that's her decision?"

He may really need to rethink this thought process. Nate had always been kind of laid back. Mostly. Nate had always been a little overprotective when it came to Ezzie, but Luke figured it had more to do with being younger more than anything else. College guys were only more filled out high school guys.

"Oh no. With the list of douche-bags she's brought around, I intend to make sure she stays single until she graduates college. Then she can date and only the guys I approve."

What the hell kind of bullshit logic was that? Ezzie was eighteen and completely capable of deciding who she wanted to date. That included him. Not someone her brother picked out. Luke crossed his arms and narrowed his eyes. "What are you going to do? Pre-screen them?"

"If that's what I have to do."

"I'm back. Oh, hi Luke." Nate's mother stepped into the room with a couple of empty boxes in her arms.

God, he'd never been more grateful for an interruption. If he had to listen to another asinine thought come out of his best friend's mouth, he might have punched him. Definitely a bad idea to tell Nate about him and Ezzie.

Luke jumped to the door and grabbed a hold of the boxes Nate's mother had been carrying. "Hey, Mrs. Donovan. Here, let me help you with that."

"Thank you. So, are you planning to spend the night here? I know Nate was thinking about it."

Taking the boxes to Nate's bed, Luke smiled. It was the perfect question and he had the perfect answer. "No. I'm gonna crash at the hotel with my parents. Nate told me he thought it was a good idea and he'd do the same."

"Oh Nate, that would be wonderful! Your father and I haven't seen much of you since we arrived."

"That isn't what I said." Nate sneered and turned to his mother. "No offense Mom, but I figured I'd crash in Ezzie's room."

"You'll do no such thing. Your sister is perfectly fine by herself. She doesn't need you hovering around," Nate's mother said.

"Mom, come on. Be reasonable. Ezzie isn't little anymore. What if some guy tries to take advantage of her while we're here?"

Nate's mother crossed her arms. "Let me tell you something, Nathan Marcus Donovan. Your sister is a hell of a lot stronger than you think.

And quite capable of fending for herself. Just a few months ago she had a situation that she handled rather well, in my opinion."

"Wait, what? What situation? And why the hell wasn't I told about it?" Nate's eyes narrowed and his nostrils flared.

Situation? Ezzie hadn't mentioned anything to him about it. And they had talked about a lot of stuff in the last few days. Not really past stuff, but future stuff for sure. Luke frowned. He kind of wanted to know about this too.

"A young man at school thought he'd get fresh and grab her behind. Your sister didn't take too kindly to that. Not that I blame her, but I'm pretty sure he learned his lesson." Nate's mother beamed.

"What the hell does that mean?" Nate yelled.

"Let's just say he was singing soprano for a while."

Ouch. Luke shuddered at the thought of his girl kneeing the shit out of some guy's bits. Right. Remind him never to piss her off. Not anymore than he already had. Speaking of? He glanced at his watch. He needed to get out of there. Heading back to his side of the room, he collected his suitcase.

Nodding his head, Nate glanced over his shoulder at Luke. "You outta here man?"

"Yeah. I'm catching a movie with some friends." It was close enough to the truth. Clutching tight to the handle of his suitcase, Luke started for the door.

"Mind if I join?" Nate began for the door as well.

Nate's mother stepped in his path. "Don't even think about it. You're going to finish packing so we can get this downstairs. I'm not spending all day getting you together."

"But, Mom!"

"But nothing. Your sister and I have done enough for you. It's time you do something for yourself." Nate's mother peered over at Luke. "Have a good time, dear."

With a quick nod, Luke waltzed out the door. That was strange, the way Nate's mother intervened and looked at him. Did she know? Nah. He had to have imagined it. No way she could know. If she had, she probably would've said something and then Nate would've definitely known. Yep. Completely imagined the look.

Ezzie focused on the steady thump of Luke's heart as he lazily stroked her arm. She liked the feel of his slick skin against her own. The two of them bundled up together under the covers was a memory she'd hold onto. It would probably be a few days before they could get together again. And for them to curl up like this, they'd have to get a hotel somewhere outside of her hometown.

He brushed a feather-like kiss to her forehead. "I was thinking, how does a picnic sound? There's a small park in Ephraim that we could go to if you want. Maybe Tuesday?"

"A picnic sounds like a great idea, but I can't on Tuesday. Matt gets back tomorrow too and he and I have a lot of decisions to make about our apartment." Not to mention she hadn't spoken to her best friend in a couple of days. They had a lot to catch up on. Thankfully he hadn't blown up her phone with a bunch of texts.

"Have I mentioned lately how much I am against you living with another man?"

Ezzie lifted her head and rested her chin on Luke's bare chest. He had to be kidding. This was Matt they were talking about, a guy who couldn't be less interested in her. "You're joking, right?"

"Oh yeah, because I absolutely love the idea of my extremely sexy girlfriend staying in another state with another man."

She covered her mouth and stifled a giggle. Okay. She shouldn't laugh, but she was amused. Ezzie blinked as a frown crossed Luke's face. Shit. He was dead serious. "Oh my god. Are you jealous?"

"What? No." Luke slipped out from beneath her arms and climbed out of the bed.

Jealous or not, she liked the view. Ezzie propped up on her side and dug her elbow into the mattress as her eyes drifted across Luke's broad shoulders down his strong back and over his round ass. He was gorgeous and all hers. She licked her top lip as she watched him bend over and yank on his boxers.

Holy shit. The green-eyed monster had really dug its heels in. Holding the sheet against her breasts, Ezzie sat up on her knees and shimmied across the bed. "You really are jealous."

Turning around to face her, Luke dropped his hands to hips. "What if I am? Wouldn't you be if the roles were reversed?"

"Probably, but I trust you. I know you would make any line clear." And if Matt had been straight, she would straight forward tell him she had no interest. Luke had stolen her heart months ago. Not that she would say anything. It was way too soon for that. Ezzie shuffled forward until she was right in front of her boyfriend.

"I do trust you. I don't trust whoever this man is you'll be living with."

No need to tease the man any further. Apparently, her boyfriend was clueless on the entirety of the situation. Hadn't she told him about Matt? Hmm, maybe not. She reached up and caressed Luke's cheek. "Trust me; you have nothing to worry about. I'm not Matt's type."

"That doesn't make me feel better. You're hot as fuck, smart, patient, kind, and you cook. I can't imagine any man in his right mind who wouldn't be attracted to you."

She'd have to remember to tell Matt that. The thought was ludicrous. Ezzie giggled. The way Luke's brows furrowed and his face scrunched silenced her. She pressed a tender kiss to her boyfriend's lips. "My dear sweet Luke, I could walk around naked and Matt would tell me to put some clothes on."

A growl rumbled from deep within his throat. "I'd kill him for even looking at you."

"Oh my god. Matt's gay." Straight forward and blunt. Crikey, she should've gone with that to begin with. As fun as it had been to torture her man, it took way too much for him to get the picture.

"Oh. That makes me—wait, how gay? Are we talking flamboyant gay or butch gay?"

How the hell was she supposed to answer that? Did it matter? Ezzie canted her head as she thought about it. Matt had grown into his body their senior year. Definitely lean and cut. Well-toned. Hmm, nope; didn't help any. "Well, he has bulked up in the last year. But he knows his designers backward and forward."

Luke sighed. "If a stranger entered the house, is he more likely to run and scream or stand and defend his home?"

"Oh. He's going to stand and defend. I promise you; I will be fine. Tell you what, why don't I arrange a meeting between you two? Would that make you feel better?"

His concern had been duly noted, but unnecessary. Not only did Matt know the girly things she didn't, he also often accompanied her in the outdoor things she liked to do. Camping, fishing ... they'd even gone to a gun range once. Ezzie grinned. She had no doubt he and Luke would get along just fine.

"Yes, but you know what would make me feel even better?"

She sucked in her bottom lip. Oh, she had a few things in mind. Wrapping a hand around the nape of his neck, she nipped at his earlobe. "Seeing me naked again? Having me writhe beneath you? Or riding you until dawn?"

Pulling the sheet away, Luke grabbed her waist and crushed her body against his. "I like the sound of all of that. But I'd really like to know when I can see you again."

"I'm game on the picnic. Wednesday work for you?"

"I like Tuesday better, but Wednesday will suffice." He captured her lips with his and sucked on her tongue. His hands slid down to her ass and kneaded her cheeks.

Goosebumps covered her body as it heated underneath his touch. Electricity coursed through her veins and her core blossomed. Eager to have him inside of her once again, Ezzie moaned into the kiss.

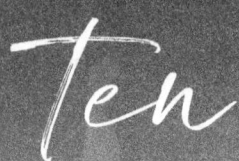

Ten

"BUT YOU SAW THE SIZE of that kitchen? Isn't that the one you liked best?"

Ezzie groaned and flopped back on Matt's bed. They had been at this for two days now. She should've expected him to do this. He showed her the videos of all the apartments he'd toured in Los Angeles. Not once did he mention money. Pick first, fret about cost after. She rubbed her temples. Crikey, her head throbbed. She hated when he pulled this stunt. "It doesn't matter. We can't afford three thousand dollars a month."

Throwing his hands in the air, Matt sat down beside her. "Why do you keep bringing that up? I already told you money is no object."

Propping up on her elbows, she glared at him. "Maybe not for you, but it is for me. That luxury complex by the university is perfectly acceptable and inexpensive."

"And tiny!"

"But we could walk to class and I can still cook and bake in that kitchen." Ezzie frowned and sat upright. Why couldn't he just accept what she was saying? It made the most sense for them to be logical in their decision. It couldn't be all about what they wanted, but what they could afford plus still have some of their desires met.

He crossed his arms. "That kitchen was a joke. What if you have to drive ten minutes or spend an hour on the bus to get to class? The Orsini is gated. It has a doorman. The kitchen is made for a chef. There are yoga classes, a lounge, plus we'll be close to downtown. You can't ask for more."

Oh no. Oh no, no, no, no. *Please tell me he didn't,* Ezzie thought. He had pushed way too hard on this place. And the way he'd spoken about it. Shit! She bet he did. "Oh, come on! You put a deposit down already, didn't you?"

Matt's green eyes widened for a second, then he dropped his gaze to the bed and picked at some invisible lint on the comforter. "I might have."

Son of a bitch! She jumped to her feet and paced from one side of his bedroom to the other. "I thought we were gonna decide on this together. Isn't that what you told me?"

"Ezzie, listen to me. I looked at all the apartments and took videos like you asked me to, but I knew we wouldn't be happy in any of them. Then I saw this one and everything was perfect. Yes, I know the rent is a bit much, but I knew I had to act. I figure you just give me what you can and I'll take care of the rest."

She stopped pacing and propped up against his dresser. This was so like him. Hell, his parents were the same way. It wasn't enough they paid for the hotel she had just spent four glorious nights in, but they had to pay for the graduation dinner too. And now this. Sure, his family didn't hurt when it came to money, but this was one thing she wanted to pay on her own. At least her part. "Matt, why do you do this? You know I can't even begin to pay you back for this past week and then you go and do this? I honestly don't know whether to hug you or smack you."

"Go with the hug. I'd agree to the smack, but I wouldn't enjoy it nearly as much as I'd like."

Cracking a smile, Ezzie shook her head. "What am I going to do with you?"

"For starters, you could stop being upset with me. Then you can accept that we are moving into a fabulous apartment, which you will adore. And finally, you can tell me all about your time with Mr. Hottie as I have yet to hear a single detail since you got back." Matt grinned.

"Touché." He made a valid point. She had focused so much on the apartment, she hadn't uttered a single word about her trip, which was surprisingly difficult given the amount of texts she and Luke had exchanged over the last forty-eight hours. Only another seventeen hours to go and she'd be leaving to see him again.

"Does this mean you are finally on board with The Orsini?"

He hadn't given her much of a choice. Either that or she'd have to check to see if any dorm rooms were available. Ezzie shuddered at the idea. Nope. Not happening. She had heard enough horror stories to last a lifetime. "Yep. I'm game."

"Good. Now tell me all about your hottie and I'll tell you all about *mine*." Matt belted out the last word in a sing-song voice.

Oh yeah. She had forgotten all about the guy Matt said he met. Hmm. What was his name? Cole? Colt? No. Colin! That was it. Now that she thought back on it though, he hadn't told her how they met. Maybe now she could find out. She'd have to remember to ask. Pushing off the dresser, Ezzie headed back to the bed and sat down. "You recall the dress I showed you? For the opera we went to?"

"The Roberto Cavalli. Uh, to die for. Please don't tell me he ruined it."

"What? No. He helped me out of it rather carefully." Ezzie giggled. It pooled at her feet. That counted, right?

"I love watching the sunset from here."

"It is beautiful."

Luke smiled. Of course, the sunset looked better with her there, not that he'd tell her that. He still couldn't fathom how he ended up with her by his side. They had only technically been together for a few days and

Ezzie made it feel like a lifetime. He shifted his gaze from the pinks and purples created by the setting sun to his girlfriend. A term he still hadn't grown accustomed to using. How long would it take for him to get there?

Would he ever get there? He had to, otherwise they'd never end up telling her family. Not that that sounded like a bad idea. Then he'd never have to chance losing anyone. Luke shook his head. Nope. He couldn't think like that. He had to stay positive about his and Ezzie's relationship. It was a good thing. Wonderful even. He might even say beautiful. About as beautiful as Ezzie was at that moment with the swirls of the soft night sky surrounding her.

Luke dug out his cell phone and tapped into his camera app. Hmm, while her silhouette was stunning, he really wanted to capture her face. "Hey, Ez?"

"Yeah?" She propped back on her hand and turned toward him.

Perfect. With a wide grin, Luke snapped a picture. He couldn't have executed that any better if he tried.

"You know that usually comes out best with two people in it." Ezzie stated matter-of-factly and crawled over to him. Snagging the phone out of his hand, she snuggled in close and flipped it to selfie-mode.

He didn't really care for photographs of himself. Luke buried his face in her hair and pressed a tender kiss to the top of her shoulder. He reached up for his cell phone and glanced at the picture she took. Talk about timing. The photograph showed the outline of his jaw, nose, and part of one eye. Nothing much there. His girlfriend on the other hand, a gorgeous smile of pure and utter bliss was plastered on her face.

"Now that's a picture."

"How can you say that? You're barely in it."

"No, but you are. And to me, that's perfect."

He didn't need to be in the picture. He only needed her in them. But Ezzie was stubborn. She'd probably try again to capture a real picture of them together. One way to prevent that. Luke set his phone aside on the blanket.

She crossed her arms. "Flattery will get you nowhere."

He sighed. Truth be told, he wasn't ready for that. Yeah, he'd almost said something to her brother about the two of them dating that past Sunday, but Nate's choice words might've affected him more than he'd have liked. Luke was pretty sure his balls had shrunk in the midst of that conversation. Now, he'd do anything to keep his relationship with her a secret from everyone, which included hiding his face in any kind of photograph. But how did he go about telling her that? There had to be a good way to explain himself.

Luke stroked her cheek. "I'm sorry. I guess ... I'm still trying to figure this out some. I like the idea of us in a picture together, but it scares me too."

She covered his hand with her own and kissed the inside of his palm. "I get that. If you need time, I'll give it to you. Whatever you need, just tell me and I can do it. I'm in no rush."

Not many women would have been so compassionate about the situation, at least not the ones he'd come across. They all would've turned the tables and questioned if it was them. But not his Ezzie. She wasn't like any other woman he'd been around. Luke brushed a soft kiss across her lips and leaned his forehead against hers. "I don't know how I wound up with someone as understanding as you, but I'm glad I did."

"Makes two of us. Now, how about we head off and find some food." Ezzie hopped to her feet, swept her denim skirt down and tugged at the hem of her white tank top.

With a quick nod, Luke stood and stretched. Man, they had been on the ground for a while. He surveyed the area. They'd been in that one spot for a couple of hours and no one had joined them, not even in the nearby surroundings. "How'd you find this place? I mean, I knew the park was big, but I didn't know there was any part of it people really didn't frequent."

"I've been up here a lot since spring break. It took me a while, but after several hikes I stumbled on this part of the park. Gave me a great view and offered the solace and peace I'd been seeking."

Four words in her explanation stuck out to him: *spring break, solace,* and *peace.* He remembered spring break she'd shown up at his and Nate's dorm room unexpectedly. Something had happened. What was it? Oh yeah. She had caught her then boyfriend in a comprising situation with one of her friends. Luke shook his head. What an idiot. Ezzie was not the type of woman you cheated on or let go. Not something he ever planned to do.

He draped an arm around her shoulders and hugged her into his chest. "Thank you for sharing it with me."

"I couldn't imagine sharing it with anyone else." She rose up on her tip-toes and pressed her lips to his.

Luke deepened the kiss until they were both out of breath and his dick strained against his fly. Panting, he scanned the area once again. Exactly how alone were they? Probably not that alone. Not that he could see anyone and it had gotten darker. But what if the park staff came upon them? He swallowed. God, as much as he wanted her right then, it was a bad idea. A bad idea.

Ezzie nipped at his earlobe. "I forgot to tell you ... I'm not wearing any panties."

"You're killing me woman." He groaned. Fuck. He was dying to get inside her. Dropping his lips back to hers, Luke lowered her onto the blanket once more. Laying her down, he peppered kisses along her neck and caressed her arm with his fingertips.

Pushing her breasts against his chest, she moaned and dug her nails into his shoulder blades. Ezzie fisted his t-shirt. Her bare hands stroked his bunched up back muscles.

Another delicious sound of ecstasy escaped her lips. God, she was driving him crazy. Luke fused his mouth to hers and captured the intoxicating noises coming from her. He cupped one of her breasts and slowly kneaded it.

How alone were they? Could they really get away with doing this here? He released the kiss and stared at her glassy blue eyes. She was just as turned on as him.

Luke swallowed. Fuck. He didn't want to stop, but this place couldn't be that secluded.

He opened his mouth and Ezzie pressed a finger to his lips. "Sshh. I promise, no one's going to see us."

It didn't take a genius to figure out why Luke had stopped. But she hadn't been kidding when she'd told him no one would catch them. They could see the lodge from their little clearing, but no one could see them. This small spot was secluded from the rest of the park. The one time she'd even try to find it from the lodge with binoculars had proven fruitless.

They were completely alone and this place deserved a good memory. Tightening her grip on his back, Ezzie tugged him closer and locked her lips with his. She shoved her hands up under his t-shirt and inched it higher and higher, urging him to lose the first article of clothing. Once it was gone, everything else would surely follow and then she'd get him exactly where she longed to have him.

With a growl, Luke sat up and yanked his shirt over his head.

She lifted her own tank up and barely got it off before his lips crashed against hers. Crikey. He felt so good! Running her hands across his broad shoulders, she worked on memorizing every single contour and every crevice. She didn't know them all yet, but nothing would prevent her from getting close and personal with every single ripple of muscle.

Goosebumps crept up her arms as Luke stroked one of her already puckered nipples. He released the kiss and nipped at her neck, then slid a bra strap from her shoulder and he sucked on the other nipple through the lace bra.

Gasping at the attention to her breasts, Ezzie rubbed her thighs together in anticipation of where they'd inevitably end up. She'd never been more grateful for locating this little spot off the beaten path. Even if—no she couldn't go there. The why would ruin the mood and she needed him too badly to do that.

In fact, maybe she should encourage him a bit more. Her fingertips skimmed the length of Luke's spine and hovered over the band of his boxers. Kicking off her tennis shoes, Ezzie grabbed his ass and squeezed.

He groaned. Reaching underneath her back, he undid her bra and yanked it free from her body. Luke took her hands in his and pushed them up over her head, then dropped his mouth to her breast again.

Crikey! His tongue lashing was driving her insane! Ezzie writhed beneath him and tried to free her arms. She had to touch him. She had to have her hands on his body or in his hair. What she wouldn't give to feel his muscles so aptly moving or the lushness of his chestnut brown, silky locks in her grip.

Keeping her arms pinned to the ground, Luke laced his fingers through hers and swirled his tongue around the other breast.

As much as she enjoyed having him right where he was, she had to have him lower. Much lower. Maybe she couldn't get her arms out of his grip, but she did have other body parts. Ezzie slid her legs from under his. Her short denim skirt restricted some movement, but not enough. Caressing his legs with hers, she wrapped them around his ass. Arching her back again, Ezzie grinded against Luke's erection and moaned.

His mouth fused to hers. He fisted her hair and stroked the length of her right leg. Luke hooked a hand behind her knee and gyrated his jean-clad cock against her core. Groaning into his mouth, Ezzie raked her nails down his bare back. Her boyfriend knew just how to torture her.

Releasing the kiss, he pressed his chest against her breasts. "Unlock your legs."

She bit her bottom lip and did as he instructed.

Luke hopped to his feet. He kicked his shoes off, undid his buckle, and unbuttoned his jeans. When she sat up to help, he pointed back to the blanket. "Lay back down or I stop."

Was he kidding? Ezzie blinked. No way was he serious. Wait. His hands weren't moving. Holy shit! He was actually serious. Fuck, that was hot! She bit her bottom lip and lowered herself back to the blanket.

The corners of his mouth pulled into a small grin and he shucked the remainder of his clothes. Completely naked, Luke knelt down between her legs. He brushed a loving kiss against her lips, then traced soft kisses along her collarbone. Suckling each nipple, he trailed a path of wet kisses down her abdomen and unbuttoned her denim skirt.

She gasped at each gentle press of his lips against her skin. Ezzie lifted her ass and gave Luke what he needed to remove her skirt.

Fuck, she's beautiful. Luke drank in the sight of his stunningly naked girlfriend. The moon offered enough light that he could see everything from her plump, pouty lips to her perfectly full breasts to her tight, round ass and neatly trimmed slit.

His dick already stood at attention, but seeing Ezzie in all her glory made the fucker rise to full mast like the City Greek Center being erected. God, he'd been pacing himself as best he could. Not that he could hold out much longer. He was absolutely ready to be inside of her.

But there was one thing he desired first. Luke leaned over and placed another kiss against her lower abdomen and then her hip. He nuzzled the top of her slit with his nose and licked between her folds. Fuck, she tasted good. So damn sweet. Like strawberries.

Rubbing her clit with his thumb, he penetrated her folds with his tongue again and sucked. She was so wet. He had no idea how long he could keep this up. Next time he'd spend a little less time on her breasts and more time with his mouth between her legs.

Ezzie whimpered and rocked against his tongue.

Desire consumed him from head to toe. He had to be insider her. Now! Luke growled and rolled her onto her belly. He licked her clit one last time and gripped her hips, then lifted her ass in the air and drove deep into her core.

He slowly pistoned in and out of her slickness. Even with as wet as she was, she enveloped him. The perfect fit, like two puzzle pieces that belonged together, their edges structured specifically for one another.

Groaning, Ezzie spread her legs further apart and leaned closer to the blanket.

It didn't seem like much, but it opened her core further for him. Luke penetrated deeper than he ever had before. Losing out to the intensity of the sensation, he wrapped an arm around her waist, propped them both up with the other and pounded into her. He couldn't hold out any longer.

Ezzie met him thrust for thrust. It didn't take long before her core tightened around his length and she came. Her release set his off. A blast of undiluted heat shot up his shaft and the most powerful orgasm he'd experienced yet combined with hers.

They both cried out in ecstasy.

Luke eased them onto their sides. He reached over to the picnic basket and pulled out an extra blanket. He draped it over the two of them and pressed a kiss to Ezzie's shoulder. This hadn't been his intention when he snagged it earlier that morning, but he was grateful he had.

Catching his breath, he lightly traced the pattern of her spine and over her left hip. He'd seen her tattoo a couple of times since they'd gotten together. The blanket shadowed part of it, but didn't entirely hide it. It was a butterfly with a halo above the antennae and a date beneath it. Quite interesting and strange at the same time.

She glanced over her shoulder. "What're you doing?"

"Just looking at your tattoo. It's beautiful." His gaze dropped to the tattoo again. Huh. He hadn't paid much mind to the fact the date was only a few months ago. Maybe it was the day she got the tattoo. No wait. That'd have to be May. Her eighteenth birthday had been the end of April. The date tattooed on her hip was mid April.

"Thanks," Ezzie muttered and looked away.

"What made you get it?"

It should be a simple answer. *No reason. Or I could even say I thought it was pretty.* But neither would be true. She had selected the butterfly and halo with great purpose. Was she ready to let him in on her secrets? Things she had kept from her brother and parents? Ezzie rolled over on her back and looked from the sparkling night sky to the chocolate hues of Luke's eyes.

She had brought him here, hadn't she? She had made that conscious decision to show him a place that meant the world to her. She had faced so much in this place. The acceptance of a difficult choice. The pain over a terrible loss. Even the idea for the tattoo had sprung from this hidden spot. So much agony she had gone through here and they had momentarily replaced all that suffering with something beautiful. The last thing she wanted to do was stain the memory they had just created with the truth behind her tattoo.

But she had to give him something. She couldn't offer a half-ass response. Hmm, maybe she could forego a reply all together. There was only one way she could do that. Ezzie brushed a soft kiss across Luke's lips and curled up against his chest. "How would you feel about spending a weekend camping together?"

A gentle sigh left his mouth as Luke caressed her shoulder. "Would it be like this? I mean ... the sleeping out in the open part."

"Sort of. We'd have our own tent, plus an air mattress. I wouldn't subject you to sleeping bags. The biggest difference is it would be on a campground."

Crikey. What the hell was she doing? Talking about camping when he'd asked about something as intimate as her tattoo. The door opened and she slammed it right back in his face. Ezzie chewed on the inside of her cheek. She should just admit the truth. But what if he hadn't noticed?

"Campground?"

She lifted her gaze to Luke's face. Although the moon gave off enough light, she couldn't see much from this angle. Would've been nice if she could tell how he was feeling about her blatant refusal to say anything about her tattoo. All she could do now was keep the conversation on track.

It wasn't like she was really hiding anything. She'd planned to mention the trip to him anyway.

"Yeah. Green River Campground. It's in Jensen. Matt and I usually make the trip, but he has graciously offered to let you go in his place."

"Really? Is there a catch?"

"Well ... no. Not really." Unless he counted her best friend doing it as a test to ensure Luke could handle ... how had Matt put it? Ezzie frowned and rolled her eyes. Oh right, her outdoor proclivities. Then again, Luke had proven he could go with the flow. She smiled.

"Oh-kay." Luke paused. "What would we do besides camp?"

"What? Oh. Uh, hiking, white-water rafting, fishing and we'd be close to the Dinosaur National Monument."

The good news ... if Luke had noted she skipped right over the topic of her tattoo, he failed to mention anything. Didn't mean it wouldn't come up later. Although she could take advantage of their alone time on the camping trip and maybe tell him then. The days between now and their trip would be exactly what she needed to gain some courage.

"White-water rafting, huh? I've always wanted to do that. All right, I'm in. When do we leave?"

"Two weeks from Friday." *Fuck.* That was way sooner than she anticipated. Fifteen days. It would give her fifteen days to gather her wits to tell Luke about her tattoo. Why the hell hadn't she thought about this earlier?

"Wow. That soon?"

Ezzie uncurled herself from Luke's arms and reached for her clothes. She had to look at this from another perspective. Forget about the tattoo. The camping trip would be a great test for them. Make sure they could properly count on one another. White-water rafting didn't just require skill, it required trust. And they had that. Right? "Yeah, I know. Isn't it great?"

"Is there anything I need to do or learn before then?" Luke sat up and snagged his own clothes.

Who the hell was she kidding? It seemed like they trusted each other, but she couldn't even tell him about her tattoo. Tugging her tank over her head, Ezzie sighed. Great way to begin a relationship—with secrets. Hadn't he asked her a question? Oh, right. She shook away the thoughts coursing through her brain and focused back on the topic at hand. "Uh, yeah. We have to get you certified for the white-water rafting trip."

"You actually have to get certified?"

"Yes. Green River isn't too bad this time of year, but the rapids can become difficult to maneuver without the proper training. And we may only have the permit for the one day, but I promise it'll be worth it." Ezzie buttoned her skirt, bit her bottom lip and eyed her boyfriend. She really should just get it over with and tell him the meaning behind her tattoo. The longer she waited, the worse it would be for both of them.

"Luke, I—"

He pressed a loving kiss to her lips and swept a strand of hair behind her ear. "It's okay. I get it. Besides, this trip sounds like a good idea ... for both of us. Now come on, let's get out of here."

"I'm telling you. It's like he figured out exactly what I was doing and decided to go with it. Keep, trash, or donate?"

Ezzie held up a silver bustier Matt helped her pick out sophomore year. They had dressed up as Riff Raff and Magenta for Halloween that year. She loved the whole space suit idea, though she could have done without the hair issues. It had taken her three days to get all the hairspray and grease out.

"Uh, keep." Matt rolled his eyes as if the question had been redundant. "He actually let you get away without any explanation whatsoever of your tattoo?"

She tossed the bustier into the keep box and nodded. "Yeah. The whole walk back to our cars and all we talked about was the camping trip."

"Are you sure he doesn't have any secrets of his own?"

"Well..." Ezzie frowned. She couldn't honestly say for certain. He had mentioned the reason he didn't date any longer. But all she knew was that something happened between Luke and his ex-girlfriend. Exactly what? She had no idea. "I don't know. Maybe."

"Could be why he let you off the hook so easily. I'm just saying." Matt shrugged and hopped off the bed.

"Whatever it is, I'll worry about that when I get to it."

"You could do the unthinkable and tell him the truth."

With a sigh, she lowered the Maroon Five t-shirt in her hands and her shoulders slumped. "What if he thinks less of me? I couldn't handle that."

Matt grabbed her hands and squeezed. "Number one, if he does, he's an idiot. It wasn't something that was in your control. Number two, he wouldn't be worth your time if he did. You are loving and the most amazing woman I know ... next to me of course."

"Have I told you how much I love you lately?"

It was like he had ESP or something. Matt always knew what to do, what to say and how to make her smile. She couldn't have asked for a better friend.

"Aw, I love you too." They hugged and Matt kissed Ezzie's cheek. "Now that my work is done, I'm off. Don't want to be late for my date."

"Where are you and Colin off to tonight?"

It had been almost a week since she and Matt returned from their separate trips. While she and Luke had been on their picnic adventure Wednesday, Matt and Colin agreed to see one another via Skype until they could be together again. It was the sweetest thing she'd ever heard of.

"We're checking out a local Jazz joint. Hopefully we can talk over the music. Uh, I can't wait to see him in person."

She canted her head and studied Matt. He had a little bounce in his step, a lilt to his voice, and a never-ending smile. He really liked this one. They should get to see one another before the two of them officially moved to California. Hmm ... a light bulb went off in her head. "You could always go visit him in a couple of weeks."

"You mean..."

"I do."

It would work out perfectly. Not just for Matt, but for her too. She wouldn't feel bad for taking Luke on a camping trip that typically belonged to her and Matt. And if Matt was out of sight, less of a chance her brother would spot him around town.

"*That* is a great idea."

"What's a great idea?" Nate asked as he stepped into the doorway.

Ezzie grinned at her brother. "Oh, nothing. We were just talking about something for our camping trip."

"I gotcha. Anything I can help with?" Nate crossed his arms.

"We're good, thank you." Matt glanced over his shoulder. "I'll text you later, Ezzie."

"All right. Smooches."

"Smooches." With a flick of his wrist, Matt walked out of her bedroom and disappeared down the hall.

Ezzie waved her best friend off and half turned her attention to her brother. He didn't drop in her room for no reason, but she couldn't fully focus on that. She still had a lot of packing to do before she moved to California. Yeah, the move was still seven weeks off. And as much as she hoped it would take its sweet time getting there, she expected it would arrive faster than she imagined possible. "What's going on Nate?"

"I wanted to talk to you about our upcoming moves."

"Oh yeah. What about them?" She spun on her heel and looked back at the closet. She didn't want to pack all of her clothes, just the ones she didn't think she'd wear for the next few weeks. Mostly the winter stuff.

"I know Mom and Dad have been planning to head to Massachusetts with me, but I thought it would be better if we took a family trip to California the week before instead."

Ezzie whirled around and faced her brother. No way he just suggested what she thought he suggested. Her brother was not absolutely trying to ruin everything. "What?"

"You know, California. Where you're moving. I want to be able to check out this apartment Matt found for the two of you. See where you're going to be living for the next four years. At least the next year."

"But I showed you the pictures he took. And the video. And the complex online. I thought you were okay with all that."

No, no, no. This would screw their entire plan up. She and Luke were supposed to have three more weeks before they revealed their relationship to her family, which would give Nate a couple of weeks to get acclimated to the idea of her and Luke dating before Nate and Luke moved to Massachusetts. If Nate insisted on going to California the week before he left for Massachusetts, then she'd have to move the entire timeline up.

"Well I was, then I realized it didn't tell me much about the people or the neighborhood. I know Matt's folks have a vineyard out that way, but I'd still like to see the town and college in person. Make sure you'll be okay there."

Crossing her arms, she shook her head. Her brother had done this her whole life. Intervened when it wasn't necessary. Butted in her business. Beat up any guy that looked at her the wrong way. One would think she couldn't defend or take care of herself or even make a decision. "No."

"Excuse me?"

"You heard me. No. I'm not a baby. I do not need my big brother playing protector and scaring off people that I don't just have to go to school with, but live around."

The over-bearing routine had gotten old. Yeah, okay, maybe she encouraged it by running to him with nearly every guy problem she ever had. But things were different. She had managed to handle most of her problems for the last couple of years without her big brother by her side. Minus the whole spring break incident.

Nate crossed his arms. "I'm not playing protector. It's my job as your big brother to look out for you."

"To what point? I'm eighteen! And not helpless. I'm quite capable of taking care of myself. I don't need you looking out for me. Plus, I'll have Matt." Hadn't they gone over all this? Maybe if she took a self-defense class her brother would get over the macho bullshit.

"You can't make every guy sing soprano. And Matt's presence doesn't do much to comfort me."

Why was she getting a sense of *de ja vu*? Oh, that's right. She had a somewhat similar conversation with Luke. Oh crap. No, no, no, no. Her boyfriend and her brother, while they shared some personality traits, they were nothing alike.

"Are you freaking kidding me?"

Frowning, Nate uncrossed his arms. "I wouldn't joke when it comes to your safety."

Ezzie threw her hands in the air. Her brother had lost his damn mind. He'd always been over-bearing, but this just pushed it to a new level. "Matt owns a gun, for crying out loud!"

"That doesn't make me feel any better. Now stop arguing with me over this. There's no point. I've made up my mind. I'm going to check everything out before I leave for Massachusetts."

Narrowing her eyes at her brother, Ezzie stomped around the stack of boxes and shoved a finger in his face. "I don't give one rat's ass if we are related or not. I'm not going to let you bully me into doing things your way. Now, get out of my room."

"Ezzie, I—"

"Get out!" A bead of sweat formed on her brow. Heat coursed through her veins and made her body burn from the inside out. She had never been so angry at her brother. If he had any common sense inside that head of his, he'd leave before she punched the shit out of him and proved she wasn't someone to fuck with.

Holding his hands up in defeat, Nate backed up and walked out of her bedroom.

eleven

EZZIE STABBED THE CHEESE FRIES from her favorite restaurant in town, Chow Hound. She'd hardly been able to eat the last few days. Today was no different. It would've been nice to enjoy a good, hearty meal, but she had to discuss the situation regarding her brother with their mother. Her mother was her only option left, which was exactly why they sat across from one another now. "I don't understand why you won't just forbid him from going."

"If Nate forbid you from dating Lucas, would you quit seeing him?"

"What?! Of course not." What kind of outlandish question was that? Had her mother's food been laced with crazy juice or something? Ezzie eyed the plate of nachos in front of her and rolled her eyes. Now who was acting like their food had been laced with something.

"Then what makes you think me forbidding your brother would work?"

Lowering her fork, Ezzie sighed and slumped in the wooden booth. No matter how many different ways she'd approached the topic over the last week and a half, her brother was convinced a family trip to California was a great idea. Logic hadn't worked. Pleading with him to trust her hadn't worked. Even Matt, a master manipulator, failed to change Nate's mind.

"I don't know, Mom. I'm just out of ideas. I don't know what else to do."

"Have you talked to Lucas about the situation? See what he thinks?"

"I may not have mentioned it yet." Not that she hadn't tried to bring up the subject. It was just every time she had; she lost her nerve. It had been her idea in the first place for them to wait to tell her brother. What a great plan that was turning out to be.

"Don't you think you should? This is something that impacts both of you."

"I know, Mom." As if she hadn't thought about that since her brother brought up the stupid idea to begin with. Ezzie shoved a forkful of the gooey, salted fries in her mouth. Their taste was off a little bit, but it kept her from saying something stupid ... or something she couldn't take back.

Her mother reached across the table and squeezed her hand. "Look, I get it. This isn't just about your relationship with Lucas, but your brother seeing you as an adult capable of making her own decisions. So, I'll make you a deal."

She swallowed the bite in her mouth. She wasn't certain she liked where this was going, but what other choice did she have? Either she accepted what her mother offered or ... or ... shit. Her only other option was to tell her brother the truth. Crikey, she was so not ready to do that.

Inhaling a deep breath, Ezzie exhaled slowly. "I'm listening."

"I'll talk to your brother, but you have to tell Lucas what's going on."

Crap. She knew she wasn't going to like it, but there was no alternative. In fact, she and Luke may have to tell her brother sooner rather than later about their relationship. Ezzie dragged a hand down her face. Whether they told her brother the truth next week or the week after that, she hoped he took the news well. Shifting her gaze back to her mother, she nodded. "Okay. Deal."

"Good. Now, when do you plan to talk to Lucas next?"

"Later tonight. We're finalizing our meeting time and place for the camping trip this weekend."

Great. She'd have all weekend long to muster up the courage to tell her boyfriend about her brother's brilliant plan. Hmm ... maybe they just didn't come back Sunday afternoon. She could enjoy living out in the woods. It'd be peaceful. Plus, they could white-water raft whenever they wanted. Well, only some of the time they wanted. Fuck. Who was she kidding? She wasn't even positive Luke would survive the weekend in the woods, let alone live out there.

"Okay then. You have the weekend to tell Lucas what's going on and I'll work on your brother over the weekend as well. Deal?" Her mother held out her hand.

Ezzie let out an exasperated breath. It was her only option left. She sat up straight and shook her mother's hand. "Deal."

Luke rolled off of Ezzie, his dick slipping out of her warm cocoon. She curled up against him and he wrapped an arm around her naked back. Lazily stroking his fingers up and down her spine, his gaze drifted to the netting at the top of the tent. Even with the dark mesh above, he caught a tiny glimpse of the night sky. The trees surrounding their secluded campsite blocked the collection of stars he'd seen earlier.

Not only were they nowhere near civilization, they were as far away from other campsites as they could be. His girlfriend had found them some little hole a way off the reservation. It was kind of nice they had their own private sector, especially with all the noise coming out of their tent over the last hour. Not as if he'd ever complain.

Their time together had been pretty damn explosive. More powerful than any time before. Almost as if they both wanted to get all their cards on the table. He almost did. Yeah, he had a secret, but he needed more time before he told Ezzie the truth about his past. Though, maybe he could get away with telling her everything but *that*.

In his gut, he knew if he ever told her, she'd ...

Luke swallowed. Tightening his grip against the small of Ezzie's back, he pressed a tender kiss to her forehead. He couldn't take the chance of losing her ... ever.

And yet after this weekend, he still could. Just depended on what happened Monday when they told Nate about the two of them dating. One of the few things they had agreed on during their drive up.

God, it had felt like one of the longest drives of his life. Then again, Sunday would be longer. They'd be going home.

Ezzie shifted her head and rested her chin against Luke's bare chest. "What're you thinking about?"

"The conversation we've decided to have with your brother."

Weren't they supposed to have another week of peace? One more week before his entire world imploded because his heart was quickly becoming hers. What the hell would happen to them once they told Nate the truth? Well, they wouldn't have to sneak around anymore. And he could lose a friend in the process. Luke sighed.

"Crikey. Can we not think about that? We have the rest of the weekend to enjoy. The last thing I want is my selfish brother to ruin it."

"I'm sorry, Ez. I know I shouldn't think about it, but I guess I'm just worried about the outcome."

Yeah, he could lose his best friend, but that didn't have his insides twisted in a knot. The turmoil over this one conversation had more to do with the thought that he could lose Ezzie in the process. He'd give anything to keep her in his life, even if meant never telling Nate the truth.

"We don't know what's going to happen or how he'll react. Plus, my mom may get him to come to his senses over California and if that doesn't happen, then Matt has a crazy contingency plan."

Luke frowned. It was bad enough she talked to her best friend, who happened to be a guy, about their relationship. But now he was coming up with back-up plans too? And what kind of plan could he have come up with that Ezzie considered "crazy?" Unless ... oh hell no! No, absolutely not. That couldn't be it.

"What contingency plan?"

"It's nothing. Besides it won't come to it."

"That's not an answer. What's the contingency plan, Ezzie?"

"Just let it go, Luke. It's stupid anyways." Ezzie swiveled away from his chest and sat up in the bed taking most of the covers with her.

His gaze raked the length of her naked back. Even with the little light provided in their tent, he could still see the butterfly tattoo on lower left hip. The halo and date stared back at him. Luke propped himself up on his elbows and bit his tongue. No. He let the explanation of the tattoo go. He couldn't do it a second time. He deserved an answer. A real one. Not some half-ass white lie. "No, damn it. Tell me the plan."

Ezzie dropped her eyes to the floor of their tent. "Like I said, it's stupid ... so there's no point in even telling you Matt's idea. Because—"

God, he was sick and fucking tired of her incomplete answers. Yeah, sure she'd told him multiple times he was brilliant, then gave him bullshit like this. Did she take him for an idiot? "The idea's stupid? Or because I just wouldn't get it?"

"Because it wouldn't work!" Ezzie pinched the bridge of her nose and rolled her eyes.

Luke sat up straight in the bed and shook his head. Fuck, he was an idiot. Of course, she didn't want to tell him the *idea*. Not because it was ridiculous, but because of the idea itself. He smirked. "Why? Because you don't think you could turn a gay man straight? Or because you don't think Matt could convince your brother he had true feelings for you?"

Her head snapped up. Ezzie shifted on the bed and narrowed her eyes at him. "Because Matt doesn't have *those* kinds of feelings for me and Nate damn well knows it. So yes, Matt telling my brother that he and I have been secretly dating wouldn't work. Like I said, it's fucking asinine!"

"That isn't the point. What if the idea is daft? This isn't the same as the tattoo. You can't just skirt around not telling me. You should've told me the idea earlier. Hell! You should've talked to me about the situation first instead of running to Matt!"

"My tattoo? What the hell does that have to do with anything?"

"Everything, Ezzie! I'm supposed to be your boyfriend. I'm the one you're supposed to run to with these things. Not Matt! And while I can appreciate, he will probably always know things I'll never know, like the meaning behind your tattoo, *this* is different. It involves me." He just couldn't sit there like none of it mattered anymore. Luke climbed off the air mattress, snagged his boxers off the tent floor and yanked them on.

He got it. Her best friend was more important than he would ever be, even if that shouldn't be the case. She would probably always run to Matt with her problems. Even if the problem involved Luke and Ezzie, she'd waltz off to her best friend first. Obviously in her world best friends outweighed boyfriends.

Grabbing his jeans, Luke chanced a glance over his shoulder. How could Ezzie just sit there and stare at him without so much as saying a single word. Looking away, he pulled on his jeans. He had to get out of there. Go for a walk or something. He had to escape her silence ... maybe even the inevitability of where this weekend apparently planned to take them.

"It's for the baby I lost."

Luke's jaw unclenched. His eyebrows rose. The blaze that had burned in his chocolate-brown eyes disappeared as his eyes widened. Shock replaced whatever anger had been written all over his face. "What?"

Why had she blurted it out like that? Why hadn't she eased into it? Because he had been preparing to storm out of the tent. And she couldn't let him walk out without knowing the truth.

All the agonizing she had done over the last couple of weeks regarding the truth about her tattoo and she spews it out without a second thought. And that one statement wasn't even all of it. Such a small amount of words and so many things unspoken within them.

Ezzie shifted her gaze from Luke to the floor of the tent and swallowed. She couldn't leave it all as it was, but she couldn't bear to look at him as she recounted only half of what he deserved to know. "A couple of weeks after Justin and I split up ... I, uh, I found out I was pregnant."

Tears prickled the corners of her eyes. She'd convinced herself over spring break it was just a stomach bug. If Matt hadn't suggested that stupid pregnancy test, she would've never ended up in that clinic. She could've ... pretended? Yeah. Because that would've lasted. For a little while.

"I wasn't sure what I was going to do. We were graduating ... heading off to college. A baby, it would've changed all that. I spent days walking around, trying to decide what to do. And I talked to Matt ... about all of it."

Talking? Ezzie smirked at her own word choice. Sure. Matt talked and she sat there in silence. She'd wound up pregnant by her cheating-scum-of-a-boyfriend. A piece of him would remain with her forever. But it was a part of her too. And that had been the clincher.

It had taken her days to come to a decision. A lot of hiding from her parents so they didn't notice the change in her appetite or how she seemed to be throwing up a lot or tired all the time. She had spent so much time at Matt's house, they could've been secretly dating. Then ... God, did she have to go there? Ezzie blinked a tear free.

"I wasn't exactly ready to be a mother and there was no way Justin was ready to be a father either. But I knew I'd never be able to deal with adoption or even think about abortion. So ... I decided to keep the baby and just figured I wouldn't bother telling him. We'd graduate before I started to show, so no big deal. Right? I could raise the baby alone."

"Ezzie—"

She shook her head. Tears rolled down her cheeks. "Please don't. You wanted to know, so I'm telling you. Please ... please ... just ... let me get this out."

She wanted to look at him so bad, but she couldn't. If he even showed one ounce of sympathy, she'd lose control. No matter how much she needed him to hold her through the ache in her heart, she had to fight through the pain—alone.

The pain she thought she'd be over by now.

Months had passed since she had miscarried. But it didn't change the anguish she had suffered. The number of nights she had cried herself to sleep. All the times she had screamed at the sky. Or the gym she had joined so she could beat on a punching bag.

Anything so she could feel a little less.

Anything to help her pretend none of it had happened.

Anything to let her return to a sense of normalcy.

Wrapping her own arms around her body, Ezzie swallowed again. It was too late to stop now. She had to tell Luke all of it. "Matt and I were hanging out one day. I'd been having some light cramps, but I thought it was normal. Then they got stronger. I'd never felt anything like it. It was like I was being stabbed. With as bad as it was ... it could only mean ... but I ..."

Crikey, it shouldn't be this hard to get the words out. She just ... she had to push through. Ezzie wiped at the tears running down her cheeks. "Matt rushed me to the hospital. He stayed with me almost the whole time, at least until Justin showed up. I found out later Matt called him and told him what was going on."

That had been the one saving grace in all of it. Justin had been a horrible boyfriend, but he'd been an extremely supportive friend. He'd proven he could be there in a moment of crisis. And she'd needed him more than she dared to admit back then. Not that it changed what he'd done.

Or how she'd been hurt by it.

The air mattress dipped down beside her. Luke brushed her hair from her shoulder and caressed the back of her neck.

Tears streamed down her face. Clutching the sheet tight to her body, Ezzie turned her eyes to Luke. "Matt knows about the tattoo because he was there when I found out I was pregnant. He knows about the tattoo because he listened to me for days about my options. Matt knows because he was there when I lost the baby and he was there holding my hand when I got the tattoo."

The tattoo had one purpose.

To celebrate and mourn a life that had barely begun.

She never wanted to forget.

Luke wrapped an arm around Ezzie and hugged her to his chest. He pressed a feather kiss to her head. "I'm so sorry you had to go through all that. And I'm sorry for being an asshole about all of it. I got jealous you were talking to him about things I feel like you should be able to talk to me about."

He was right. She should be able to talk to him about it. None of her previous boyfriends cared, but Luke wasn't like them. Any of them. She had to remember that. Ezzie swallowed again. This was a first for her, but something she could handle.

"I'm sorry I went to him about our situation. I've just gone to him for so much over the last four years, I guess, I'm not used to anyone else besides him wanting to be there for me."

"I want you to talk to me about these things, but I promise if you need to talk to him too or even first, then I will try not to get so apprehensive about it." Luke kissed her forehead.

She let the beat of Luke's heart wash over her. The rhythm reminded her of a steady crash of waves clearing out all the toxins. Swiping the tears from her eyes, she inhaled and exhaled deeply. There was a middle ground for them there. Something they both had to do to make their relationship work.

"Maybe we both need to make an effort. I'll try talking to you more and you try being a little less anxious."

"I can live with those terms." He tightened his hold around her.

Luke brushed a soft, loving kiss to her forehead one last time. "Yeah, I can definitely live with those terms."

Rubbing the back of his head, Luke lifted his knuckles for the third time to knock on the front door of the Donovan residence. The news he and Ezzie had received the day before on their way back from their trip altered their plans to sit down with Nate. Apparently Ezzie and Nate's mother had talked Nate out of going to California. At the time he'd been fine with not telling Nate about his and Ezzie's relationship. If only his heart had gotten onboard with his brain.

He spent half the night tossing and turning over the deceit. He couldn't keep lying to his best friend. It was time he manned up and admitted the truth. Yeah, it meant he'd be risking his relationship with Ezzie, but it was a chance he had to take because the more time he spent with her, the more time he wanted to spend with her.

Now if only he could guarantee his past wouldn't cause any problems between them, but one step at a time.

Right. One step at a time. Fuck. He should probably deal with that first. Shouldn't he? Luke sighed and spun on his heel. The front door opened

"Luke? Hey, man. What're you doing here?" Nate asked.

Shit! Too late to run. He had no choice, but to tackle the situation. Just not head on. Luke turned back around. "I'm here to talk to you."

Nate crossed his arms. "Really? Looked like you were leaving."

"Nah. I was just going to get a map out of my car. Figured we'd need it."

He hadn't come unprepared. Well, only partially unprepared. He was completely unprepared for a necessary conversation with Nate. But Luke had planned ahead. The two of them were moving to Massachusetts in less than a month and they still hadn't hashed all the details out, which worked in his favor.

"For what?"

"So we could get the last of everything worked out for our new place. I know we still have time, but I also know how slowly you pack." It wasn't a lie, even if they still had plenty of time to get the last few details together, Luke liked to be ready. And checking on Nate's packing progress served as a great excuse.

Uncrossing his arms, Nate shook his head. "I swear I'm coming along, but you're welcome to come in and check."

"I'm just messing with you. You set yourself up for it. I mean, don't get me wrong. I do want to see where you're at, but mostly I figured we'd hang out for a bit."

Grinning, Luke stepped into a house he knew almost as well as his own. He'd spent enough time there to learn the layout. Not much beyond that though. Before now, he'd been afraid of running into Ezzie, so he avoided the house a lot. Certainly not something he had to do now. Instead if he showed up and she was there, he had to control himself and be mindful of his facial responses. Not that he had to fret over that today. They'd texted earlier and she planned to go shopping with Matt.

Nate started down the hallway. "Touché. As for hanging out, I've got time. I have to leave in about thirty to pick up Becca."

"Oh yeah? You guys going out tonight?" Hmm, if he knew exactly where Nate would be, then maybe he could actually take his girlfriend out to dinner somewhere around her hometown. It would be nice not to have to go to another town for a date.

"Yep. It's her birthday, so I'm taking her to Tamarisk." Stopping outside a bedroom, Nate pushed open the door and gestured toward the inside of the bedroom. "Is this progress enough?"

Luke poked his head inside and glanced around. There were about six boxes stacked alongside one wall. Most of the posters, pictures, awards, books and other knickknacks he knew his best friend had had all been taken down. Not all of it packed, but it was at least off the walls.

Luke nodded. "You're further along than I expected. That's good."

"Got most of it done this past weekend. Not that I had much of a choice. My parents threw a wrench into my plans and forced me into it."

"How so?"

"You know how I told you I wanted to go to California so I could see this place my sister was moving to?"

He followed after Nate toward the dining room. "Yeah. I thought you guys were all set for that."

"Apparently that's a no go. I guess my parents can only afford to take time off to help me move, not both of us. They keep telling me not to worry about Ezzie since she has Matt's family to help, but I have this sneaking suspicion that there's more going on."

There was, not that he was going to confirm or deny Nate's suspicions. At least not yet. "I can't imagine your parents hiding something from you."

"No, not my parents. My sister. I think she's dating someone. And for some reason she's hiding this guy's identity from me." Nate stopped in front of the refrigerator. "You want a beer?"

"Sure." *Oh hell.* Luke swallowed and sat at the dining room table. This was not the direction he imagined this conversation would go. He may end up telling Nate the truth today after all. Only if he had to; he really needed to talk to Ezzie first.

"Okay. What if she's dating someone? What does that have to do with the move?"

"I don't know. I keep thinking she's conned our parents into believing she doesn't need any help so she can spend more time with this guy. Except my sister isn't the manipulating type." Nate grabbed a couple of bottles of beer out of the refrigerator and joined Luke at the dining room table.

"So, what you're saying is that you tried to manipulate the situation in hopes your sister would reveal whoever this secret boyfriend of hers is?"

And this is why they were studying to become lawyers; then at least their innate ability to manipulate the situation to their advantage could be used in a positive manner, something Luke had discovered pretty early on in his and Nate's friendship.

"Exactly. I need to make sure he's a decent guy. You know, not like us. Guys like us don't date girls like my sister."

Luke frowned. He didn't like the direction the conversation had taken. No way Nate meant to say something that sounded so derogatory. Yeah, when Ezzie first mentioned the idea of the two of them dating, he tried to push her away. He even said he wasn't good enough for her. But somewhere over the last month his thought process had changed. Nate had to mean something else. "Guys like us?"

"Yeah. I mean, come on, we both play the field."

"Don't you have a steady girlfriend?"

Hadn't they discussed Becca not fifteen minutes ago? And her birthday celebration? Some way to "play the field." And as for him playing the field, Luke hadn't played the field in months. He hadn't even slept with another girl since before spring.

"I do, but that doesn't mean I'm gonna stay with her forever. Don't get me wrong, Becca's great, but she isn't exactly marriage material. My sister is and she deserves a man who's going down that road."

It all made perfect sense. Nate didn't think Luke was the marrying type. Maybe for the last few years he hadn't been. It didn't mean that was still true. Not that he had imagined what life would be like if he one day married Ezzie. Nope. Not a big blue house to match the color of her eyes. He hadn't dreamed about kids with her either. One boy, one girl. At least five years apart. Luke hadn't thought about any of that. Taking a sip of beer from the bottle, he leaned back in the chair and eyed his best friend.

"What makes you think I'm not the marrying type?"

"Dude, you haven't even dated anyone since Jessica. And unless I'm missing something, kind of hard to think about getting married if you aren't even dating someone."

God, Jessica. He still hadn't told Ezzie about that. Maybe that didn't make him the marrying type. If nothing else, it certainly made him hypocritical. He got so upset the other day over the meaning behind her tattoo and he hadn't even been able to bring himself to tell her the truth about his past. One that he was more reluctant every day to share.

Silently, Luke sighed. "You're not missing anything."

His best friend was right.

He wasn't the marrying type.

And that was the kind of man Ezzie deserved.

Twelve

PROPPED UP AGAINST THE PURPLE, plush pillow on her bed, Ezzie turned to the next page in the photo album she'd discovered amongst her things. Her eyes fell to a picture of her and her brother. Her in a bathing suit and denim shorts and her brother in a t-shirt and shorts. Each of them had a water balloon in hand. She grinned. That had been a fun day.

How long ago had that been? Maybe five or six years ago.

Had they been celebrating something? Or had it all just been in fun? She couldn't remember exactly who or what started the water balloon fight, but by the end Nate had been soaked from head to toe and she had been half way dry, not something her brother appreciated a whole lot, especially when she'd teased him.

Oh, what had she said?

Nate had been … what? Sixteen? Ezzie flipped the picture over and scanned the back for a date. It only had the year: 2007. Meant her brother would've been … seventeen.

Oh yeah. That's right. It was his birthday and she had said, "Are you sure you're not a seventeen-year-old snail? Slow and slimy."

Ezzie snickered. Her witty repertoire needed a lot of work back then. Of course, she was only thirteen at the time. It had been pretty good for her age. It had certainly improved over time. Too bad she couldn't say the same for her relationship with her brother.

She swept her thick, dark locks over her shoulder and sighed. Something had happened in the last few days. She had no idea what, but whatever had gone on put a further drift between her and her brother. Yeah, he had finally agreed not to go to California, but she hadn't meant for him to stop talking to her altogether. She knew he meant—

As if she had summoned him, Nate knocked on the open bedroom door. "Hey, sis. Mind if I come in?"

"It's a free world." Ezzie smirked and slammed the photo album shut.

Why should she feel guilty about the two of them not being on speaking terms? She hadn't done anything wrong. Okay. She hadn't told him she and Luke were dating, but aside from that, Nate pretty much knew everything else. Well, that wasn't entirely true either.

Ugh.

Could her two sides find a happy medium here?

Nate shoved his hands in the pockets of his jeans and rocked back and forth on his heels. "So, what are you doing?"

"I was looking at old photos, if you must know." Frowning, she tucked her hair back behind her ear and climbed off the bed. She walked over to one of the near-empty boxes and set the photo album inside atop the few stuffed animals she had packed away.

"Oh. Well, I wasn't trying to interrupt."

"You aren't. They're a distraction anyway and I still have a lot of packing to do." That was a bold-faced lie. Ninety percent of her bedroom had already been packed and she wasn't leaving for a few weeks.

Had it really been five weeks since she and Luke started dating? Hadn't they agreed to tell her family about their relationship after four weeks? And now they were at five? How had the time gone by so fast?

"Ezzie, come on. We both know that's not true."

He was right. Not that she'd openly admit that. The lavender walls had been stripped of all her posters. She'd taken them down first. They were in a cylindrical container by her empty closet. All the books from her two bookcases had been packed in about five small square boxes. Even her desk had been cleaned off and packed up. The only thing that was left was the sheets, white comforter, and pillows from her bed. And the few knickknacks she still had in her bathroom.

With another sigh, she glanced over her shoulder. "What do you want Nate? You didn't come in here for small talk, so spit it out."

"I wanted to apologize. I know I've been giving you the cold shoulder the last few days and I'm sorry for that. I guess … I'm just not accustomed to you keeping secrets from me."

"What're you talking about? What secrets?" Ezzie crossed her arms and faced him. Sure, it was a stupid question, but she had to know what her brother believed she was keeping from him. After all, there was more than one thing he didn't know about.

"Look, I know you're dating someone. And I'm fairly certain that's why you don't want me to go to California with you. I just wish you'd let me meet him before you go trotting off with another asshole."

Another asshole?

Granted, some of her choices in men hadn't been all that stellar, but only one of them truly fell into the asshole category. And he had partially redeemed himself, not that her brother knew anything about what happened after her and Justin's breakup. Still, none of her other ex-boyfriends had been bad. The relationship just hadn't worked out for one reason or another.

Ezzie narrowed her eyes and glared at her brother. Did he think she was incompetent when it came to men? "You do realize I'm quite capable of choosing someone for myself?"

"I do. You just don't have the best track record."

"Excuse me?"

Her brother had to have lost his damn mind. No way in hell he heard a word that came out of that crap-pile he called a mouth. Nate might as well have called her stupid for all the bullshit he just spewed.

Grinding her jaw, Ezzie uncrossed her arms, balled up her fists and stepped closer to her brother.

"Come on, Ezzie. You can't honestly believe any one of your last three ex-boyfriends have been great choices. I mean, Derek was a compulsive liar, Richard was constantly demeaning you, and then Justin, the guy who cheated on you; well, he must have been the cream of the crop."

Oh hell no! Who the hell deemed her brother better than any of the guys he had mentioned?

Closing the distance between the two of them, she got in Nate's face. "First of all, not that I owe you any damn explanations, but most of what you just spewed is utter bullshit. Derek only lied about his home life and that's because he was ashamed of his background. As for Richard, he didn't demean me; he was just a sexist pig. In fact, ninety-five percent of the jokes he cracked, I heard from you first. Don't you dare go acting all high and mighty like you're Mister-Fucking-Perfect."

"I never said I was perfect and I'm not trying to come off like I am. The last thing I want is for you to date a guy like me."

Well didn't that force her steam down a couple of notches.

Talk about taking five steps back. Ezzie inhaled and exhaled a deep breath. She had to calm down a smidge, especially after a comment like that. But wait, Nate only said *he didn't want her to date a guy like him.* He didn't say he believed she wasn't.

"You think the guy I might be dating is like you?"

"For all I know he could be."

"Well you don't have to worry. He's nothing like you."

The words came out of her mouth before she could even stop them. Not that she had included Luke's name, but she had definitely admitted to secretly dating someone. Too late to take it back now.

Then again, she wasn't sure she wanted to. She was quite proud to be Luke's girlfriend. He was a good man.

"Good. I look forward to meeting him. Soon."

Narrowing her eyes, Ezzie glowered and stomped over to her bedroom door. "You'll meet him when I'm damn good and ready to introduce him and at the rate you're going, that will be never. Now, get the hell out of my room."

Stretching his arm, Luke held the door open to their hotel suite and Ezzie walked in past him. The last couple of hours with her had been deafening. She hardly said a word during dinner. Something was obviously on her mind, but he hadn't been able to get her to talk about whatever had been bothering her. Not that he'd wanted to push too hard. He didn't want to get into a fight, but he absolutely wanted her to talk. Maybe with no one around now, they could do just that. If not tonight, well, then he had all weekend to get her to tell him what was going on.

He used his foot to prop open the door, grabbed both of their suitcases and entered their room. It was a fairly nice hotel. Not the five-star high-end he had grown up staying in, but close enough. The room was clean. The door opened into a small living area with a tan couch and chair across from a television. In the middle of the suite was a marble counter with a coffee machine on top and a small refrigerator underneath. Directly across from the kitchen area, if it could be construed as one, was the bathroom.

Luke shook his head at the layout and rolled their suitcases into the bedroom, on the other side of the pint-size kitchen/bathroom. The king-size bed appeared to be the best part. Several pillows covered the white comforter and made it look welcoming. As long as it was comfortable, they'd be set.

"Can we talk?" Ezzie asked.

Turning around, he faced his girlfriend. Not exactly the first words she'd spoken all night, but more than anything she'd said in the last few hours. But definitely what he'd been hoping would happen.

"Yeah, sure."

Her gaze dropped to the carpet and she kicked at it with the toe of her white Converse. "I know I've been kind of quiet and I'm sorry for that. I didn't mean to take all of this out on you and I kind of feel like I have."

"Ez, look at me." Luke placed his forefinger beneath her jaw and gently guided her chin up until her sapphire blue eyes met his. "You have nothing to feel guilty about. You've done nothing wrong. I don't care you were quiet. Sometimes you need to sort things out in your head before you can lay them out on the table."

"I know, but the argument Nate and I had was days ago. It shouldn't have still been impacting me."

Argument? Had the California thing come up again? No. After his talk with his best friend he figured it had become a non-issue. Unless ... fuck. Nate probably asked about her *secret boyfriend.* God, Luke really hoped that wasn't the case. He wasn't ready to jump on the bandwagon and tell Ezzie's family about their relationship.

"What did you two fight over?"

"My excellent choice in men." Rolling her eyes, Ezzie sighed. "Nate has figured out I'm seeing someone and according to him, my previous choices in men prohibit me from picking out a good, decent man for myself."

"Please tell me he didn't suggest he pick one for you." Luke frowned. He hadn't meant to say that, especially since he hadn't exactly told Ezzie about Nate's grand idea. Too late to take it back now. Maybe his girlfriend wouldn't think anything about it.

Ezzie narrowed her eyes. "No. He only said he wanted to meet this boyfriend of mine. What would make you think he'd pick a guy out for me?"

Open mouth and insert foot. Great job, asshole. Fuck. Luke dragged a hand down his face. How the hell did he explain this? The truth? His girlfriend was already upset with her brother anyway. No harm, no foul. Right? Right. If only he felt better about turning on his best friend.

"Nate might have mentioned it in passing."

"I'm sorry. What?"

That could've come out a lot better. Maybe he needed to try a different approach. After all, he didn't entirely disagree with Nate's previous assessment of everything and that kind of sucked. Luke gripped the back of his neck. The stubble from his recent hair cut brushed against his hand. "Look, I know he has a weird way of showing it, but he's just worried about you. He wants to make sure whoever you pick is someone who deserves everything you have to offer."

"Except he didn't say any of that. He actually said I have poor taste in men. But that isn't the point. You're great and we're happy together. That's why I think we should tell my family we're dating."

Fuck. Fuck, fuck, fuck. Luke rubbed the back of his head. He'd known this was coming. He just kept hoping for a little longer. Or that they'd keep their relationship a secret until ... god, he had no clue. Until what? He graduated. Yeah, because that would happen. No matter what, he needed more time. As soon as they told her family, he knew exactly what would happen. He'd lose her.

"Can't we just wait another week?"

"Luke, we're already past the time we originally agreed on. We've been together, what, almost six weeks now? Nate is leaving for Massachusetts in a week and I'm leaving for California the week after that. Don't you think we've put this off long enough?"

There was no good answer to that question. Spinning on the ball of his foot, he walked over to the king-size bed and sat down on the edge of the mattress. For all the time he longed to have with her, he had to face the facts. She deserved better than him. Pressing his elbows into his thighs, Luke slumped. "We don't have to tell them. I already know what Nate thinks."

"What? How?"

"He talked to me about his suspicions. I didn't tell him that I'm your *secret boyfriend*, but he made his feelings about me as your boyfriend clear."

He didn't have to tell her that Nate lumped him into the group of losers she'd previously dated or flat out said how Luke would never be marriage material. From the moment he and Ezzie decided to give their relationship a chance, he knew it would end one way. After what he'd done to Jessica, the last thing he deserved was to be happy, as Nate had fondly reminded him.

"I'm confused. If you didn't tell him you're my boyfriend, how did he tell you how he felt about you as my boyfriend?"

God, why couldn't she just accept a simple answer? Why did she have to know the specifics? It wasn't like the details mattered. The bottom line was that he was no good for her. Maybe that was the problem. He hadn't given her enough to see the big picture. With a deep sigh, Luke hung his head. She'd left him no choice. He had to go there.

"Because he described me as a non-relationship kind of guy. And he's right."

"What? I don't ... why would you say that?"

Luke looked up at Ezzie. She had taken a step back from him. Good. This was good. God, it may have been right, but there was an ache in his heart that hurt like no pain he'd ever known before. But he had to do this. He swallowed. "Because it's true. I don't do relationships. I don't know why I thought things with you would be different."

Her eyes widened and a single tear rolled down her cheek. "Are you ... are you breaking up with me?"

Ezzie shook her head and backed up. Her hand rested on the handle of her suitcase. "No. You know what? Don't answer that."

"Ez—" Luke stood.

"Just don't." Tightening her grip on her suitcase, she started for the hotel room door.

"Where are you going?"

"Away from here! Not that you should care based on what you've just said. Right? You're not a relationship kind of guy? That's utter bullshit and you know it! Don't even bother trying to explain or even defend it. I get it. You're a coward. A coward, Lucas Jonnihan. You have true feelings for me and you can't even admit them to yourself! Instead you stand there and spew whatever is necessary to get me to leave! Well, congratu-fucking-lations! You got your wish." Ezzie walked out of the hotel room.

The door slammed shut behind her. Luke balled his fists up. It took every ounce of willpower he had not to chase after her. Letting her go was the right thing to do. Not that it made it hurt any less. But he had to—

"Fuck."

He sprinted across the room and threw open the door. He stepped out into an empty hallway and ran down the hall to the elevators. He rounded the corner just as the elevator doors closed. Tears prickled the corners of his eyes. What the hell had he just done?

Placing a hand on the closed elevator doors, Luke inhaled and exhaled a deep breath.

The right thing.

That's what he'd done.

The right thing.

"He hasn't reached out at all?"

The last thing she wanted to talk about was the fight she had with Luke three days ago. Three long ass fucking days of complete silence. Not a single text. Not one phone call. Not one time of him showing up on her doorstep. No apologies. No explanations. No nothing. Not that she really expected anything.

Still, she had hoped Luke would come to his senses. Ezzie rolled over onto her back and fluffed the white pillow behind her head. Brushing her hair from her face, she glanced at Matt. "Nothing."

"I know this is probably the last thing you want to hear, but you deserve better. If he can't crawl out of his ass and act like the man you deserve, then fuck him. You don't need him."

"Crawl out of his ass, huh?" Ezzie stifled a giggle.

He certainly had a way with words. At the same time, she couldn't dispute the truth. Not that it changed how she felt. The last few weeks with Luke had been different. She'd seen the change in his self-esteem. What he had pulled back at the hotel ... it was like someone else had swooped in and taken over his body. They were his actions, his words, but there had been a struggle in those chocolate brown eyes of his that he hadn't been able to hide.

"Well, he isn't up my ass and he most certainly isn't up your ass. The only option left is that he's up his own ass."

Ezzie shook her head. If nothing else, he had at least succeeded in making her feel a little better. Her heart still hurt, but her best friend made it a little easier to deal with. "Matt, sometimes, I have no idea what to do with you."

"Easy." Matt grinned. "Take me shopping."

"I can't afford your shopping sprees."

He spent money like there was an endless supply. Kind of the same way Luke spent money. She had gone shopping one time with Luke. Okay, two times if she counted the day they had together in Busch Gardens. Both experiences had been quite different. One, she purchased items for other people. The other, she'd been looking for something for herself, a business casual dress for a meeting she had with the dean of the culinary department within her first few days of classes.

For every dress she tried on, Luke insisted she model it for him. After each outfit, she'd strutted out of the dressing room as if she had been on a runway. She had thoroughly enjoyed herself. In the end, she had selected a bright blue pencil skirt with a white and multi-colored polka dot blouse and a pair of bright pink sandals. He had told her it accentuated her eyes.

Then out of nowhere, Luke paid for it all. She had her own money to spend and he'd taken care of it without a second thought. It had taken her multiple, declined, offers to pay him back and several thank yous to accept what he'd done.

She'd never had that—with anyone. And yeah, she was only eighteen. She'd probably have it with someone else. But she didn't want anyone else.

She was in love with Luke. Ezzie bit her bottom lip and looked to Matt. "Tell me what I'm supposed to do. I don't know how to deal with this."

"Well," he paused. "You have three choices. One, wait for him to come to his senses. Two, reach out to him first and just be as honest as you can be. Three, we can hop in the car today and take a road trip to California."

"I—" The smell of something rancid infiltrated her nostrils, like a week's worth of stale milk had been left out. "Crikey, what is that—" A wave of nausea hit her like the crashing tide. Ezzie jumped to her feet and ran straight into Matt's bathroom. She yanked the lid up just in time to spew her guts out.

Not that she had a lot in her stomach in the first place. She'd been queasy all morning, so she hadn't eaten much of anything. Throwing up what little had been in there, Ezzie sat down on the tile floor and flushed the toilet.

"Are you okay?"

"Yeah. I think so." She took a second to get to her feet and headed over to the sink. Turning on the faucet, she cupped her hands and rinsed her mouth out with water.

"You sure?"

"Yeah." Ezzie nodded and rinsed her mouth out one more time. "Probably just a stomach bug or something."

"Stomach bug? You sure that's it? Because the last time you hopped of my bed like that you ..." Matt let the statement drift off.

Switching off the faucet, she raised an eyebrow, reached for the towel and dried her face. "I what?"

"You were pregnant."

Lowering the towel from her face, Ezzie's eyes widened. She couldn't be pregnant. Yeah, they hadn't used condoms since the club, but she'd been on the pill for months now. It was supposed to prevent pregnancy. Right?

She blinked. "Oh god."

Luke stared at the endless tunnels being explored on the television. He hadn't paid much attention to what was going on. The only thing he could tell anyone was that some kind of secret documentation had been discovered and it had been used to search unexplored tunnels. Anything beyond that? Not a clue.

Snagging his cell phone off the coffee table, he pulled up Ezzie's number. His thumb hovered over the call button. Hanging his head, he set the cell phone back down and leaned forward digging his elbows into his thighs.

God, he'd really screwed up. He hadn't gone past the elevators that night and he hadn't made a move to reach out to Ezzie either, not that he hadn't started to multiple times. Even if he got her on the phone, what the hell was he supposed to say?

The sound of the television shutting off caught his attention. He looked up at his mother who stood there with her arms crossed and the remote in one hand.

"Sorry. Was it too loud?"

"Son, you barely had the sound on. I'd simply like to know what is going on with you."

"Nothing's going on, Mom. I'm fine."

If there was one thing he could count on, it was his mother's willingness to accept his lies. Didn't mean she wouldn't offer help if he asked for it. Not that he ever wanted to talk about his relationship issues with his mother. He'd go to his father first for advice.

His mother uncrossed her arms and set the remote on the coffee table. "Lucas Daniel Jonnihan, I'm quite certain I've taught you to never lie. Of which I have no doubt that you are not fine as you have spent the last three days moping around the house watching nothing, but the History channel. Now, I presume this has something to do with Esmeralda, so why don't we try this again. What is going on with you?"

If he hadn't known any better, he would've sworn his mother had just read his mind. Not only had she figured out he was lying, but she even managed to figure out the person involved in his lack of desire to do anything. But how could his mother know that? He hadn't told either of his parents about their relationship.

"What makes you think it has to do with Ezzie?"

"My dear, if a man is moping it always has to do with a woman and since she's the only one you're dating—"

"Dating? What would make you say that?" His eyes widened at his mother's word choice. Where had she gotten the idea that he and Ezzie were dating? It didn't matter that it was true or at least that it had been true. He wasn't sure what they were at the moment.

"Two reasons. One, I saw the way the two of you looked at each other on the flight home after your and Nate's graduation. Two, I've seen a new light in those brown eyes of yours over the last month and a half. Something that only happens when a man is in love."

"Mom!"

Luke hopped to his feet and walked around the sofa. He wiped his sweaty palms down the legs of his jeans and headed into the kitchen. Who the hell said anything about love? He hadn't even confirmed he and Ezzie were dating ... had dated ... and his mother goes and tosses out the "L" word? No way was he in love with Ezzie. Because no man who was in love with her would hurt her the way he had. No man in love with her would've been so willing to let her go, no matter how much pain he suffered because of it.

"You can deny it all you want, but it doesn't make it untrue."

He peered over his shoulder. His mother had followed him into the kitchen. God, why couldn't she just drop it? Who was he kidding? This was his mother. She pushed gently and slowly ebbed every ounce of problems out of people. It was just in her nature. One of the reasons he'd avoided her for weeks after the whole Jessica incident. He stopped in front of the kitchen island and dragged a hand down his face.

"Fine, Mom. Yes, Ezzie and I dated, but it's over. I ended it. That's all you need to know."

"Let me see if I understand. You've been moping around here for the last few days because you broke up with the one you love. I'm not buying it."

"I never said I loved her!" Luke slammed his hands down on the island. That was the problem, wasn't it? He did love her. Not that he should, but he hadn't been able to stop it. Though he wasn't positive he would've wanted to either. She was everything he ever hoped for and nothing he deserved. That was the bottom line.

His mother crossed her arms and narrowed her eyes.

Gripping the back of his neck, he sighed. "Look, Mom. It doesn't matter if I love her or not. I don't deserve her and that's the truth."

"Why? Please explain to me why you are undeserving of a good woman loving you. Because I guarantee she loves you too."

"Because I don't." God, he didn't want to go into this. He didn't want to explain what happened four years ago. Talking about how he'd hurt Jessica was the last thing on his mind.

"Why?"

"Because I don't." He looked around the kitchen and his mother for an escape route. He had to get out of there before he said something he'd regret later.

"Lucas Jonnihan that is *not* an answer. You want me to drop it, then give me a real response. Why don't you deserve Esmeralda?"

"Damn it! Because of what I did to Jessica!"

Thirteen

THREE PREGNANCY TESTS AND A visit to the clinic later confirmed her best friend's theory. She was pregnant. About six weeks. If Matt hadn't said anything or if she hadn't thrown up, it would've been a couple of more weeks before she even realized it. Her last period had been lighter than normal, but she hadn't given it much thought. The birth control pills regulated her period, not the flow.

Ezzie lazily strolled across the parking lot back to Matt's car. She wasn't in a hurry to head home. There were so many things to figure out. Most importantly—Luke. Where did they stand? How would this impact their relationship? How had she managed to find herself in this situation again? Maybe she just needed to abstain from sex all together. Seemed to be the only sure-fire way to prevent pregnancy.

"You gonna be okay?" Matt depressed a button and unlocked the car doors.

"I don't know."

Eventually she'd be okay. Right then, all she wanted to do was curl up in a ball and pretend her life wasn't a complete and utter mess. Her boyfriend, if she could call him that, wasn't talking to her; hell, he may have broken up with her, she really didn't know. She was supposed to be leaving for college in a couple of weeks. And to top it off, she now had to worry about a baby.

She climbed into the car and her cell phone beeped. Probably her mom trying to find out when she planned to be home. Never, if she had her way. She dug her cell phone out of her purse and pulled up the text message. Ezzie blinked.

Matt put the key in the ignition and started the car. "Who is it?"

"It's Luke. He wants to meet." She read over the text message again.

Hey Ez. I'm sorry about the other night. Can we meet downtown to talk? Now?

Part of her wanted to scream, *"Yes!"* and the other part of her wanted to yell, *"No."* Did this mean he was ready to admit the truth about his feelings? Did he want to work out their relationship? Or did he plan to really call it quits? So many different ways meeting him could go. Now there was the baby to consider too. Luke's baby.

No way she could make this decision on her own. She had to talk it out. She turned to Matt, opened her mouth and snapped it shut. It had been natural to seek her best friend's advice, but truth be told, he couldn't help her make this decision. It wasn't his place. She needed to do the right thing and tell Luke about the pregnancy, even if their relationship was coming to an end. He deserved to know the truth.

Ezzie tapped out a response and looked to her best friend. "You mind if we head downtown?"

"We can do that. Guess this means you're going to tell him?"

"Yeah. I think so."

Yes. I'll meet you.

Luke read the text message a second and third time to ensure he hadn't dreamt Ezzie's answer into existence. With all he had put her through over the last few days, and yet she was still willing to give him a chance to explain. She truly was an amazing woman. And maybe he didn't deserve her, but that really wasn't his call.

Setting his cell phone down on the metallic table, he lifted the cup of iced coffee to his lips. He sipped on the sweet and slightly bitter concoction. It was just the thing he needed to perk up after the self-induced solitude he had endured. His mind had to be sharp and clear for the conversation that lie ahead.

He didn't just have to explain himself; he had to dredge up the past. He had to reveal everything he had been hiding from Ezzie, all the details regarding the pain he'd caused Jessica had to come out.

That was not something he really wanted to talk about.

But in order to move forward, he had to let go of the past. That meant addressing it with the one person who mattered the most to him in this world. Dragging a hand down his face, he sighed and returned the cup to the table.

"Luke? Luke Jonnihan? Is that you?"

His gaze flipped to the woman who stopped in front of his table. If the long, curly, blonde hair hadn't given away her identity, the deep-set sky-blue eyes would have done the trick.

Luke blinked and sat up in the metal chair he currently occupied. Not quite what he had in mind when it came to dealing with his past.

"Jessica?"

"One in the same. How long has it been? Three years?"

"Four," he stated. Surely, he didn't need to remind her of the last time they'd seen one another. They hadn't exactly parted on the best of terms. Not that he blamed her for that. It had been entirely his fault.

"Right. School parking lot. Silly me. How could I forget?" She lightly smacked her forehead.

"Jessica—"

"Unless you're going to apologize, don't waste your breath. I don't even know why I stopped." She spun on the ball of her black pump and started walking away from the table.

He hadn't asked for it, but this was an opportunity he couldn't pass up. Luke jumped to his feet and chased after his ex-girlfriend. He grabbed the crook of her arm. "Jessica, wait!"

"What?" Yanking her arm from his hold, she turned half-way around and partially faced him.

"I'm sorry. I didn't..." Luke paused. No way those two words would go far enough. The only way he could do anything to make up for his actions back then was if he owned up to them. All of them. "I didn't handle the pregnancy very well. And I didn't handle the miscarriage any better."

Crossing her arms, Jessica faced him all the way. "You didn't handle anything. You gave me money and then left me to deal with everything alone."

"I know. I'd say I was scared and definitely not ready to be a father, but that's no excuse for just walking away. I'm sorry that I wasn't there to help you through it all. I don't know if that will ever be enough, but I do hope that one day you can forgive me."

A weight lifted from his upper back.

He really had carried the guilt of his actions four years ago with him all this time. Until that point, he couldn't have even said he'd forgiven himself. He'd refused to date another woman as punishment for leaving his ex when she needed him the most. It's why he had only ever slept with them ... until Ezzie. Luke rubbed the back of his head, then dropped his arm to his side.

"I did forgive you. A long time ago. I had to; otherwise I'd never be able to move on with my life. I'm not going to say I wasn't angry because I was for a while. I eventually found the strength to let it go, but thank you for apologizing. It means a lot to me." She uncrossed her arms and hugged him.

He wrapped his arms around her without a second thought. It was unexpected, but he took it as a good sign. If his ex-girlfriend could forgive him for the wrong he'd done to her, then maybe his current girlfriend could do the same.

Luke released his hold of Jessica and smiled. "I'm glad I ran into you."

"Me too." Jessica planted a kiss on his lips.

Ezzie rounded the corner and froze. She spotted some blonde woman making out with a dark-headed guy. For a second, they looked like any other couple on the sidewalk. Except she recognized that head of hair. She'd threaded her fingers through it enough times to know it the way she knew her own body. Her heart stopped in her chest and dropped to her stomach. It was like she'd hopped on a rollercoaster ride that had an unexpected fifty-foot fall.

Digging the knife in a little deeper, Luke's chocolate brown eyes lifted. Meeting her stare, his eyes widened. Tears streamed down her cheeks. She turned around and ran back toward the blue sedan parked twenty feet away.

"Ezzie! Wait!" Luke called out.

Refusing to hear him out, she kept going and didn't stop until she got back to Matt's car. Yanking the passenger side door open, she climbed in and slammed the door shut. "Go."

"Hey. What happen—"

"Please just go," she whispered.

Weeping, she sagged in the cushioned bucket seat. It was Justin all over again, only worse. And she'd caught Justin having sex with a friend. The difference was the place each guy held in her heart. Her feelings for Luke were stronger than they'd ever been for Justin.

Not questioning it further, Matt pulled out into traffic. "Any particular direction?"

She shook her head. Right then, she didn't care where they went. She didn't care about much of anything. What was the point?

The car his girlfriend had gotten into took off. Luke gripped a chunk of his hair. This wasn't supposed to happen! They were supposed to be making up. She wasn't supposed to run off. *Damn it!* He glanced back at his ex-girlfriend. "Why the hell did you do that? Why'd you kiss me?"

"I thought you wanted me to."

"No! Fuck! I just thought for five seconds I could make amends for the way I hurt you. I have a girlfriend. One I love very much."

And one who just so happened to see him and another girl kissing. Shit! How the hell was he going to fix this one?

"I'm sorry. I didn't know. Not that it should be a big deal. She doesn't have to know."

"She fucking saw it!"

Whatever his ex-girlfriend thought didn't matter. Dismissing Jessica's response, Luke headed for the crosswalk. He had to go after Ezzie and find some way to salvage their relationship. Eyeing the red-handed signal, he checked both directions and jogged across the street. There was no time to wait.

He got in his car and sped off toward Ezzie's house. It was the only place he could think to go and the one place he really hoped to find her at.

Ezzie stared out the passenger side window. Her tears had subsided some time ago. Not that she could say exactly how long ago her eyes dried up. She had no idea how long they'd been driving. She hadn't bothered to count the number of trees they'd passed or the various buildings she'd seen in the distance. The road they were on wasn't important. It didn't matter. All that mattered was that she had gotten as far away from Luke as possible.

"Are you going to tell me what happened back there?"

She shook her head. Funny. She told Matt everything. There hadn't been a single secret between the two of them, yet she had no desire to tell him this. Because it validated the concerns he'd expressed weeks ago. Of all the boyfriends she had prayed he'd be wrong about; Luke had been one. And the most important.

"Okay. Well, obviously you didn't talk to him. But I can assume you saw him, otherwise you wouldn't have run back to the car the way you did."

Tears prickled the corners of her eyes. *Fuck*. Sniffling, she wiped at her face. She wasn't going to start crying again. It didn't do a damn thing to make her feel better, it only made her face all puffy and splotchy. Not that she cared what she looked like right then. Hell, she may never care what she looked like again. No way she planned on dating another guy. And she certainly wouldn't sleep with anyone else, not with how easily she wound up pregnant.

Why did Luke have to do this to her? She could've dealt with a simple break up. It would've hurt like hell and would be painful to deal with, but it would've been a hell of a lot better than him kissing another woman and it would've complicated their situation a little less.

Matt gasped and narrowed his eyes at her. "You saw him with another woman, didn't you?"

Her eyes widened at his guess. She should've known he'd eventually figure it out. Chewing on her bottom lip, Ezzie shifted her gaze back out the passenger side window and sagged in the seat. "Yes."

"Oh my god! Ezzie, I'm so sorry."

Shaking her head, she swallowed the saliva building up in the back of her throat. It was the only way to stave off the tears. If she thought on it too much, she'd start back up and she had other things to worry over. Not that she wanted to think about them now. Luke had ruined that. Partially twisting in the passenger seat, Ezzie glanced over at Matt. "I don't get it. Is there something wrong with me?"

"Oh honey. There is absolutely *nothing* wrong with you. It's on them for fucking up. Not you."

If only she believed him. His words had conviction, but she was the one who had chosen to date these guys; the guys who chewed her up and spit her out when she no longer suited their needs. So there had to be something wrong with her. She just didn't know what.

"I have an idea. Why don't we make our trip to Los Angeles a road trip? Our bags are already packed. We can swing by each of our places, grab our suitcases and hit the road. Everything else can be delivered by the movers."

"Are you serious?"

Sure, she'd been living out of a suitcase for the last couple of days, but it hadn't been so they could take off at a moment's notice. It had been in preparation of their move. Leave then? What would they do? And how would they pay for everything? She didn't have extra money for a road trip.

"As serious as a shopping trip."

That was pretty serious in Matt's book. Ezzie blinked. There wasn't any reason not to go. They had two weeks before classes started, plus she could use the time to figure out how to handle things with Luke. And her family. She hadn't even thought about that. At least this way, there'd be no chance they'd figure out she was pregnant until she was ready to tell them.

"Okay. Let's do it."

"Yay! I love a good road trip. And I'll be sure we have loads of fun." Matt grinned, pulled off to the shoulder and made a u-turn.

Luke stared at the red stoplight. He'd gone to Ezzie's house and she hadn't been there. It had taken some convincing, but he'd gotten her best friend's address and checked there too. Yeah, it had been a shot in the dark, but it was one of the only other possibilities he'd been able to come up with, at least the one that made the most sense.

Not that she'd been there either. He'd driven by a couple of her favorite hangouts. The coffee shop. That rib shack they'd had their first date. The rafting store she'd taken him to for gear. He'd been running around for nearly two hours, which didn't include the multiple unanswered phone calls and texts. But he wasn't ready to give up. Not yet. His only hope was that she had returned home by now.

He turned right and drove down a street that held his heart in its hand. Parking alongside the curb of Ezzie's house, he sighed in relief. Her jeep, which hadn't been there an hour earlier, sat in the driveway. This was a good sign. He shut off the ignition and climbed out of his car.

The front door opened. Nate stepped onto the front porch and stopped. "Hey, man. What are you doing here?"

Last time he'd come prepared with an excuse. This time he didn't have one ready. Of course, he could just state the truth. Except that would likely lead into a slew of questions he couldn't answer before speaking to Ezzie. Left only one route.

Luke cracked a smile. "I just wanted to come by and see how your packing was coming along."

"I had to put it on pause for a second, but no worries. I'll be done before the week's end." Nate walked over to Ezzie's jeep and popped open the trunk.

His smile faded. Pause? He didn't like the sound of that. And why had Nate gone over to the jeep? Luke headed up the driveway and stopped a few feet from the jeep. Inside the trunk sat a stack of empty boxes. This wasn't good.

"Oh? Um, how come?"

"Ezzie asked me to pack the last of her things for her."

Fuck! Gripping the back of his neck, Luke tried to massage the tension building in his muscles. Explaining things to his girlfriend, if he could even still call her that, had just gotten harder. But how much more difficult was the question. "She say why?"

"I don't know all the details. All I know is whoever this douche-bag is that my sister was dating broke her heart, so she and Matt took off together. Guess they decided to road trip it to California."

"She's gone?"

The question popped out of his mouth before he could stop it. Luke frowned. He'd been prepared to fly to Los Angeles if necessary. Ezzie had given him the address to the apartment she'd be staying in a few weeks back. But if she was taking a road trip, there'd be no way to tell for sure when she'd get there. And he had his own classes starting soon.

"Yeah. She took off about twenty minutes ago."

Dragging a hand down his face, Luke slumped against the jeep. The last thing he expected was for her to up and disappear on him. He figured he'd have to apologize and explain. Really tell Ezzie everything. But with her gone, how was he supposed to fix their relationship?

"You okay, man?"

No. Not really, but I guess this is what I get for pushing her away. Luke lifted his eyes to his best friend. What he wouldn't give to get some support right then. But if he told Nate the truth, he risked losing all he had left.

Plastering a smile to his face, Luke nodded. "Yeah. I'm all right."

The storefront sign read "Available for Rent." Rubbing her slightly rounded belly, Ezzie bit on her bottom lip and eyeballed the dusty windows. Obviously, it had been abandoned a while ago. It was a lot of glass, but she could handle cleaning around classes. That wasn't a big deal. Not to mention Matt had already volunteered his and Colin's services for clean-up crew. The store sat in the perfect location too. Right across from the college. Her only concern was that the inside hadn't held up over the years.

"You ready to go in?" Mitchell asked.

"Lead the way." She gestured and watched as the real estate agent unlocked the front door. His ass made for a nice view. She may have decided not to date anyone, but she wasn't blind and her sex drive had gone a little crazy these days. Something about second trimester hormones. Made abstinence tough, but not impossible.

Her family had been mostly understanding when it came to her pregnancy. Nate questioned her once a week about the baby's father, but she'd stuck to her story; a one-night stand. She just shifted the timeline a little. It was the most believable and simplest lie she could come up with after her and Luke's break-up.

She hadn't spoken to him since she'd left Utah, nor told him about the baby. It had been a tough decision, but the more she'd thought about it, the more she realized it was best Luke didn't know about the baby. That way he could focus on his education and future, and not the right thing.

She hadn't told her brother about her and Luke's relationship either. As long as the baby looked more like her than Luke, she'd be okay. Only fourteen more weeks before she found out. If her son happened to look like Luke, well, she'd reconfigure her decisions.

Mitchell held the door open. Placing a hand beneath the crook of her elbow, he escorted her inside the inner sanctum of the vacant store. "Be careful."

A jolt shot up her arm. Ezzie snapped her arm from his hold and purposely put some distance between the two of them. *Focus on the store.* That's what she needed to do. If she did that, she could keep her body from betraying her. *Focus.* She turned her attention to the checkered pattern floor. It would have to go. Wood floors suited her purposes better. She looked to her right. Placing her hand on the empty glass case, she smiled.

She could easily see it filled to the hilt with all kinds of different pastries: small lava cakes, vanilla croissants, berry muffins, and more. Beside it sat a long, empty freezer intended for different flavored ice cream. Just beyond that was the swinging door that led to the kitchen where the magic happened. Ezzie glanced over her shoulder. She'd have a few tables where people could share treats and a couple of couches for lounging. She already had the best name picked out for her bakery. It would be called, And Dessert Too.

"It's perfect. I'll take it."

BONUS
Content

EZZIE FORGETS HER PHONE

MATT EYED THE TIME ON his watch and glanced down the hall. Ezzie's bedroom door was still closed, which was weird. Her door was always open after she left for school. Didn't she have a class in like fifteen minutes? She should be gone already.

Maybe she overslept. She'd done that twice last week. He scooped the last of the cereal in his mouth and set his bowl in the sink. Rinsing it out, he dried his hands and headed down the hallway. Matt knocked on the door and poked his head in through the doorway.

Sure enough, she was passed out. Her mahogany hair splayed across the lavender pillowcase. One leg hung off the bed, outside the covers. He snickered. As adorable as she was laying there, she was going to be late for her first class. "Ezzie!"

She bolted upright. "What? What?"

"Are you skipping class today?"

"What? No." Ezzie looked at the time on her clock and jumped out of bed. "Shit!"

"I'll toast you a couple of Pop Tarts while you get ready."

"Thank you!" She scurried from one side of her bedroom to the other.

Good lord, pregnancy had turned her into a walking disaster. Shaking his head, Matt strolled back to the kitchen. The only good news, it would take her less than five minutes to get dressed, ready to walk out the door. And toasting her some breakfast would take, maybe three.

Pop Tarts weren't her normal staple food, at least not recently. She was usually up before him, in the kitchen making her yummy, super cheesy, omelets. That should've been his first clue she'd overslept. She hadn't been in the kitchen. Neither had the sink been full of dirty dishes.

The dining room table hadn't been set either. Ezzie had gotten to putting out place mats and silverware before they sat down to eat. It had been as empty as the gym on a Friday night. That should've been another clue.

They each had their own bathrooms, so that wouldn't have helped any. And she took a night-time shower like he did. Of course, he also showered in the morning too. Matt dropped one strawberry and one cinnamon Pop Tart in the slots of the toaster.

Not only had their breakfast routine changed in the last month, his best friend's taste buds had also gone a little wonky. Which was exactly why he had picked up a box of each flavor when he was at the store the other day. He never knew what kind of day it would be.

Or what kind of mood she'd be in for the day. It was a good thing he was gay. He'd never have to deal with pregnancy hormones.

Again.

Ezzie darted into the kitchen, set her phone down on the kitchen island and grabbed the carton of milk out of the refrigerator. She unscrewed the top.

"Don't you dare drink straight from the jug!" Frowning, Matt snaked a plastic travel cup and thrust it in her face.

"Ugh. I don't have time for this."

"Well, do it anyways. I don't know where your germs have been lately." That wasn't entirely true. He knew she hadn't seen anyone since her break-up with Luke. Still, she could've kissed some random stranger when he wasn't around.

"Crikey, you're a pain in my ass." Ezzie poured milk into the travel cup and crammed the jug back into the refrigerator.

The toaster popped and tossed up two Pop Tarts. He tore a paper towel, removed each warm, gooey, flaky pastry, laid them on the paper towel and handed it over. "Yeah, but you still love me."

"Ugh." With a groan, she shoved a pastry in her mouth and ran out the door.

Rolling his eyes, he unplugged the toaster.

Ding!

What the hell? Matt turned around and noticed the cell phone Ezzie had left on the kitchen island. *Shit!* Picking it up, he eyeballed the text message that had come through.

It was from Luke.

Ez, I know ur still mad at me, but pls call. I really need to talk 2 u.

Had she spoken to him? He thought they hadn't talked since their break-up. Matt scowled. No way had Ezzie lied to him about something like that. Not with everything they'd supported one another on and been through together.

All their various relationships.

Her pregnancy and miscarriage.

The tattoo she'd gotten.

Every bully he'd faced in high school.

There had to be something he could do about this. He couldn't stand by and do nothing, while she tried to get over this asshole. His best friend and the child she carried deserved better.

Matt nodded to himself. There was something he could do. He just wouldn't tell her he found it. Tucking the cell phone away in his pocket, he put the toaster away and walked to his bedroom on the other side of the apartment. He put the phone on silent, placed it in the third drawer of his nightstand, collected his backpack and left.

EZZIE CALLS LUKE

EZZIE LET HERSELF INTO HER and Matt's apartment. He wasn't back from school yet, which was a good thing. She really wasn't in the mood to talk. She headed straight back to her bedroom and shut the door.

A boy.

That's what her obstetrician said. When the doctor had pointed out the gender, all Ezzie had been able to do was stare.

A girl she could've handled. It would be a miniature version of herself. Not Luke. How was she supposed to handle that?

What if her son not only looked like him, but acted like him too? No one in her family would be able to overlook that. Sure, her mother knew, but no one else did. She had yet to tell her brother or her father. Because once she told one, they would blab to the other.

She flopped back on her bed. What the hell was she going to do? Maybe she could stick with her *stranger* lie and prayed her son didn't look like Luke or that her brother and father couldn't tell if he did.

There was one other option.

Chewing on the inside of her cheek, Ezzie dug her cell phone out of the back pocket of her denim shorts. She stared at the new Android in her hand. He wouldn't recognize the number. She'd lost her original phone and had to get a new phone number when she switched carriers. That's what Matt told her, plus the guy at the store had told her the same thing.

Still, maybe he'd answer.

Only one way to find out.

Ezzie dialed the number she'd remembered by heart months ago. *Here goes nothing.*

The phone rang once … twice … three times. "Hello?"

A female answered. Ezzie eyeballed the number. No, she'd dialed it correctly. But it was a woman who picked up Luke's line.

Not him.

Some woman.

Ezzie swallowed. She opened her mouth—

"Hello? Is someone there?"

No. She couldn't do it. She couldn't respond to this woman. Ezzie hung up the phone.

Had Luke moved on? It had been 12 weeks since they split-up. No. It wasn't possible. He couldn't have gotten over her that fast.

Then again, he had been a player. Her brother's girlfriend had told her that. Ezzie rolled over to her side. Tears rolled down her cheeks.

Of course, he had.

It was the only thing that made sense.

Luke flipped through the case he was studying for his Criminal Law class. Who knew first year law classes could be so intriguing and brutal at the same time? At least it kept his mind busy. And he was only two months into his courses.

Knock! Knock! Knock!

He snapped his head in the direction of the door. Who the hell could that be? He wasn't expecting anyone. And Nate wasn't even there. Luke hopped to his feet and strode across the apartment. He opened the door and cocked an eyebrow. Had he forgotten all about a study night? "Hey,

Melanie. What are you doing here?"

"To give you your phone back. At least I hope it's yours." She held out a sleek black Android.

"It looks like mine, but how'd you get it?" He took the cell phone from her and entered his pass code, which it accepted. Wait a second. If she had his phone, then whose did he have? Luke glanced over at his desk.

"I think I grabbed yours by mistake when I was over here the other night. Our phones look the same."

Waving her in, he walked back to his desk and collected the cell phone that had been sitting there quietly for the last few hours. He eyed the Android. Huh. He hadn't even noticed that he hadn't been able to get into it for the last day or so.

Shit. Did that really mean he hadn't called or texted Ezzie in two days? No. That couldn't be right. He'd reached out every day since the day she left Utah.

Luke typed in his pass code, but the phone told him it was wrong. He blinked. He absolutely hadn't attempted to contact her in nearly two days. Shaking his head, he handed Melanie her cell phone. "Sorry."

She shrugged. "For what? I'm the one that mixed them up. I'm just glad I realized it before you answered any calls from my girlfriend."

"I'm sure that would've been awkward." He grinned.

"Oh, I don't care about that. She would just never let me live it down."

"I gotcha." God, he couldn't believe he hadn't called Ezzie in two days. Had he been that busy he hadn't even thought about it? Or was reality beginning to sink in? It had to be the first because he didn't want to imagine a world where she wasn't in his life.

"Anyways, thanks for this." Melanie held up her phone and started for the front door. She paused in the doorway. "I almost forgot. A private number called your phone like an hour ago. I answered the call, but nobody said anything."

A private number? He didn't know anyone who would have a secret phone number. Maybe they had dialed his number in error. "Thanks."

"Sure thing. I'll see you in class." She left.

EZZIE TELLS NATE

"I CAN'T DO IT." EZZIE walked away from her cell phone. It had been two days since she'd called Luke. She hadn't heard from him at all. Her only conclusion: he wanted nothing to do with her. That was fine. She and her son didn't need him. They'd be perfectly fine on their own.

Not that she had much of a choice now. She'd mustered up the courage to tell her *parents* about her pregnancy. Her mother had done a great job pretending to be upset. Her father on the other hand, he hadn't faked anything. He'd been genuinely angry she hadn't told him sooner and disappointed that she had *no clue* who the father was.

One person in her family remained. And she wasn't ready. She couldn't do it. She couldn't tell her brother.

"Don't you think it's kind of too late for that?" Matt gestured to her growing belly.

She swore she had ballooned out of nowhere. Okay, that wasn't true. Her jeans had stopped fitting weeks ago, but she discovered rubber-bands and long t-shirts worked great. "And? It's not like I'm going to see him anytime soon. I can put it off for another day or so."

Matt crossed his arms. "Actually, you'd probably have a couple of hours until your dad tells him. If he hasn't, already."

"I really hate you, right now." Ezzie frowned and shuffled back to her phone. Crikey. This shouldn't be so hard. She was just going to have to be tough and not reveal everything to her brother. Inhaling and exhaling deeply a couple of times, she shook her hands out and FaceTimed her brother.

The line rang twice. "Hey, Ezzie. I was just thinking about you."

"Oh? Anything in particular?"

"Yeah. I realized Thanksgiving is a couple weeks away and I didn't know if you were planning to fly home for the holiday."

"I really hadn't thought about it." That was complete and utter bullshit. She had thought about and thought about it some more. It was kind of what made her decide to tell her family about her pregnancy. Either that or she showed up with a belly the size of a small ball and yelled, "Surprise." She didn't think her family would care for that.

"You should. I wouldn't mind seeing my baby sister for a bit. And I'd be totally up for taste-testing any new recipes you've come up with."

She shook her head and giggled. "What? Don't get any home cooked meals there?"

"Yeah, well … Becca doesn't exactly cook and Luke … he's good at ordering out. So, no, I don't get anything home cooked."

She didn't want to talk about Luke, think about him, or even hear about him. Not that she could tell her brother that. Rubbing her brow, Ezzie swallowed the words on the tip of her tongue. She had to focus on the reason she'd called her brother. "Well, I might be persuaded to come home for the holiday, but before I do … I need to tell you something."

"You know you're my favorite sister, right?"

"I'm your only sister."

"All the more reason you should come home for Thanksgiving."

"Fine, but I really do need to tell you something first." Fuck, she was so over him kissing ass. Honestly, all she wanted to do was get this out.

"Okay. Shoot."

Right. Just tell him. Just say the words. I'm pregnant. Why weren't the words coming out of her mouth? Shit. This really was harder than she thought it would be.

"Ezzie? You okay?"

"Um, yeah. Sorry. I guess … I'm just not sure how to tell you this." Sure, she was; she had practiced this speech ten times over the last couple of days. *I'm pregnant. I don't know who the father is; it was a one-night stand about three and half months ago.* It sounded so easy when she thought about it like that.

"You're not hurt, are you?"

"What? No. Nothing like that."

"Did you get married?"

"Really? Married? Why would you even think that?" Talk about an out-of-nowhere possibility. Marriage was the last thing on her mind. Next to last thing.

"That only leaves … Ezzie, please, please, don't tell me you're knocked up."

Rolling her eyes, she scowled. Why did he have to be so crass about it? It completely demeaned everything beautiful about the little boy growing inside of her. "I wouldn't use that terminology, but something to that affect."

Nate sighed heavily. "Okay. Just tell me one thing. Well, two things. One, who's the father? Two, where is he in all of this?"

"Yeah, about that." This conversation was going downhill fast. And it was about to get worse. Not because she had to lie about the next part, but because of the crap she was going to feed her brother. If she and Luke had parted ways differently, if she still didn't care about him … her story would be very different.

"Don't tell me you haven't even told this guy yet? Or is it that douchebag you broke up with? You know, the one you never told me about."

Pinching the bridge of her nose, Ezzie groaned. For crying out loud, this had been more difficult than telling her father. She had to get it all out at once. Otherwise, she'd chicken out. "No. My ex-boyfriend is not the father. I hooked up with some guy about a month after Matt and I moved here. I met him at a club one night. All I know is his name is Daniel. I have no way to contact him, so, technically he doesn't know he's going to be a father. Which would make him not involved at all."

"How the hell could you sleep with some random stranger? And why didn't you use protection? Not just because this could happen, but you could get STDs too!"

"First of all, we did practice safe sex. Second of all, condoms are not 100% foolproof." Only part of that was true. She and Luke had used condoms the first few times they were together. Then at the club and after, they'd foregone the condoms in lieu of her birth control. She'd kind of forgotten about the anti-biotics she'd been on that cancelled out her birth control. Too late to think about that now.

Ezzie dragged a hand down her face. "Can't you just be happy for me? No matter how this baby came into the picture?"

"I'm sorry, sis. I'm trying, but all I can see is some guy taking advantage of you and I just want to kick his ass."

"Despite what you think, I am a grown woman and I can take care of myself. So, believe me when I say, no man has taken advantage of me. I promise you that." And none ever would. She was too smart for that.

"I know you can." Nate paused and stood still for a minute. "Have you told mom and dad?"

"Yeah. A couple of hours ago. Neither of them is thrilled. Mom said she was too young to be a grandmother and Dad; it was kind of like talking to you." Again, another partial lie. Their father's reaction had gone fairly similar to her brother. As for their mother, she'd found out about a month ago and while she did say she was too young to be a grandmother, she was also happy about it. Something about how it was kismet. Whatever that meant.

"What can I say? We're protective of you."

"Yeah, well, you can both be a little less protective. The two of you have taught me well." Protective was being nice. Her father and brother had been overbearing most of the time. She'd been grateful when her brother had gone off to college in Virginia Beach. The leash she'd been on relaxed, a lot.

"If you think you being pregnant is going to make us less protective, you've got another thing coming. We might get worse. In fact, I should probably text Matt and see what kind of food you're eating. How far along are you? I might need to research what would be a good diet to follow."

Crikey. She had to open her big mouth. Ezzie grumbled. What the hell was wrong with her? No. She wasn't going to have her brother texting her best friend and making her life difficult. Thank god, she was further along than what she planned to tell her brother. "To answer your question, I'm 14 weeks. As for you texting Matt, if you do, I swear to God, I will disown you. You won't have to worry about being an uncle because you won't have a sister. Got it?"

"Alright. I promise not to text Matt. I'm just worried. That's all. A baby is a lot of responsibility to tackle on your own."

"I know that, but I have it handled. I've got Matt and his family here, plus Mom has offered to spend a couple weeks with me after the baby is born. I have thought about all of this and I'm preparing for it." Not to mention, Beverly had volunteered too, but she didn't think it was wise to mention Luke's mom. Then her brother would want to know why and that would mess up her perfectly constructed lie. Luke's mother wasn't supposed to know, but her mother had opened her mouth and told the woman about the baby.

"Good. That's good. Listen, I've got some homework to do, so I'm going to let you go, but I'll see you in two weeks. Right?"

There was something going on inside her brother's head. She could see the wheels spinning and the steam pouring out of his ears. "Yes. I'll clear it with my doctor and if he says it's okay, I'll make flight arrangements. Okay?"

"Alright. I love you, sis."

"I love you, too."

Nate hung up the phone and opened the door to his apartment. He had homework all right. It was called dig through his sister's social media accounts and find the fuckhead that knocked her up. Sure, she said it had been a one-night-stand, but she was notorious for selfies. He'd bet his in-progress law degree she had a photograph in there somewhere.

"Hey, man. A couple of us ..." Luke paused. "You alright? You look like you just failed a test or something."

Failed a test? Yeah, he'd be upset, but nothing like this. Failed test could be recovered from. This was fucking life altering. He dropped his laptop bag by his desk and flopped down in the chair. "I wish it was that simple. I could deal with that."

"What could be worse than ... oh, did you and Becca have a fight?"

"God, no. And please don't wish that on us." He pinched the bridge of his nose. That on top of his baby sister being pregnant, no way he could deal with that. Shit. Maybe he should just tell Luke. The guy saw Ezzie like a sister. If anyone would understand how he felt, then Luke would.

Nate dug his laptop out and fired the machine up. Time to play *find that bastard.* "I just got off the phone with Ezzie. She's pregnant."

"I'm sorry, what?"

"I know. I can't believe it either. She's eighteen and knocked up by a guy whose name she doesn't even know." No, wait, that wasn't right. His sister had told him a first name. That was *so much* better than not knowing a name at all. Nate glanced over his shoulder.

Luke's eyes bugged out. "Wait, what?"

"She told me she got together with some guy a couple of months ago. And all she knows is his first name." The log-in window on his laptop came up. He typed out his password and proceeded to access his social media accounts. All he had to do was search through his sister's posts online.

No way. It couldn't be true. Luke stumbled backwards and slumped onto the couch. It had to be a load of bullshit. It had to be. He just wasn't sure which part.

None of it made any sense. Ezzie wouldn't lie to Nate of all people about being pregnant. But hooking up with a stranger? He couldn't believe she'd do that either. If that was the case, only one option remained.

She was pregnant with his child.

Then why wouldn't she tell him? Any secret he knew she'd kept from her family had been to protect them. Who would this protect? Him?

Luke gripped the back of his neck. There had to be more to this story. More information for him to glean an accurate picture. "Did she, uh, how far along is she?"

"Fourteen weeks. You know, she may still be able to get an abortion."

Balling his fists up, he swallowed the anger bubbling up his throat. How in the hell could his best friend even suggest that? "I'm going to pretend you didn't say that. I know this is your sister we're talking about, but you know damn good and well she's not that kind of person."

"I know." Nate sighed. "She's eighteen. She still has her whole life ahead of her."

"And what? You think a kid is going to ruin that?" When the hell did his best friend become so negative? Luke took in a calming breath and focused back on the first answer to his question. Fourteen weeks; definitely not his unborn child. They hadn't been together in over four months. Over four months since he'd spoken to her. Over four months since he'd heard her sweet voice. Over four months since she'd walked away with his heart.

"Honestly, I don't know. Ezzie has always been mature for her age, but is she ready for the responsibility of a child?"

"She helped raised you, didn't she?" Luke smirked. He shouldn't tease Nate, but he couldn't help it. It was the only way to prevent the tears from falling. This was not how he imagined his life. He never once thought he and Ezzie would go this long without talking, connecting … nor had he for one second believed she'd wind up carrying another man's child.

"Ha, ha."

Luke stood. He needed air. Or at least away from there. He couldn't stay in the apartment any longer. Talking about this hurt too much.

Disappearing into his bedroom, he grabbed his gym bag and headed for the front door. "I'm going to head to the gym for a bit. I'll catch you later."

LUKE GOES TO CALIFORNIA

SURVEYING THE TALL BUILDING, LUKE wiped his clammy palm down the front of his jeans. He'd come all this way to see her; there was no turning back now. Inhaling and exhaling a deep breath, he walked through a set of glass doors.

A huge, elegant lobby welcomed him. He slowly made his way across a shiny, tan marble floor. It had some kind of intricate design, but he couldn't make out exactly what. Though if he hadn't known better, he'd swear he just stepped into ancient Rome. All the gold, oranges, and blue in the design on the floor in front of a long front desk screamed money.

He glanced to his left. There was a small sitting area with an exquisite oriental rug. It was one of those that a person could spend hours studying provided the vinyl covered chairs and burnt orange couch were comfortable. At least he was alone.

For a second.

One of the glass doors between the two white columns in front of him opened. The young man nodded at him as he strode on by. Luke quickly snapped a hold of the door handle before it shut all the way. He eyed the empty front desk one last time, then continued through the second set of doors to the elevators.

Ezzie had given him the address months ago. And it was probably best she didn't know he was coming. There'd be no way for her to hide or ignore him.

The elevator doors opened and he slid in. Luke depressed the button for the sixth floor and shoved his hands in the pockets of his denim jeans. He had no idea what to expect. Other than Ezzie being really pregnant. It had been over a month since he'd learned of her pregnancy, which was part of why he'd decided to make this trip.

With all of the dead ends Nate had found trying to locate the guy who had impregnated Ezzie, Luke had to wonder if she had really lied. What if she had made up some cockamamie story about the father to protect him? What if she had lied about the length of her pregnancy? It was completely plausible. The only way he'd find out was for him to see her himself.

The number six lit up and the elevator door released him from his hold. He exited onto the sixth floor and turned to the right. The online map hadn't offered him a lot of insight. He hoped this was the right direction.

Wiping his hands on his pants again, he strolled down the hallway until he reached the apartment number Ezzie had given him. Luke took in one more deep breath and knocked on the door.

The apartment door opened and on the other side stood a guy nearly six feet tall. A pair of bright, emerald green eyes stared at him. He didn't normally notice those things in a guy, but he didn't care for a good-looking guy answering Ezzie's door.

Wait, maybe—Luke caught a glimpse of Ezzie's mahogany hair and round belly just past the dude in the doorway. She hadn't seen him yet. As fast as he spotted her, she stepped out of his view. Where'd she go?

"Can I help you?" The guy asked as he closed the door.

"Um, yeah, I'd like to talk to Ezzie."

"I'm sorry. She's not available."

"What? I just saw her." Luke gestured toward the shut door that stood between him and his future. He blinked. Wow. After all this time he didn't even realize he still thought of her that way. Good to know he could surprise himself.

"I didn't say she wasn't here. I said, she's not available."

Luke frowned. This guy was really starting to piss him off. What the hell was the difference? Especially when he'd seen her as clear as the stars in the sky. He'd have to try another approach. "Maybe we got off on the wrong foot. I'm Luke and I'm sure if you tell Ezzie I'm here, she'll want to see him."

"I'm well aware of who you are and I can promise you, she doesn't want to see you."

Well, that made one of them. He had no clue who this guy was, other than a dickhead. Obviously, it was someone who at the very least knew Ezzie, but beyond that he couldn't say he recognized him at all. Trying not to be standoffish, Luke shoved his hands in his pockets. "Who are you to say what she does and doesn't want?"

"I'm her best friend and roommate, but if you must know why I can say with complete and utter confidence she wants nothing to do with you, then I'd tell you it's because she's inside with her boyfriend. Now, you found your way in, I'm assuming you can find your way out." Matt stepped back into the apartment, shutting the door once again.

Luke stared at the door. In a matter of seconds, he knew two things. One, the guy's name who had stood between him and Ezzie. She'd told him all about her best friend. At one point, Luke had even accused the guy of being secretly in love with Ezzie, not that he'd said anything to the guy's face.

The second thing, the second he could've dealt without knowing. Ezzie had started dating. She had moved on … without him.

Maybe it was a lie.

He lifted his knuckles to knock on the door again, but stopped. There had been another man in the apartment. He'd hardly noticed him, but Luke recalled the guy had been close to Ezzie.

She had moved on.

Swallowing, tears rolled down his cheeks. Luke lowered his hand and shuffled back toward the elevator.

"Honey, will you tell her hot sauce will only make the chili better?" Colin said.

Bearing a wide grin, Matt held his hands up. "Oh no. If I have learned anything over the years, it's to not argue with any of her recipes and stay out of the kitchen when she's cooking."

"Or baking!" Ezzie chuckled and shook her head. Matt's boyfriend really had been out to prove her wrong. She told him that when it came to the kitchen, Matt would side with her. No matter what.

"Ugh." Colin threw his hands in the air.

She shouldn't be amused, but it was the funniest thing she'd heard in days. It was one of the reasons she liked having Colin over for dinner. He constantly made idiotic suggestions to the person going to culinary school. Whatever. At least he was entertaining. "Hey Matt, who was at the door?"

"Jehovah's witnesses."

"How'd they get past the guard?" Wasn't this one of the many reasons they'd moved into this upscale apartment? To avoid unwanted guests. Ezzie spun on the ball of her foot to stir the chili again and paused. Her son started tumbling around in her belly. If she didn't know any better, she'd swear he was a freaking acrobat. Once he finished using her bladder as a football, she stirred the chili and tasted a small bite.

"I think it's that new kid on duty tonight. You know how he likes to disappear from his post."

Hmm, not yet. Her bladder would have to hold on for a few minutes. Ezzie dug around for some red pepper flakes and salt. "They really need to do something about him. It's rather tiring. At least you got rid of them quickly this time."

"Yeah. I just told them my pregnant mistress and gay lover were all godded out."

With a snicker, she added a little bit of both seasonings to the chili and tested it one last time. Perfect. "Dinner's done. Why don't you guys set the table, while I go pee?"

"Didn't you just go like five seconds ago?" Colin asked as he traipsed back into the kitchen.

"Yes, well, this kid is like his father. He thinks my body is a playground." The words had come out of her mouth before she could stop them. Neither of them would've cared about the snarky comeback, but they would—

"Eww," Matt and Colin said simultaneously.

"That is so gross. We don't want to think about that," Matt added on.

She giggled all the way to the bathroom. Her hormones were a bit all over the place, which made her miss Luke more on days like today. Ezzie shook it off. She had to accept he wasn't in her life.

And that he probably never would be.

The phone call and unanswered letters had made that quite clear. Ezzie wiped the tears from the corners of her eyes and rubbed her belly.

They would be okay.

They had to be.

DELETED
Scenes

When I originally wrote this scene, I started from Ezzie's point of view. I thought I was showing her frustration, but I was really missing a lot of the inner-struggle Luke was facing, so I changed it.

EZZIE SCANNED HER BROTHER'S SIDE of the room and inwardly groaned at all the packing that still had to be done. Why couldn't he manage one simple task? Unfortunately, the answer was her and their mother. The two of them had spoiled the guy for far too long. Maybe they should've stopped years ago. Yet there she stood with an open box on his bed, carefully organizing and packing his books.

Biting on the inside of her lip, she stole a quick glance of Luke's side of the room. The man certainly had skill when it came to putting things together. Last night had been weird. Had he been off kilter or something? First the welcoming arms, followed by the world's best embrace, during which she was pretty sure he'd sniffed her. Only to end with him quiet for the entire car ride to the hotel. Yeah, it hadn't been a long drive or anything. Maybe fifteen minutes tops, but how could he flip the switch like that?

One second, he's grateful she's there and trying hard to hide his reaction to her presence. And the next she might as well not have even existed. How could Luke go back and forth between the two with such... ease? Whatever. She had three days to corner him if she had to. After the hug at the airport, she was certain he was attracted to her. The dorm room door opened and Ezzie opened her mouth to chastise her brother on his lack of cleaning habits. Except it wasn't him. She hadn't needed to check to confirm her suspicions.

Luke had his own unique smell. Like fresh clean air. Reminded her of home. Ezzie looked over to the door. There hadn't been a whole lot of time last night to really admire how much he'd physically changed over the past year. Dark brown hair. Soft brown eyes. Thick thighs. Broad, well-defined shoulders. Plus, the strong jaw-line. Even in a t-shirt and jeans he was sexy as hell. She swallowed to wet her parched throat. At least she hadn't drooled. "Hey."

"Umm, hi. Where's, uh, where's Nate?"

"I sent him for some breakfast. Figured it was the least he could do since I was up at the butt-crack of dawn." Although she hadn't planned for any time alone this morning with Luke; things obviously worked out in her favor. To her surprise, the door closed and he entered the dorm room.

He gripped the back of his neck and crossed over to his side of the room in three long strides. Barely glancing in her direction, he placed two packages on his bed. "Can you tell him I got his cap and gown?"

"Yeah." She sighed and turned back to the box in front of her. Folding the flaps shut, she chanced another peek at him.

Caught staring, Luke quickly looked away and headed for the door. "Thanks."

"You're leaving?"

"Yeah. I've, uh, got some things to do before, uh, before I pick up my parents."

"Sure, you aren't just avoiding me?" She'd been here for two days in the spring and he'd done exactly what she accused him of now. If he intended to run from her, she deserved to know.

Luke paused with his hand on the doorknob. "I'm not avoiding you."

"Bullshit." She'd push whatever buttons she had to for him to admit the truth. Calling him on his crap was the most logical place to start. Ezzie padded closer to him. With his back to her, she folded her arms across her chest.

Luke spun around and faced her, but dropped his gaze to the floor.

"Will you please let this go?"

"No. You ignored me the last time I was here. I have a right to know what the hell is going on, especially after the way you hugged me last night." She had to take advantage of the opportunity presented. Who knew for certain when or if there would be another chance? He could do everything in his power to avoid her until her parent's arrival. At which time, her plan of seduction would likely go up in smoke.

His eyes lifted to hers. Their normal brown had darkened to the color of rich chocolate. A melting pot of pure yummy. "Ezzie, now is not the time for this conversation. Your brother could walk through the door any minute."

"All the more reason for me to ensure there will be time to have it." Screw the talking. He stood in front of her and stared at her like he wanted to devour every inch of her body. Ezzie stepped closer to him. She gave him five seconds to make a move. His inhale of breaths quickened. Resting one hand on his chest, she gripped the back of his neck with the other and lightly brushed his lips with her own.

His arms locked around her shoulders and his lips crushed hers. Slowly Luke plied her mouth open. The instant their tongues met; heat coursed through her body straight into her core. Passion and desire consumed the depth of the kiss. Their lips slowly parted. His forehead pressed against hers. They both panted and inhaled the shared air from their lingered kiss. While it confirmed their feelings for one another, it also left her hungry for more.

Luke pulled back and brushed his thumb across her cheek. "I don't want to avoid you."

"But?" The wonderful moment they'd shared and he has to go and ruin it with, well she had no clue. Obviously, there was a but on the end of his statement. Ezzie turned around, glared at him and waited for his answer.

He stepped around her and paced the length of the room. His eyes remained glued to the carpeted floor as he walked past both beds, stopped at the mini-fridge and turned back toward the door. He lifted his gaze to her and dropped his hands to his hips. "Shit, Ezzie. Just shit."

"Well stated." There were no other words. And no other options. His one-word response covered the situation they'd found themselves in. She could see the mixed emotion in his beautiful eyes. Would they get more confused if he knew everything she'd planned? Maybe she should walk away. No. The silence sucked. But the lack of answers was worse. She had to wait it out.

Hanging his head, he dragged his hand down his face. "I'm sorry, Ezzie. I —"

"Luke, just stop. If you aren't going to give me any real answers then stop. I don't want excuses. To think, you know what, never mind." She snatched her purse off her brother's nightstand and stormed toward the door. Her mind was racing. So many possibilities and they'd all disappeared in such a short time. Matt had been right to think the whole thing would blow up in her face.

Hands roughly grabbed a hold of her, spun her around and shoved her back into the door. Luke leaned into her body; his well-muscled chest pressed into hers. His lips crashed against hers and practically devoured her on the spot. One of his hands slipped to her ass and squeezed. The other yanked the ponytail tie from her hair. With her hair flowing loosely around her shoulders, he fisted in her hair in the palm of his hand. His entire body exuded heat.

With this scene, I didn't just start from Luke's point, but I expanded on his and Ezzie's time in Busch Gardens. While I've never actually been, I did a lot of research online to check out all the different places that they could've gone and what they could've tried. In the end, I decided to slim it down to what was necessary.

WHISTLING, LUKE WALTZED DOWN THE hall to Ezzie's suite. Last night had gone better than he'd expected. Though he could've done without admitting the truth to her. Maybe she'd agreed to friendship, but how long would that last? For either of them. However long it lasted, at least they'd had fun. More fun than he'd had in a long time.

They'd discussed the dynamics of *Ted* 2 versus *Ted* 2 on their way to the movie theater. A great start to the evening. Truthfully, he hadn't minded their lack of interest in *Ted* 2. Even though they'd ended up with an hour before their movie started, he still wouldn't have changed one thing about last night. Between games, popcorn, a good horror flick and the perfect company, celebration of his graduation couldn't have gone better if he'd planned it.

Waiting for the movie to start, they'd spent some time in the game room. And that had been great. They'd located a couple of pinball machines side by side. Challenge issued and accepted. Three rounds and he'd lost every single one of them. Ezzie distracted him in the best way possible. Not that he'd shared that little tidbit. Watching her kick his ass in those heels, the plum colored dress and his jacket, well, he'd won in his own silent way.

Still, he had to redeem his manhood. He'd really thought he could best her at a shoot 'em up game. Yet, she'd racked up more dead zombies than he had. And the surprises kept on rolling.

Kicking back in the theater's luxury seats with a bucket of buttered popcorn and soda, they'd watched the third chapter of *Insidious*. She'd made a few snide comments during the movie, but he'd happily accepted the jokes and cracked a couple of his own. Shocking the hell out of him, she hadn't screamed once. She'd grabbed his arm several times throughout the movie, but that had been her biggest reaction. All in all, he couldn't complain one bit about how the night had gone. Even if it had started a bit on the rocky side.

Clutching a bag of breakfast in his left hand, Luke knocked on the door with his right. How late had it been when he'd dropped her off last night? Two? Three in the morning? Thus, the reason why he'd followed his instincts and swung by Panera on the way to the hotel. As long as Ezzie was ready to go, they should hit Williamsburg around ten. Plans with his parents weren't scheduled until seven, so they'd need to be back by five at the latest. Plenty of time for their destination.

The door opened. Ezzie's gaze landed on the Panera bag in his hands. "I hope this means you're feeding me."

"Yep. You about ready?" As a peace offering, he handed the bag over to her. She looked, well, hot, but mostly prepared to leave. Her hair had been thrown into a ponytail. Another pair of way too short shorts. White graphic t-shirt with the words *I do not care at all.* The t-shirt alone garnered a small chuckle. Luke slipped into the hotel suite and shut the door.

Taking a bite of the soufflé, she half nodded and lifted one barefoot off the floor. She traipsed into the living room and plopped down on the couch. "I just have to put my shoes on."

"Good. What about the checklist I sent you? Everything in your backpack ready to go?"

"All together." She took another bite of the soufflé and picked up a piece of paper. Holding the paper out she pointed to the backpack on the couch.

While she ate and put on shoes, he scanned the list. Everything had a neat checkmark beside it including an item he hadn't listed. "Two bottles of water?"

"Based on your list, I figured we'd need them." Ezzie gestured to the kitchen counter. A couple of large bottles had been stationed there ready to grab and go.

Had she meant both bottles for herself? Or had she considered him? He had an odd question, but he had to know her specific reason. "Why two?"

"One for you, one for me. Should always stay hydrated." Tugging a sneaker on, Ezzie raised an eyebrow as if he'd asked a stupid question.

He grinned and gathered her backpack off the couch. She was different all right. Most of the women he'd met were only concerned with the outside package. And every single one of them had let him into their bed because he looked good. It was the one place he'd ever go with those women. He wouldn't let another woman into his heart. But Ezzie... she honestly cared about him. The whole package. Was there a way? Could he be good enough for her? Even if only for a weekend? "Good point."

"Does this mean you'll tell me where we're going?" Sneakers in place, she hopped to her feet with bag in hand. A wide smile crawled on her face and she waggled her eyebrows.

"Not on your life."

Lacing her fingers in one another, she batted her eyelashes at him. "Aww, come on. Not even a hint?"

"Nope. Now grab the waters and your key. We have to go."

"Ugh. Pain in my ass." Ezzie smirked. She tucked her room key into the back pocket of her denim shorts. Holding tight to the bag with her bagel she collected both bottles of water and held them in the crook of her arm.

Not really, but he could be. Shaking the image from his head, he grabbed her hand and they walked out of the hotel suite.

Of all the places he could've taken her to, he selected the one place she'd wanted to visit since her brother travelled to Virginia for college. Busch Gardens. And his timing couldn't have been better! It was the last weekend of the Food and Wine Festival. The last two days and it would go away until the following year. She stepped through the turnstile and stole a quick sidelong glance at Luke. They walked a little further into the theme park and she took it all in.

Shops to her right. Theater to her left. A huge clock towered over them in the middle. Her eyes widened at the detailed replica. She rushed over to the clock and lifted her eyes all the way to the top. It stood so tall! How many feet had it stood? At least thirty for sure. This was so amazing! Even if it wasn't the real Big Ben, it sure looked like it. She could really be in England. Beaming a huge smile, she glanced at Luke. No longer could she contain her excitement. Ezzie threw her arms around his neck and hugged tight. "Thank you! This is awesome!"

"You're welcome, but you haven't seen anything yet."

"Yeah, but I'll never forget this." She kissed him on the cheek. Releasing her hold, she dropped to her feet and gazed at him. He had no idea what this meant to her. Then again, the amount of joy shining out of those brown peepers of his, maybe he knew exactly what this meant. Tearing her eyes away from his face, she bit on her bottom lip.

Clearing his throat, Luke gripped the back of his neck. "So, umm, what country should we start in?"

"Here, or we could go see Ireland. Or head to Scotland. Ooo, or what if we went to France. Or maybe... " Ezzie dug her cell phone out of her back pocket and scanned the map on the Busch Gardens app. She'd downloaded it the second the roller-coasters came into view. There were so many things for them to do, but they wouldn't have time to complete the whole park. Still she had to make a decision.

"Or?"

Grinning widely, several options ran through her brain. How could she choose? Especially with such limited time. She glanced at her watch. Five hours, forty-seven minutes and counting. The most logical route would accomplish something for the two of them. Though they'd both likely enjoy everything they tried. "We'll hit the shops in England. Candies are a must! Then we can head to Scotland, check out the Clydesdales and take a ride on the Loch Ness. After, we'll head off to France from some food tasting, then more roller-coasters in Germany."

"Sure you haven't been here before?"

"Positive. I'm just good at organization. Now, let's not waste any time."

"No arguments here." Luke grabbed her hand and they walked together toward the land of sweets.

They climbed off *The Battering Ram* and Ezzie loosened her hair. She brushed the fly-aways free and gathered her hair into a ponytail once again. "Not as good as the roller-coasters, but fun as hell."

"We still have about an hour. Where to next?" They stopped at the lockers and collected their belongings. Luke ushered her toward the center columns so they were out of the way. The day had been, to coin her earlier phrase, amazing. With all the food they'd tried throughout the park, they hadn't really had to stop for lunch. Which meant more time to enjoy the rides. And Ezzie had been a real trooper. She'd gone on every single roller-coaster without complaint. Hearing her joyous squeals with every plunge had been the best *thank you* he'd ever received.

She'd purchased a couple of beer steins in Germany, one for her brother and one for him. Though he'd disagreed with her insistence on buying him anything, she'd refused to listen and gotten it anyway. Stubborn ass woman drove him crazy. Yet he'd cherish the item, simply because she picked it out. In Ireland, he'd picked up a couple of crystal champagne flutes for her mother and a Guinness mug for her father. Ezzie had crossed her arms and rolled her eyes at the pieces he'd chosen. The only reason he'd managed to even get the items was because he'd, reluctantly, agreed to split the cost.

Left his parents and her. Whatever he got for her had to be special. Something that matched her personality, including her stubborn nature. Guess her pig-headedness matched his own. It was okay. All day, he'd experienced her will. He'd been able to leave his past behind; escape who he'd become. Be someone else. A real man. One she'd be happy to have by her side.

Digging her phone out of her back pocket, she scanned the app and checked their surroundings. "Well, there's a couple of shops here we could hit. The *Bella Casa* has some beautiful masks. I think you're mom would like that. Plus, there's a few more stops for the food tasting."

"Ugh. I don't think I can eat another bite. You can taste the food and tell me how it is."

"Wimp."

"Call me all the names you want. I won't try anything else." He chuckled. Had she really challenged him on food? He'd miss their banter. No. No need to think about Monday. For the rest of the weekend, he'd be someone else. The guy she deserved.

Giggling, she hooked her arm in his and dragged him along. On their way to the shops, they passed an artist doing caricatures. Ezzie slowed her paced and stopped. "You up for it?"

"Umm..." Part of him wanted to say no. It wasn't as if he hadn't liked the idea, it was, well, a strange way to make a memory. The artists always made their subjects look cartoony. He gripped the back of his neck and peered at the beautiful woman standing next to him. Ezzie had the best smile and hadn't cared if it was goofy. Maybe he shouldn't either. And if he agreed to her request, he could have a moment of them together. A small piece to carry with him.

Taking encouragement in her smile, Luke nodded. He laced his fingers through hers and they trekked the short distance to the artist. One stool. Hmm. They set their bags down and he handed two twenties over to the guy. Grinning at the artist, he hopped up in the chair and wrapped his arms around Ezzie's waist. "Two pictures. Nothing too silly."

Few people shocked her. When she'd suggested the caricatures, she'd truly expected Luke to politely decline. Not only had they gotten their picture done, but they'd gotten in together. She eyed her copy of the drawing and carefully tucked it in a bag with her other purchases. Pure bliss. And this moment would remain embedded in her brain for years to come. She'd never forget the feeling of Luke as he held on tight. Or the warmth of his chest against her back. The ache in her cheeks from the smile that refused to leave her face. Memories of a lifetime.

The day wasn't over yet. She walked hand in hand with Luke and stopped. Peering into the shop window, Ezzie studied the display. "Do you think your mom would like a mask like one of these? They're really pretty."

"She does have that China Hutch she's always putting things in."

"Like collectibles?" Shaking her head, Ezzie softly chuckled. It was so cute the way he knew things, but had no idea at the same time.

Luke smirked and dragged her inside. He gestured to a pretty purple and white mask on the right wall of the shop. "What about this one?"

"No. I need a mask that screams Beverly Jonnihan." None of the masks lining either wall spoke to her. Every gift she'd selected had been chosen with great care and precision. Her insight into people told her exactly what they needed. It made gift-giving difficult. Mostly because she was extremely finicky. No item she'd ever gifted had been returned. And she'd not start with a whimsical selection. She crossed the small shop to where the artist hovered over a new piece.

Taking in the few details she could of the new design, she watched as the artist worked. White mask. Sparkling teal swirls. Feathers around the crown. Patiently, Ezzie waited while he finalized a masterpiece. Her phone chimed. New text. A few minutes wouldn't hurt. She absolutely had to see the finished mask before she could be certain. The man straightened and her eyes locked onto the completed product. "It's perfect!"

"You like?"

"Yes. I'd like to buy that mask, please."

"Of course." The artist carried the piece to the check-out counter. He rung her up.

Pausing beside her, Luke draped an arm over her shoulder. "Find something?"

"What do you think?" Ezzie handed the artist/cashier her credit card and picked up the mask for Luke to see. A wide grin formed on his face. His response said it all. This particular piece was an excellent choice for his mother. With her purchase done, she tucked her credit card into her back pocket and collected her bag.

"We should go into the artisan shop next door."

"Good idea. I might be able to find something for Becca there."

He cocked an eyebrow at her. "I was thinking we could find something for you there."

"Me? I don't need anything." Hadn't the day at Busch Gardens been gift enough? There would be nothing he could possibly find that would top what she'd experienced thus far. This trip had been a dream come true. In ways she hadn't even imagined. A place she'd love to come back to. Go on rides they hadn't had time to get on. Visit shops they'd passed. Take more photos of the two of them together. Even if she'd already taken a ton.

"Of course, you do. I've searched in every shop we've walked into, but I haven't found anything that, well, that's unique, like you."

Her? Unique? He must've hit his head somewhere. Or maybe he'd bounced around too much on that last ride. Ezzie selected a pair of handmade flower earrings. Perfect for her brother's girlfriend. "Seriously, you don't have to get me anything. This has been enough."

"I do. Now stop arguing with me." Luke had to find the perfect gift for her too. She had to know how special she was to him. And despite what their future held; she'd taken up space in his heart. The memories would always be there, but he wanted something physical to mark the occasion. He studied the various necklaces and earrings. None of them appeared as unique as Ezzie. Frowning, he walked deeper into the shop. There had to be... hmm, maybe.

His gaze landed on a handmade *Tiger Lily Pendant Necklace*. A store person rushed over to assist him. Taking in the details of the pendant, he pointed it out. "May I see that?"

"Yes, of course." The clerk removed the necklace from the glass display and laid it out for Luke to inspect closer.

Ezzie stepped beside him. "That's really pretty, but honestly I don't need anything else."

"We could argue over this, but you'd lose. Just like I did when it came to the beer stein." Raising an eyebrow, he peered at Ezzie. Would she put up a fight? He was prepared to battle it out until she relented.

She rolled her eyes and threw her hands in the air. "Fine. I give."

"I love winning. I'll take it." He smiled more at Ezzie than at the clerk, but it worked both ways. Gloating wasn't required. The look of defeat on her face was enough. Luke purchased the necklace and accepted the bag.

Heading for the door, she muttered something about mules. He only caught part of what she'd said before she stopped at the exit and glanced over her shoulder. "Okay. Now, we just need something for your dad and we're set to go.

"Almost makes me think we should search a little more. Maybe another hour." Draping his arm around her shoulders again, he pressed a feather kiss in her hair and they left the shop.

Smirking, she shook her head. "You were the one who said we had to leave by four."

"We do. Oh well. Another time. As for my dad, what about that food shop you wanted to hit?" She'd mentioned the last food stop on their list a short bit ago. No way he'd fit anymore into his stomach. Hell, how could she? Where had it all gone? It was almost as if Ezzie had a hollow leg.

"The only thing they'll have besides food is wine."

A bottle of wine. Yeah, his dad would love that. Luke escorted her toward the final food pit. "That'll work."

"Seriously? I thought you'd be more creative."

"Oh, I am. After all, we're in Italy. It'll be one of their finest wines. And he'll treasure it more than anything else I could get him from here." Which was entirely true. His father wouldn't care for a sword or something from one of the rides. The man had fairly simple, but extravagant, tastes.

"I feel like this is cheating."

The gift she'd selected for his mother had been great. Pegging his mother wasn't hard. Technically, of the two, his father should've been the easier one to read. Still, she got an A for effort. Luke grinned. "Trust me, it's not. Now, do you know what you want to eat?"

"I don't know. The Tiramisu sounds delicious, but so does the cannoli. But I don't want to look like a pig and get both."

"Not that you'd ever look like a pig, I think you should splurge and get both." Even putting away food the way she had, she was gorgeous. Nothing could ever make him see her differently.

"On one condition. You have to take a bite of each."

Gripping the back of his neck, he groaned. She was trying to kill him. Or make him so sleepy, they'd never make it to meet his parents. And that was a no go. His mother would strangle him if they missed out on dinner and the theater. Luke stroked his chin and stared at Ezzie. One bite. He could handle one bite. Besides, how could he say no to her? "Deal."

"Then I'll get both."

When I originally wrote this scene, Ezzie wasn't just seeing past Luke's façade, she was recognizing some of her own concerns. In the end, I simplified this a bit without losing the on-going battle between them.

EZZIE COULD STILL TASTE HIS lips on hers. Afraid to move, she kept her eyes shut and hung there suspended in his arms. What if she woke up and this was a dream? No. It couldn't be. Not with the way he spoke. She replayed his words in her head. Luke had never been so ... sincere or honest. Had she cracked his wall? No way it had fallen so easily. The last two days had proven that. But perhaps it was the rift she'd been searching for.

Slowly she opened her eyes and looked up into his chocolate brown eyes. Hunger swirled with another emotion in them. Not that she could pinpoint—that wasn't true. It just wasn't something Ezzie ever expected to see in Luke's eyes. Fear.

God, she understood that. Giving herself to him scared the shit out of her. Not the physical part, but the emotional. He could turn out to be like all of her other ex-boyfriends. But the connection she shared with Luke was nothing she'd experienced before. While that frightened her too, the idea of never taking a leap with him terrified her more.

Did they share that same fear? Or did his stem from something deeper? Ezzie bit on her bottom lip. Only one way to find out. "Give me one good reason why."

With a sigh, Luke straightened his body and released his hold on her.

He gripped the back of his neck and nodded. "Okay, but can we at least talk in your room?"

Cold air rushed against her bare arms and back. Her spine tingled from the sudden change in temperature. She missed the heat that poured off of him, but it was best they get things settled before going to a place of no return. "Yeah, we can do that."

Inhaling a deep breath and blowing it out, Ezzie brushed the skirting of her dress out and crouched down to collect her clutch. She grabbed the key card to her room, stood up and faced the door. Unlocking the door for the second time, she pushed open the door and walked in. Setting the key card and her clutch on the kitchen counter, Ezzie glanced over her shoulder as Luke sauntered into the room and shut the door.

If all they were going to do was talk, she needed some distance. Stepping into the kitchen, she headed to the refrigerator. Ezzie eyed Luke again out of her periphery. His broad shoulders tensed as he stopped in the kitchen entrance and shoved his hands in his tuxedo pants. Obviously, this wasn't easy on either of them. While a good stiff drink would probably help them both relax, it wouldn't help them resolve anything. She got into the refrigerator and dug out two bottles of water. Letting the door swing shut behind her, Ezzie held out one of the bottles to Luke. "Here."

"Thanks." Luke accepted the bottle, popped the cap and took a couple of swigs.

Following suit, she leaned against the kitchen counter and returned the top to the bottle. Ezzie dropped her gaze to the floor. Great conversation they were having. She frowned. This got them nowhere. It was up to her to get things going. Lifting her eyes back to Luke, she opened her mouth—

"I don't want to lose you Ezzie. I know that isn't much of a reason or really a reason at all, but I'm not sure how else to explain it. I just … I can't imagine my life without you in it."

"I feel the same way, but I need more than that. You've been back and forth so much over the last couple of days, I don't know what you want anymore. And I can't keep doing it." It was exactly why she told his mother she was done. Emotions be damned. Her heart deserved more than the roller-coaster she didn't agree to ride.

Luke dragged a hand down his face and sighed. "You're right and I'm really sorry about that."

She held up her hand. Not another fucking apology. No man had ever apologized to her this much. "Stop apologizing. It doesn't do any good if you have no idea what you're apologizing for. Or if you just can't admit it. I don't know. You'd think I presented you with pie and cake, but you can't or won't decide which one is right. I'm not sure. All I know is you need to figure it out."

"I feel like all I have are apologizes and I wish I could give you more. You deserve that."

So did he. God, why couldn't he see that? What girl destroyed his self-esteem? A question Luke would probably never answer. One amongst the many things he refused to share. And she couldn't keep holding out hope that he would one day. Ezzie eyed Luke and shook her head. "Just go."

"I ..." He grabbed the back of his neck and squeezed. "Please don't do this. Please give me a chance."

"To what? Apologize some more? I'm tired of apologies. I want real answers and you can't seem to do that. So please ... just go." Ezzie hung her head as tears prickled the corners of her eyes. Her heart ached. The last thing she wanted to do was watch him walk out the door. But she would only set herself up for an endless cycle of hurt if she let him go the way he had been. She couldn't continue to play the role of the fool.

The last deleted scene is another one where I flipped the point of view. This seemed a little out of the ordinary for Luke and it seemed more prudent for Ezzie to see this.

COMING UP BETWEEN EZZIE AND the dickhead, he wrapped an arm around her waist and dropped his lips to hers.

The kiss was meant to be quick and to the point. But the second their lips touched; all sensibility left his body. His tongue entangled hers and Luke deepened the kiss as if she was the oxygen to his lungs.

Grabbing a hold of his shoulders, Ezzie pulled him closer.

Releasing the kiss, Luke brushed his nose against hers and looked Ezzie straight in the eyes. She needed to know how much she meant to him. And the time apart from her had put things into perspective. "Sorry I'm late."

"You must be the guy," a red-head lingering behind Ezzie yelled over the din.

Luke shifted around, but kept Ezzie close to his side as he eyed the woman before him. She didn't look familiar. How did his girl know her? They couldn't have met in the last couple of days. He and Ezzie had spent a lot of time together. Unless they met while she was out shopping with his mother. Or on the plane. A small smile tugged at the corners of his mouth. The seatmate. He grinned and nodded. "You must be the friend."

The red-head held out her hand. "That I am. Natasha Stovyck, but my friends call me Tasha."

"Luke Jonnihan. Ezzie's boyfriend." He shook the extended hand. His girl stiffened a touch in his grip. Luke curled his fingers around Ezzie's hip as if it was second nature. He hadn't meant to throw her off. His name and title flew out of his mouth before he had a chance to stop it. Now that he'd said it, he sure as hell didn't want to take it back.

"Nice to meet you."

"Yeah, you too. Mind if I borrow my girl for a few?"

"Not at all."

He dipped his chin appreciatively to Tasha and escorted Ezzie off the dance floor. Luke glanced around. They really needed somewhere private to talk. His gaze paused on the back rooms. It was a bad idea to take her into one of the *stalls*, but it would be one of the quieter places. Threading their fingers together he peered over his shoulder to Ezzie. "Come with me."

TO BE CONTINUED IN...

REignited

WHEN EZZIE WALKED AWAY FROM Luke, she never thought she'd keep the truth from him for so long. Five years later, falsely accused of a crime, she returns home seeking help from her brother—never expecting Luke to come through her parents' kitchen door or waltz back into her life. Now if only she can prove her innocence without reigniting a flame she buried long ago and avoid whoever is after her in the process.

LUKE PRIDES HIMSELF ON BEING prepared for anything, inside and outside the courtroom—until he sees the woman who stole his heart and disappeared with it has kept quite a secret. Despite the shock and anger of seeing Ezzie again and the child he knew nothing about, he can't turn down the challenge of clearing her name. If only he can do it without losing his heart a second time and keep both of them alive.

ABOUT THE AUTHOR

BRIGIT ROSÉ lives in a world of romance. She has taken her life experience and made it into one endless love story. When she's not breathing the air of hearts and kisses, she's singing loudly and off-key, hanging out with friends, or playing with her 2.5 fur babies. She can usually be found with a margarita in one hand and a twist of lime in the other, exactly the kind of stories she likes to read and write. If you'd like to know more about Brigit, you can find out more on her website.

BRIGITROSE.WORDPRESS.COM

OTHER WORKS BY BRIGIT ROSÉ

LOVE'S WORTH SERIES
UnHinged
ReIgnited

FAIRYTALE RETELLINGS
Grace's Beast

Under Krys Fenner

DARK ROAD SERIES
Addicted
Damaged
Avenged

THE GUARDHIAN SERIES
Awakened
Disillusioned

COMING SOON

Burned (Dark Road Series)
ReUnited (Love's Worth Series)